Fallen

BOOK THREE
THE SISTERS
OF KILBRIDE

JAYNE CASTEL

WINTER MIST
PRESS

A woman running from her past. An outlaw determined to triumph over his. The twisted clan-chief who hunts them both. Redemption and healing wounded hearts in Medieval Scotland.

Sister Coira has a secret. She once worked in a brothel and was the favorite plaything of the MacKinnon clan-chief. But since fleeing the hardship of her old life, she has made a new one for herself—as a nun.

Unfortunately, the past has a way of catching up with you.

Coira's new identity is put in peril the day the leader of an outlaw band turns up badly hurt at the abbey. The clan-chief has put a price on his head, and although she can't turn an injured man away, Coira knows his presence at Kilbride will put them all in danger.

Craeg MacKinnon has tainted blood. He's the clan-chief's bastard brother. Driven by vengeance, Craeg has become a thorn in his half-brother's side—stealing from him and giving his wealth to the poor.

Despite that she knows she shouldn't, Coira finds herself irresistibly drawn to the outlaw. Likewise, Craeg can't keep away from the enigmatic yet alluring healer who has saved his life—a woman who is forbidden to him.

But as the clan-chief closes in, and the Black Death ravages the Isle of Skye, both Coira and Craeg's lives will be changed forever.

.

Historical Romances by Jayne Castel

DARK AGES BRITAIN

The Kingdom of the East Angles series
Night Shadows (prequel novella)
Dark Under the Cover of Night (Book One)
Nightfall till Daybreak (Book Two)
The Deepening Night (Book Three)
The Kingdom of the East Angles: The Complete
Series

The Kingdom of Mercia series
The Breaking Dawn (Book One)
Darkest before Dawn (Book Two)
Dawn of Wolves (Book Three)
The Kingdom of Mercia: The Complete Series

The Kingdom of Northumbria series
The Whispering Wind (Book One)
Wind Song (Book Two)
Lord of the North Wind (Book Three)
The Kingdom of Northumbria: The Complete Series

DARK AGES SCOTLAND

The Warrior Brothers of Skye series
Blood Feud (Book One)
Barbarian Slave (Book Two)
Battle Eagle (Book Three)
The Warrior Brothers of Skye: The Complete Series

The Pict Wars series
Warrior's Heart (Book One)
Warrior's Secret (Book Two)
Warrior's Wrath (Book Three)
The Pict Wars: The Complete Series

Novellas
Winter's Promise

MEDIEVAL SCOTLAND

The Brides of Skye series
The Beast's Bride (Book One)
The Outlaw's Bride (Book Two)
The Rogue's Bride (Book Three)
The Brides of Skye: The Complete Series

The Sisters of Kilbride series
Unforgotten (Book One)
Awoken (Book Two)
Fallen (Book Three)
Claimed (Epilogue novella)

Epic Fantasy Romances by Jayne Castel

Light and Darkness series
Ruled by Shadows (Book One)
The Lost Swallow (Book Two)
Path of the Dark (Book Three)
Light and Darkness: The Complete Series

Awoken, by Jayne Castel

Published by Winter Mist Press

ISBN: 978-0-473-54757-8

Edited by Tim Burton

Cover photography courtesy of www.shutterstock.com
Map by Jayne Castel
Celtic cross image courtesy of www.pixabay.com

Visit Jayne's website: www.jaynecastel.com

***

To my wonderful readers—this wouldn't be possible without you

***

Map

Death leaves a heartache no one can heal,
Love leaves a memory no one can steal."
—*From an Irish headstone*

Prologue

I Will Die First

*Dunan broch
MacKinnon territory,
Isle of Skye, Scotland*

Winter, 1338 AD

COIRA LAY UPON the bed and thought about the best way to kill him.

She could lunge for his dirk.

Or she could reach for the heavy iron poker lying next to the hearth.

This was her chance, and yet she didn't take it. She'd swing for murdering a clan-chief anyway—so it was just as well that she lacked the courage to act upon her thoughts.

The young man in question—Duncan MacKinnon—was getting dressed a few feet away, whistling a smug tune as he laced his braies and reached for his léine. Now that his lust had been slaked, he had no use for her.

Coira watched him go through his usual routine, hate cramping her belly.

Every part of her body hurt.

She lay naked on her side, resisting the urge to curl up into a tight ball—resisting the urge to whimper. Instead, she breathed shallowly. Her gaze never left the tall, broad shouldered figure who pulled on his léine—a loose shirt laced at the throat—before buckling on his belt.

He was handsome, yet she'd soon learned that the clan-chief's good looks hid much that was rotten beneath.

Running a hand through his short brown hair, MacKinnon then fixed her with his storm-grey gaze, and an arrogant smile quirked his mouth.

"That was a delight," he drawled. He then circuited the big bed, to where he'd heeled off his boots earlier in a hurry to disrobe so that he could plow his favorite whore. As he passed her, MacKinnon slapped Coira's naked bottom. "Ye always give a man good sport, don't ye?"

Drawing in a slow, measured breath, Coira squeezed her eyes shut. Rage, hot and prickly, rose up within her. Hate thundered in her breast; her heart pounded painfully against her ribs. She took one deep breath, and then another. Her fingers clutched at the tangled sheets upon which she lay.

She didn't answer him. And she knew he wouldn't care.

MacKinnon didn't visit her for conversation.

She listened to the scuffing sounds while he pulled on his boots and then his heavy tread as he left the chamber, the door thudding shut behind him.

After that she heard the creak of the floorboards while the clan-chief walked across the landing and descended the stairs to the lower levels of *The Goat and Goose*, Dunan's most popular brothel.

Still lying upon the bed, Coira squeezed her eyes shut even tighter. A tear managed to escape nonetheless, trickling down her temple and onto the sheet beneath. However, it wasn't a tear of despair, but of fury.

Today, on this bleak winter's morning, she'd had enough.

I will never suffer that man's touch again, she vowed. *I will die first.*

Slowly, she opened her eyes and pushed herself up into a sitting position. Glancing down at herself, Coira tensed when she saw the raised red welts on her breasts, belly, and thighs. As usual, he'd been rough—pummeling, squeezing, and pinching her body as he rutted her.

Coira rose to her feet, swaying slightly as her head spun from the pain that knifed between her thighs. Out of all the men who visited this brothel, MacKinnon was the one she dreaded the most. Few of the customers were gentle, but the clan-chief delighted in hurting her, in humiliating her. Trembling, Coira wrapped her arms around her torso. This time had been one of the worst.

Her gaze dropped then to where a rumpled, dark robe lay pooled at the foot of the bed.

A nun's habit. It was one of MacKinnon's peculiarities. Part of what got him really excited was for her to dress up as a nun. He went into a frenzy at the sight of it, his gaze gleaming with lust when he ripped the habit off her.

Coira had no idea why such a guise excited him. But she preferred not to delve into Duncan MacKinnon's motivations. She didn't want to think about the man at all.

Bile rose in her throat, and she swallowed hard.

It's time. I'll not suffer this life any longer.

Moving stiffly, for each step pained her, she walked to a corner of the chamber and pushed back the heavy curtain, to reveal a wash bowl and a collection of kirtles hanging against the stone wall. The gowns mocked her, like brightly colored butterflies.

She got to keep little of the coin she earned at *The Goat and Goose*, but Maude, the woman who ran this place, liked her lasses to be dressed well. The brothel had a reputation, and the old woman wanted her whores to do her proud.

Coira flushed hot then, and she thought of how she would have liked to take an iron poker to Maude as well as MacKinnon. The woman knew what a beast he was, but she didn't care. In the three years Coira had worked in this place, Maude had never shown her the slightest softness, sympathy, or consideration. She was merely a body, to be sold for silver.

Her feelings didn't matter.

The desire to reach out, tear those kirtles down, and rip them to shreds with her bare hands flooded through Coira. However, she fought the urge.

Now wasn't the time for revenge. She had to get out of here.

She hobbled over to the wash basin and cleaned herself as quickly as she could manage. All the while, her teeth ground with pain. The water came away bloodied, but she preferred not to examine what MacKinnon had done. There would be time for that later. Once she had washed, Coira reached for a dun-brown léine and the plainest of all the kirtles—a gown of jade green. She donned the léine first, an ankle length tunic that fell softly over her bruised body. The kirtle went on next, lacing up over her aching breasts. It hurt to pull on her leather ankle boots, but she would need them for what lay ahead.

Finally dressed, Coira then sank to her knees in the corner of the alcove. Using the handle of her hairbrush, she pried up a loose floorboard. Underneath was all the wealth she possessed. Three years of awful work, and only four silver pennies shone dully up at her.

But it was better than nothing.

Amongst the pennies, something else gleamed: a small silver ring, tarnished with age. Coira's throat thickened at the sight of the item of jewelry; it was the only link she now had with her parents. The ring had belonged to her mother, and Coira would have worn it if she wasn't afraid of Maude. The woman was worse than a magpie.

Coira reached down and picked up the ring, her vision blurring as memories of her mother surfaced. She'd been so wise and strong—and taken too young.

Coira slid the ring upon her right hand, her fingers curling into a fist.

Today, she'd remember her mother as she took back her freedom.

Retrieving the pennies, Coira replaced the floorboard and rose to her feet. She then took a heavy woolen cloak from its peg behind the door and left the bed-chamber.

It was a loathsome place, for although it was her home, and where she slept each night, the room had never been Coira's sanctuary. It was the place where men used her—day in, day out. Sometimes it felt as if the walls were closing in.

Out on the landing, Coira paused a moment. Three other closed doors surrounded her, and behind the nearest one, she could hear a man's groans as he took his pleasure, followed by a woman's giggle.

Coira's throat closed. She never wanted to hear those sounds again.

On trembling limbs, she descended the rickety wooden staircase. Her bed-chamber lay upon the top floor of the brothel, and she passed two other levels on the way down to the common room. On the way there, she heard further sounds of coupling—cries, grunts, and groans. The noises, which had been commonplace for so long now, made her pulse race once more. *The Goat and Goose* would forever haunt her nightmares.

Maude was downstairs, presiding over the busy common room. A few men reclined in chairs around the fire, tankards in hand. A girl, not yet old enough to service customers, circled the room with a jug of ale, while an older lass perched on one of the men's knees.

Hot male gazes raked over Coira as she stepped onto the sawdust strewn floor.

"Where do ye think ye are going, lassie?" Maude barked. A portly woman with a florid face, Maude's low-cut kirtle showed off a fleshy cleavage. She'd once worked as a whore in her younger years, but these days the woman ran this brothel. Maude had a mane of thick blonde hair, now laced with silver, and small, sharp green eyes that missed nothing. That jade gaze narrowed now as it swept over Coira's cloaked form. "I have another customer for ye."

Maude motioned toward a hulking man in the corner who was watching Coira with a hungry stare. A chill slithered down Coira's spine, and suddenly it was difficult to breathe, difficult to swallow.

I have to get out of here.

Meeting Maude's gaze, she forced herself to speak calmly. "I've just seen MacKinnon." Coira paused there, her gaze holding the older woman's. Maude knew that she was in no fit state to see other customers directly after the clan-chief had visited her. She hoped she wouldn't need to spell it out, especially in front of the common room full of men. A squeal intruded then, as the whore wriggled on a customer's lap. Her name was Greer, a foolish goose of a girl who had only recently joined the brothel. The man had a hand down the front of her kirtle and was groping roughly.

Coira's legs started to tremble then, and she was glad that the long skirts and cloak hid her fear.

"I'm off to see the herb-wife," she continued, "for a poultice."

Maude's mouth thinned, her eyes narrowing further. Coira thought that she might refuse her, that her lust for silver would be too great. But then she gave Coira a brisk nod. "Hurry up then. As ye can see, we're run off our feet this morning."

Coira nodded back, relief crashing over her. All she cared about was getting out.

A biting wind gusted down the fetid alley outside the brothel. It bit into the exposed skin of Coira's face and dug through the layers of clothing she wore. Glancing up at the sky, she noted that that it was grey and stormy. Bad weather was on its way. It wasn't a good day to travel, but she would do so nonetheless.

It hurt her to hurry her stride, to make her way hastily out of 'The Warren'—the tightly packed network of alleyways of Dunan. Above it all rose the grey bulk of the broch, threatening against the stormy sky. MacKinnon's lair.

Reaching the busy market square before the North Gate, Coira worked quickly. She bought herself some oatcakes and cheese for the journey, and then made her way toward the gate itself, where she joined the trickle of travelers out onto the road beyond.

The wind was harsh beyond the fortress, battering the high stone walls that surrounded Dunan and tugging viciously at Coira's cloak. Despite the chill morning and the dank smell of an approaching storm in the air, cottars still worked the fields around the MacKinnon stronghold. This time of the year, many of the fields lay fallow, but it was a time to enrich the soil, to dig in compost, and there were plenty of hardy greens, such as kale and cabbages, which grew all year round.

Coira hesitated only a moment in front of the gate, before she turned left and took the road that circuited Dunan. She'd already made her decision about which direction she was headed in: west. North would take her into MacLeod lands and to the port village of Kiltaraglen. But there was nothing there for her but a life just like the one she was fleeing—and she had no intention of ever working in a brothel again.

Instead, she took the road that headed into the depths of the wooded vale behind Dunan. Tall, dark pines spread up the hillsides, their pungent scent lacing the chill air. This road would take her to the wild western shore of Skye, and the only place upon this isle that could give her sanctuary.

Kilbride Abbey.

Warmth spread through Coira's belly at the thought of her destination and the safety that awaited her there.

It was an irony really, after she'd worn a habit for MacKinnon's pleasure just a short while earlier. She was not pious and hadn't been brought up in a god-fearing family. Her parents had died when she was barely ten winters old, both from a deadly fever that had raged through the isle one winter. They'd left her an orphan, and for a while, every day had been a struggle against starvation. Finally, desperation had brought her to

Maude's door. She'd been taken in, first as a servant, and then, when she grew into womanhood, as a whore.

After what she'd endured during her twenty winters, she found it hard to believe in God. If such a force existed, it was cruel indeed and cared nothing for her happiness.

But the abbey wasn't just a place where pious women could live in contemplation. It was a sanctuary from a world that was both harsh and cruel. Coira had heard that the abbess of Kilbride was compassionate, and that she'd given many women shelter and a new start.

Drawing her cloak close against the howling wind, which now had spots of rain in it, Coira lowered her head and walked toward the mountains. And as she did so, she touched the small silver ring upon her right hand, tracing its intricate decorations with a fingertip.

The ring gave her strength; it made her feel as if her mother was watching over her.

For the first time in years, Coira looked toward the future with hope.

Ten and a half years later ...

1

Uncanny

*The village of Torrin
MacKinnon territory,
Isle of Skye, Scotland*

Summer, 1349 AD

"DO YE THINK I have the plague?"

The old man's raspy voice filled the smoky cottage, and Coira heard the note of fear in it.

Straightening up from where she'd been mashing herbs together with a small wooden pestle and mortar—creating a comfrey poultice that she would rub upon his chest—Coira met his eye. "Ye have the grippe, Colin ... and it's settled upon yer lungs. But it's not anything more serious."

"But how do ye know?" The farmer's voice rose as he pushed himself up against the mound of wool-stuffed pillows.

"The pestilence has not yet reached this corner of Skye," Coira replied evenly. "And the symptoms are different to what ails ye."

Over the past year, Coira had heard tales from travelers and visitors to the abbey about the dreaded sickness, some of them conflicting. However, she didn't want to frighten her patient with the details.

"But what *are* the symptoms?" Colin pressed.

Coira heaved a sigh. "Chills and weakness of the limbs ... and terrible cramps to the belly," she murmured, "and then, as the illness takes hold, dark pustules appear on the body."

As expected, Colin visibly blanched at this description. Coira had to admit that the symptoms did sound ghastly; she'd been on the lookout for them ever since the plague—which had wreaked havoc over Europe, England, and Scotland—had crossed the water to the Isle of Skye.

She was as sure as she could be that no one in Torrin had yet shown signs of it.

"Even so," Coira continued when Colin didn't respond, clearly cowed, "we must take care that yer lungs do not worsen. I will spread this salve upon yer chest, and ye must drink a special tea that will help clear the mucus and lessen the aching in yer limbs."

Colin nodded, meek now that he'd been assured he was not infected with plague.

Coira worked deftly, administering the salve and then wrapping the old man's chest. Behind them, his wife fussed over a pot of what smelled like mutton stew over the hearth.

"It's nearly time for the noon meal, Sister," the old woman said as Coira started packing her things away in her basket. "Will ye not join us?"

Coira flashed her a grateful smile and picked up her staff, which she'd leaned against the wall. "Thank ye for the offer, Alma, but I can't stay ... a few chores await me at the abbey, before I can sit down to eat."

It was true. She'd noticed her supply of herbs was getting low. She'd need to gather some more in the abbey's sprawling gardens before joining the other nuns in the refectory for the noon meal.

Leaving the stone cottage, Coira stepped out into a narrow dirt street. The air was soft, cool, and damp—a balm after the reek of peat smoke indoors. The smoke wasn't good for old Colin's lungs either, but like most folk in the village, he lived in a one-room dwelling that gave him no respite from it.

Coira hitched her basket against her hip and made her way through the cluster of dwellings, heading south. Torrin perched near the edge of a cliff-face, with a small kirk presiding over it and arable fields to the back. In the decade she'd lived here, Coira had gotten to know the locals well. They were hard-working and generous with what they had, if a little small-minded and superstitious at times. She'd done her best to tend their ailments, and had grown fond of many of them.

A gentle smile curved Coira's mouth as she left the village and took the narrow road down the hillside. A shallow wooded vale lay before her, and in its midst sat the high stone walls of Kilbride. From this vantage point, she had a wide view of the surrounding landscape. A rugged coast stretched south, to where a green headland jutted out into the sea; and although she didn't bother to look over her shoulder, she knew that the charcoal shadow of the Black Cuillins, Skye's most dominant mountain range, rose to the north. To the east, the bulk of other great mountains thrust up into a veil of low cloud. This was a mountainous isle, and Coira had grown very fond of this corner of it.

Kilbride felt like a world away from the hardship she'd known as a child and young woman. She felt safe here, protected.

A soft summer rain started to fall as she walked, a cool mist that kissed Coira's skin. She inclined her face up to it, closing her eyes a moment. Over the years, she'd gotten used to having her head covered by a wimple and veil, but her face was still exposed to the elements.

The road led her down the hillside, in amongst copses of birch and hazel, before the high walls of Kilbride loomed in front of her. The peaked roof of the kirk rose above it all.

Despite that Kilbride Abbey was a place of sanctuary, of peace and worship, its austere appearance made it off-putting. The abbess had increased this unwelcoming air by employing men from Torrin to dig deep ditches around the base of the walls, making them even harder to scale should anyone dare. Huge gates, made of iron and oak, barred Coira's way—although as she approached, she noted that they were ajar and a black robed figure awaited her.

Drawing nearer, Coira recognized the nun as Sister Mina: a novice who was due to take her vows of perpetuity that autumn. She had a sensitive face and wide grey eyes that were huge this morning.

As Coira drew near, Sister Mina rushed forward to meet her. "Sister Coira! Ye must come immediately!" the young woman gasped.

Coira abruptly halted, tension rippling through her. "What is it ... what's happened?"

"There's a man here ... he's badly injured ... and is delirious with fever."

Coira frowned, snapping into her role as healer. "Where is he?"

"We've taken him to the infirmary," Sister Mina replied, her slender hands clasping before her. "He's in a bad way."

Coira gave a sharp nod and moved past the novice. "I shall go to him now."

Not looking to see if Sister Mina followed her, Coira strode across the wide yard that stretched out inside the gates. Before her rose the steepled kirk, while the various outbuildings—dormitories, the abbess's hall, the chapter-house, guest lodgings, the refectory, the kitchen, and store houses—flanked it either side. Her long legs ate up the ground, and moments later she heard the patter of Sister Mina's sandaled feet as she attempted to keep up with her.

The infirmary was a narrow, low-slung building made of stone that sat behind the kirk. There was room inside for six sleeping pallets. One of the older nuns had recently been laid up there for a while after suffering a fall, but she'd just returned to her usual lodgings, leaving the infirmary empty once more.

Only now, Coira had a new patient.

Two tiny windows let in pale light, illuminating the tall figure sprawled upon the pallet in the far corner. Even as she approached him, Coira could see from the sharp rise and fall of the man's chest that he was suffering.

However, when she drew up before the bed, and her gaze alighted upon his face, Coira forgot all about the reason she was here.

She froze, a cold sensation creeping out from her belly and numbing her limbs.

That face. It was as if a ghost had just risen up before her.

"Sister Coira?" Sister Mina had stopped next to her. "Is something wrong?"

Coira didn't answer. She couldn't. Her attention didn't waver from the man who lay before her, eyes closed, his handsome face gleaming with sweat.

"He was conscious when we brought him in," the novice said after a few moments, perhaps thinking that Coira was merely shocked by his state. "But he's worsened since then."

Coira was grateful he wasn't awake. The last thing she wanted was those iron-grey eyes to open and stare up at her.

And yet, as the initial shock faded, Coira realized that maybe she was mistaken.

This wasn't the man who'd caused her to wake up in a cold sweat at night for the first couple of years after she left Dunan. This wasn't the beast who'd hurt her, humiliated her.

Aye, the lines of this man's face were similar to those of Duncan MacKinnon's. Yet his hair was shaggier, wilder than the clan-chief's, and his physique more heavily muscled.

She'd also last seen MacKinnon only a moon earlier, when he'd arrived at the abbey looking for Lady Leanna—the novice he'd abducted and then lost. She didn't remember the clan-chief sporting a long, thin scar that slashed vertically from his temple to cheek, just missing his left eye. It was an old scar, silvered with age.

Coira exhaled slowly. This wasn't Duncan MacKinnon—although the resemblance was uncanny.

"Did he give his name?" she asked finally, surprised at the slight tremor in her voice. Even after all these years, MacKinnon could still rattle her.

"None that I heard," Sister Mina replied. "We found him alone ... sprawled on the ground before the gates. He was muttering, but most of it was incoherent. I think Mother Shona managed to get some sense out of the man, before we carried him in here, but I didn't hear what passed between them."

Coira nodded, only then daring to move closer to her patient. Setting down her basket, she lowered herself onto a stool beside the pallet.

That's how they'd found her too—over a decade ago. Her flight from Dunan hadn't gone well. A few hours after fleeing the stronghold, a winter storm had blown in, bringing with it sleet and a freezing wind that had chilled her to the marrow. She'd plowed on though, leaving the road and scrambling cross-country to avoid anyone who might be searching for her. Night had fallen swiftly, and she'd been forced to find shelter, crouching shivering under the lee of a boulder while the wind screamed across the exposed landscape. The next morning she'd awoken with an aching body and a fever—and by the time she reached the abbey, she'd been staggering. It was the abbess herself who'd found her crumpled before the gates.

"Ye said he was injured?" she murmured, running her practiced gaze down the length of his strong body. He was clad in a leather vest and plaid braies wet with sweat.

"Aye ... there's a festering wound to his left flank. I checked under his vest, but it's all bandaged up."

Coira nodded before reaching down and deftly unlacing the vest. As the novice had said, a bandage had been wrapped around his chest. It was filthy, and Coira could see a dark stain on the left-hand side. Drawing a knife from her belt, she carefully cut away the bandage.

A putrid stench immediately filled the infirmary.

Mother Mary preserve him … this doesn't look good.

Behind her, Sister Mina made a gagging sound, before she muttered something incoherent under her breath.

Stifling the urge to clap a hand over her mouth, Coira straightened up. "Open the windows," she ordered, "and fetch me some vinegar, a clean cloth, and a bowl of hot water … quick as ye can."

Grateful to have an excuse to flee the stench of rotting flesh, Sister Mina did as bid, leaving Coira alone with her patient.

Staring down at the wound upon the man's left flank, Coira's mouth pursed. It looked to her as if the man had sustained a battle wound—an arrow most likely. The offending item had been removed, but looking at the red, swollen sore, and the pus leaking out of it, she knew the wound had soured. Angry red lines now stretched out from the injury, a bad sign indeed, as was the fever that had brought the man to his unconscious state.

She'd have to work hard, if he was to be saved.

2

Taking Risks

COIRA ROSE TO her feet and stretched her aching back. She'd lost track of time, of how long she'd been bent over the injured man, cleaning and then dressing his wound. She'd missed the noon meal, and Sister Mina had come and gone with steaming bowls of water, clean cloths, and bandages as the afternoon slipped by. But now she was done.

Heaving a sigh, Coira glanced down at the man's sleeping face. He was still fevered, and had started to twitch and thrash about. However, his wound was now clean. She'd do her best to dress it regularly, but the rest was up to him.

She wondered if her care had come too late.

Covering her patient up with a light blanket, Coira left the infirmary. Outside, a misty rain continued to fall and a low mantle of cloud had settled over the abbey, closing them in. Sister Mina approached, a slight figure through the gloom, carrying a pile of clean linen.

"Is it done?" the novice asked, her gaze flicking over Coira's shoulder to the closed door of the infirmary. "Will he live?"

"It's too early to tell," Coira replied, her voice heavy with fatigue. "The next day will be crucial. If his fever rages, then he may lose the fight." She massaged a tense muscle in her shoulder then. "I'm starving ... is it time for supper yet?"

"Not for a while, although I'm sure ye can get some bread and cheese in the kitchens," Sister Mina replied. "But before ye do, ye had better go and see Mother Shona. She's asked that ye pay her a visit once the patient is tended to."

Coira nodded. However, she wished she could have gotten herself something to eat first. She felt light-headed from hunger. "Very well, I'll go to her now," she replied. "Please stay with him for a while ... fetch me if his state worsens."

Coira found the abbess in her hall. At this time of day, Mother Shona often shut herself away for a period of study and quiet contemplation, while the nuns took an opportunity to rest before the last of the afternoon chores and Vespers.

Mother Shona was seated in a high-backed chair by the hearth, where a lump of peat glowed. She motioned for Coira to enter.

Crossing the floor, Coira lowered herself onto one knee before the abbess. Mother Shona then made the sign of the cross above Coira's bent head. Once she'd blessed her, the abbess gestured to the seat opposite. "How is he?" she asked without preamble.

"Very ill," Coira replied. "I removed a splinter of wood from an arrow wound to his left flank, which had caused the problem ... it should have been attended to long before today."

Mother Shona nodded, her brown eyes shadowing. She was a small woman with a deceptively gentle demeanor that belied the steel underneath. Around twenty years Coira's senior, the abbess was the strongest person Coira had ever known. Thanks to her, Coira had grown hardy, both in body and spirit. She had learned to defend herself, and had found solace in her life as a Bride of Christ.

"Did he speak to ye?" the abbess finally asked.

Coira shook her head. "He was in a fever sleep when I attended him ... and remains in one."

"He was delirious when we found him earlier," Mother Shona replied, her expression still veiled, "but I managed to glean his name."

Coira frowned. "Sister Mina told me ye all didn't know his identity?"

"I decided some news is best not shared," the abbess replied with a wry glint in her eye. "The name 'Craeg the Bastard' is not one to be bandied about in these parts."

Coira went still, the cold, fluttery feeling she'd experienced upon entering the infirmary at noon returning.

"No wonder I recognized him," she whispered.

The abbess's face turned stern. "I'm surprised the others didn't. The similarity is striking."

For a moment the two women merely watched each other. The intense look upon the abbess's face made Coira tense. Sometimes she swore the woman could read minds. Mother Shona was the only soul in the abbey who knew her history, knew that she'd fled the life of a whore. However, she didn't know the whole story—that Coira had run from Duncan MacKinnon's brutality.

She didn't know that Coira's heart had nearly stopped when she'd set eyes upon her patient.

"I heard there was a skirmish ... to the south ... around a month ago ... between MacKinnon and outlaws," Coira said, breaking the brittle silence between them. "The outlaw leader has likely been carrying the wound since then."

Mother Shona shook her head. "It's a miracle he still lives."

Coira let out a long exhale. "Aye ... but it's a risk having him here. There's a price on that man's head that would tempt many. If MacKinnon ever discovers him here, all of us are in jeopardy."

"I'm aware of that," the abbess replied. Her voice was unusually weary. "But he came to us out of desperation. We couldn't turn him away."

Of course they couldn't. Coira had never refused to tend anyone, and had been pleased to hear that MacKinnon's bastard brother was causing the clan-chief so much trouble of late.

However, keeping him at Kilbride was another matter. Here, he risked bringing the wolf to their door.

"So, what should we do?" Coira asked, almost dreading the answer.

"We will keep him here, out of sight." The abbess now adopted a determined expression that Coira knew well. "Unfortunately, news of an injured man's arrival has already spread through the abbey, but no one beyond its walls knows he's here, yet. If he survives his injuries, as soon as he's able, he will have to leave."

Coira nodded. Mother Shona's decision didn't surprise her. Neither of them was going to turn an injured man away, and yet the sooner they rid themselves of Craeg the Bastard, the better.

After supper, Coira discovered that she couldn't settle. She'd filled her belly with bread, cheese, and onion broth; slaked her thirst with a cup of ale; and tried to rest—but she found that she was full of nervous energy.

Instead, she decided to practice with her quarter-staff.

Having MacKinnon's half-brother here at Kilbride had put her on edge. It didn't matter how much she steeled herself before visiting Craeg, every time she set eyes on the man the likeness between him and MacKinnon made a shiver slide down her spine.

However, unlike the clan-chief, Craeg was loved rather than reviled by the people of this territory. There were a number of stories about this man that had almost become folklore upon Skye. Despite that he was a criminal, Craeg had recently become a savior figure for the folk here, the only one who'd stand up against the clan-chief's iron fist. His behavior was audacious and foolhardy to the extreme. He boldly attacked supply wagons, couriers, and even MacKinnon's own men, stealing food and silver, most of which he gave away to the poor. MacKinnon had been hunting him for a while now, but Craeg always seemed to slip free of his net.

Maybe this time he wasn't going to be so fortunate.

Outdoors in the misty gloaming, Coira noted that tension had turned the muscles in her neck and shoulders into planks of wood. The evening chores had been done and Compline completed, and the abbey had just entered the Great Silence—a period of quiet reflection during which the nuns did not converse until after Mass the following morning.

The Great Silence was actually Coira's favorite time of day. And usually at this hour, she was happy to rest upon her sleeping pallet—but not this evening. Returning briefly to her tiny cell in the building next to the dormitories, Coira retrieved her quarter-staff—a six-foot stave fashioned of ash with pointed iron tips.

This was her weapon of choice.

Upon arriving at the abbey, it hadn't taken Coira long to realize that all wasn't as it seemed. Aye, the abbess was a pious woman who took her service to God very seriously, and expected the nuns to do the same, but she was also an enigma. Like Coira, she appeared a woman who kept secrets.

Even so, Mother Shona had revealed some of her past to the nuns. Over the years Coira discovered that the abbess had once been a novice in a convent in Lismore upon the mainland. One summer, brigands attacked the convent, raping and slaughtering any nuns they found there before burning it to the ground. Shona had been spared that day, for she'd been out collecting herbs when the attack had taken place. Terrified, she'd fled into the forest, and had been on the verge of starving when a group of outlaws found her and took her into their fold.

Coira wasn't sure what had happened afterward, for this was the part where the abbess had been vague, but it appeared that the outlaws had taught the young nun how to defend herself. Eventually, she'd left the band and traveled to the Isle of Skye, where she'd entered Kilbride Abbey. Years later, when she was elected as abbess,

Mother Shona had determined that the nuns under her care would always be able to defend themselves, and had set about teaching them all skills that were highly unusual for a nun—abilities that she'd kept secret from her fellow sisters for years.

Over the years, Coira had learned to fire a bow and arrow, throw a knife, handle herself with a sword, and defend herself with her hands if the need arose.

But wielding the quarter-staff—a weapon that could be as dangerous as a sword—was the skill she'd focused on. Coira carried it with her whenever she left Kilbride's walls, which was often because she needed to collect particular healing herbs in the woods, and attend the sick and injured beyond. To the folk beyond here, it looked as if she carried a staff to help her walk upon the uneven terrain, but the Sisters of Kilbride knew differently.

Coira was lethal with a quarter-staff.

She walked to the wide yard before the shadow of the kirk now and stood for a few moments, legs planted hip-width apart as she centered herself.

Around her, it felt as if the mist had closed in further still. The oil lamp that Coira had brought, and placed down on the ground a few yards behind her, only illuminated a limited space. She couldn't even see the surrounding walls of the abbey. It mattered not though; she could still practice, even in the fog.

Swinging the quarter-staff around in an arc, Coira started through a series of drills. She could have done them in her sleep, for they were movements that she taught all the young nuns who'd entered the abbey after her. These days, she and Mother Shona shared the duty of training the others.

The wooden stave whistled and swooshed through the air as she spun it around. She shifted stance then, holding the staff two-handed—attacking, feinting, and parrying, as if an opponent stood before her.

She went through the drills, again and again, her mind completely focused. For a short while, the rest of the world receded. Her past ceased to exist, and all the problems that had plagued the abbey of late disappeared as well. She'd lost two friends recently, both of whom had been very dear to her. Coira knew that a woman who dedicated herself to serving Christ shouldn't cling on to earthly relationships, but she'd been very close to Sisters Ella and Leanna.

Fortunately, both women were still alive. However, due to extreme circumstances, they'd left the abbey for new lives. And although Coira kept herself busy at Kilbride, she sometimes felt an ache in her chest whenever she thought of Ella and Leanna. Without them here, she sometimes felt very alone.

Finally, the sweat pouring down her face and back, Coira finished her practice. She was breathing hard, yet the tension had now eased from her neck and shoulders, and the muscles felt loose.

I needed that, she thought as she turned, retrieved her oil lamp, and headed toward the nun's quarters. Yet halfway there, she halted. She'd intended to return to her cell, where she'd retire for the evening. But something prevented her.

Instead, she turned and made her way around the back of the complex, to where the infirmary stood, shrouded in mist.

Her patient would be alone.

She couldn't leave him like that—not tonight. Not when his life hung by a thread.

With a heavy sigh, Coira entered the infirmary. It was dimly lit by the glow of the hearth at one end and a flickering oil lamp on the low table next to the only occupied bed.

Craeg the Bastard lay sprawled upon his back, his breathing deep and even as he slept. He wasn't thrashing now, which could be a good or bad sign, depending on how his body was responding. Lamp aloft, Coira approached the sleeping pallet and peered down at his bandaged midriff. They'd removed his vest, leaving him naked from the waist up. Examining the bandage, she was pleased to see there hadn't been much seepage—that there was no tell-tale yellow stain from pus. That was a positive sign.

Satisfied that she had done all she could for the moment, Coira set down her lamp and pulled up a high-backed wooden chair next to the bed. With a sigh, she sank down onto it and clasped her hands before her.

All she could do now was pray.

3

Just a Man

CRAEG AWOKE TO a dull throbbing pain in his side and a raging thirst.

He opened his eyes slowly, for although the room in which he lay was dimly lit, his eyes still stung from the candlelight.

For a few moments, his vision was cloudy and blurred, and then his surroundings sharpened into focus.

And the first thing he saw was an angel standing over him.

A woman with a face that looked as if it had been sculpted by the hand of the master: strong patrician features, and high cheekbones, with a full, beautifully drawn mouth. But the thing that really caught his attention was her eyes. They were an unusual color—violet—and framed by dark arched eyebrows. Truly, he'd never seen such beauty.

An instant later though, he realized he was not looking up into the face of an angel, but a nun. Those angelic features were framed by an austere white wimple and a black veil. She was tall and broad-shouldered for a woman, and her body was shrouded in a heavy black habit, girded at the waist with a leather belt, where a small wooden crucifix hung.

A jolt of surprise made Craeg catch his breath.

He wasn't dead and being attended by one of heaven's angels after all—although in retrospect, after the life he'd lived, he was much more likely to have been sent to the depths of hell—but very much alive.

Craeg tried to remember how he'd gotten here. He could remember telling Gunn and Farlan to return to the others, before he'd finished the journey to Kilbride on his own. He also recalled staggering through the trees, to where the austere walls of Kilbride Abbey rose in an impenetrable barrier against the outside world. He'd barely made it to the gates, and hadn't had the energy to reach for the heavy iron knocker to alert them to his presence. Instead, pain, fever, and a crushing fatigue had slammed into him like a charging boar, and he'd collapsed upon the dirt before the gates. An instant later darkness had taken him.

Staring down at him, the nun's lovely face tightened a little. Those unusual violet eyes widened.

"I'm so thirsty," Craeg croaked. "I can't swallow."

With a brisk nod, the nun moved away, and returned an instant later at his side with a wooden cup. Craeg found he was propped up on a mound of pillows, and as such, when the nun raised the cup to his lips, he was able to take a sip, and then another, without choking. The ale that she fed him was watery, yet it tasted like the sweetest mead to his parched mouth and throat. He could have gulped it down, but since he knew it would only make him ill, he prevented himself.

With a sigh of relief, Craeg sank back against the pillows. Then, dreading what he might see, he lowered his chin to look down at his left flank.

Unlike the last time he'd seen it, when the bandage had been filthy, stained with blood and pus, and stinking like the devil's toenails, it now looked clean, although the dull throb set his teeth on edge.

"How is the wound?" he asked dreading the answer. Craeg knew he'd been a fool to leave it as long as he had; the last month had been fraught as he and his band had narrowly escaped capture again and again. There had been no time to think about himself. A chill settled in his belly as he remembered just how awful the wound looked last time he had dared uncover the bandage.

"Much better than it was," she replied. Her voice was as lovely as her face. It had a low, husky quality to it, and its timbre soothed him. "The souring came from a splinter of wood that hadn't been removed." She paused here, those startling eyes narrowing. "From an arrow, I take it?"

Craeg nodded. "I took the wound around a moon ago, and it started to trouble me a few days later." He halted there, his eyes closing as he braced himself for bad news.

"Don't look so worried," the nun continued, her tone rueful. "Ye might live yet, outlaw."

His gaze snapped open. "I might?"

She nodded, the edges of her sensual mouth lifting in the barest hint of a smile. "Last night was the most dangerous time, and ye passed it. Now, if I can keep the wound clean, and help it to heal, ye will live and continue to be a thorn in yer brother's side."

Her dry sense of humor made Craeg smile. "I see ye know who I am?"

The nun nodded, breaking eye contact with him. She then took the wooden cup from him and set it down on the table next to the pallet.

"The people of this territory have much to thank ye for," she said, her voice soft now as she started to sort through what appeared to be a basket of herbs. "Last winter ye gave silver to the folk of Torrin after MacKinnon robbed them. They'd have starved otherwise. Because of ye and yer band, they have hope."

Her words, strangely, made warmth spread out from the center of Craeg's chest.

He knew that many folk living upon MacKinnon lands saw him as some kind of savior figure, but he never spent much time dwelling upon the fact.

The truth of it was less pretty.

He didn't do this for them, but for himself. Revenge fed him, drove him—it was his beer and bread. However, he prevented himself from telling the nun this. Despite that he'd only just met her, he realized that he wanted this stranger to think well of him. Odd really, but he did.

"I need to take a look at that wound," the nun informed him, her tone changing from warm to cool in an instant. It was almost as if she realized the conversation had become too familiar. She was now trying to distance herself from him.

"Go on then," Craeg replied.

He fell silent, observing as she approached once more and deftly cut away his bandage. He noticed as she did so that she had beautiful hands with long, nimble fingers. When she had removed the bandage, he forced himself to look upon the wound.

It still wasn't a pretty sight. The flesh around the wound was badly swollen, although the red lines that had scared him into making the journey here had started to fade a little. Thank the Lord that the wound no longer stank. It was red and angry looking, but there was no pus, and it no longer had a putrid appearance.

The nun bent close, her cool fingertips gently prodding the inflamed skin around the injury. She then glanced up, and their gazes fused for an instant. "I'm going to have to wash it again, she informed him. "It's going to hurt."

He nodded, steeling himself. "I'm ready."

She hadn't been lying. When the vinegar poured over the wound, red-hot pain exploded down his left flank. Craeg gritted his teeth, his hands clenching by his sides as he bit back a groan. The first jolt of pain receded, followed by waves of burning agony that seemed to pulse in time with his heartbeat.

"Sorry about this," she murmured, meeting his eye once more. Craeg saw that she meant it to, for her gaze was now shadowed. "The vinegar removes the evil humors."

Craeg nodded, not trusting himself to speak. He'd taken a few wounds over the years, but even the one on his face hadn't hurt as much as this did. He didn't want to embarrass himself over it though, so he kept his jaw clamped shut.

"I'm curious," the nun said, as she continued her tortuous work. "How is it that ye and yer band have eluded MacKinnon for so long? I'd have thought there were only so many places ye can hide."

She was trying to distract him, he realized. All the same, Craeg appreciated the gesture.

"The heart of MacKinnon lands is a wild place," he replied through clenched teeth. "There are many hidden corners where few men have set foot ... I have discovered them."

"The people of this land must truly love ye," she replied with a shake of her head. "But don't ye worry all the same that one of them might betray ye?"

Despite the red-hot agony that pulsed down his left side, Craeg's body tensed. One of his men already had, barely a month earlier. However, this wasn't the time to discuss it.

"Not really," he grunted. "MacKinnon has done a fine job of making himself the most hated man upon Skye."

"He has," she agreed, "but silver has a way of making folk forget such things."

Their gazes met, and he saw the keen intelligence in those violet eyes. An instant later the nun rose to her feet and wiped her hands upon a damp cloth.

"That's done for now," she said with a half-smile. "Ye did well."

Somehow Craeg managed a wan smile of his own. "Aye, thanks to ye distracting me. I'd tell ye that ye have the gentlest touch this side of the Black Cuillins... but I'd be lying. I've never been in so much pain."

Her mouth curved then into a proper smile, and if Craeg had thought the nun was beautiful before, she was positively radiant now. That smile illuminated her face like winter sun emerging through a bank of frozen fog. For a moment Craeg merely stared at her, entranced. Eventually, when he spoke, his voice had a slight husk to it. "So as ye will know, my name is Craeg. May I know yers?"

The nun's smile faded, although her eyes were still warm. "I am Sister Coira," she replied.

Coira stepped out of the infirmary into the misty dawn and raised an unsteady hand to the center of her chest. As she suspected, her heart was racing.

Mother Mary ... it's like looking upon MacKinnon's twin.

The man had been civil and respectful in his manner, so different to the clan-chief. But it didn't matter that Craeg wasn't his brother, he still unnerved her. The similarity in their looks was eerie—although she'd noted a few differences.

Firstly, his eyes. She'd expected them to be grey, like Duncan MacKinnon's. But the eyes that stared back at her this morning were a deep moss green—as different from MacKinnon's as mid-winter was to mid-summer. Even shadowed with pain, there had been wry humor and a large dose of arrogance in them, which wasn't surprising. She hadn't met a warrior who wasn't arrogant.

His voice was markedly different to MacKinnon's as well. It was much lower and deeper. Just like his eyes, the outlaw's voice held a warmth that the clan-chief's had always lacked.

And yet, standing outside the infirmary, Coira struggled to regain her equilibrium.

She wished there was another healer in the abbey— another nun who could help him besides her.

Goose, Coira chided herself. *He's just a man. Ignore who he is and treat him like any other*. She walked away from the infirmary, and toward the refectory where bread and beer would be served to break the nuns' fast.

Truthfully, she had no appetite. She usually enjoyed all her meals, for she worked hard and was rarely idle during the day. But this morning, her encounter with the outlaw had left her shaken.

Her only solace was that she didn't think the man had picked up on her reaction to him. He was in too much pain.

Lost in brooding thoughts, Coira circuited the complex, and was about to join the flood of nuns who were entering the refectory, when the clang of iron echoed across the yard.

Coira's step faltered. Someone was at the gates and had just let the knocker fall.

Kilbride had visitors.

Glancing around her, she saw that a few of the other nuns had halted, including Sister Elspeth, one of the older women who'd been here long before Coira's arrival at the abbey. The nun wore an expression of constant disapproval, her small mouth pursed, her eyes narrowed. She drew herself up now, irritation vibrating through her thin body, and when she spoke, her voice held a querulous edge. "Who dares bother us at this hour?"

Coira didn't reply, as she realized the question was probably rhetorical. With a huff of irritation, Sister Elspeth picked up the long skirts of her habit and hurried across the dirt yard toward the gates. Without thinking, Coira fell in behind her.

Once she reached the gates, Sister Elspeth drew open the small window that sat at eye-height. Coira couldn't see what the older nun was looking at, but judging by the way Sister Elspeth went rigid, she hadn't liked what lay beyond.

"Who is it?" Coira whispered.

Sister Elspeth ignored her. Instead, she stepped back and started unbolting the gates. "Help me, would ye?" she snapped.

Irritated at having orders barked at her, Coira reluctantly stepped forward and aided Sister Elspeth. Together they gripped one of the heavy wooden and iron gates, and hauled it back.

A thin, milky mist breathed in, its tendrils twisting like crone's hair. A jingling sound filtered through the damp air then, and a harsh command cut through the dawn. "Open the gates ... I have business with the abbess!"

Coira's breathing slowed. *The Saints preserve us ... I know that voice.*

She peered through the fog, where shadowy figures now emerged. The nearest was a lanky, round-shouldered figure: a monk garbed in black who'd just knocked upon the gates. Behind him clustered a group of his fellow monks, who suddenly parted to admit a heavyset figure atop a pony.

Only, it wasn't a pony but a mule. The creature was bedecked in bells, ornaments, and tassels; the bells tinkling as the burdened beast swayed forward. The man astride it wore a truculent, pinched expression, as if his arse pained him.

Coira heaved in a deep, steadying breath, even as her belly dropped.

Father Camron.

The Abbot of Crossraguel was paying them another visit.

4

Thwarted

Dunan broch
MacKinnon territory
Isle of Skye

DUNCAN MACKINNON SLAMMED the goblet down upon the table, his gaze fixed on the blond man standing at the foot of the dais. "This isn't good enough, Broderick ... the bastard can't have disappeared into thin air!"

A tense silence settled upon the Great Hall of Dunan—retainers and kin swiveled in their seats, their attention settling upon their clan-chief. Everyone was halfway through their noon meal of blood sausage, braised leeks, and hefty loaves of oaten bread when MacKinnon's right-hand, Carr Broderick, had entered the hall.

MacKinnon glared down at the warrior, irritated that his outburst hadn't moved the man at all. His rugged face was set in an unreadable expression. Although not overly tall, Broderick made up for it in breadth and strength; his stocky frame was pure muscle. His close-cropped blond hair just added to his severe, unyielding appearance.

"We've combed yer lands over and over again," Broderick said when the silence between them started to crackle with tension. Like his expression, his voice gave nothing away. "There's no sign of the outlaws."

"But I saw my bastard brother take an arrow in the side," Duncan exploded. "He'll be injured ... he won't have gone far."

"Maybe he's dead?" A cool female voice interjected then, and MacKinnon swung his gaze left to where a dainty woman with rich brown hair piled up onto the crown of her head had just spoken. Undaunted by her brother's outburst, Drew MacKinnon's sharp grey-eyed gaze met his. "Have ye not considered that?"

"I'll not believe Craeg's dead till I see his rotting corpse with my own eyes," Duncan snarled back.

"Lady Drew has a point," Broderick rumbled. "That might be why we can't find him ... he's buried under six-feet of dirt somewhere."

Broderick hadn't moved from his position. He waited before the raised platform at the end of the Great Hall, where the clan-chief and his kin took their meals. The warrior stood, legs akimbo, in an arrogant stance that grated upon MacKinnon. His previous right-hand, Ross Campbell, had been an arrogant man too, but he'd also been clever with words, and had known how to ease a tense situation or offer explanations that would appease MacKinnon.

Carr Broderick was charmless and disarmingly blunt at times. Duncan watched the warrior, gaze narrowed. Campbell's betrayal had made the clan-chief wary of the men who served him. He knew the two men had been friends, and initially after Campbell had run off with the woman Duncan had planned to wed, Lady Leanna, the clan-chief had suspected Broderick of somehow aiding them. However, the man had been off fetching a priest for the marriage ceremony when the incident occurred.

MacKinnon's attention shifted back to his sister. He didn't trust her either. Drew swore that on the night Campbell and Lady Leanna escaped the broch, she'd heard nothing. Duncan didn't fully believe her at the time—and he still suspected she was hiding something. However, he had no proof against her.

The memory of that humiliating night still burned within him, and his chest constricted whenever he recalled it. He'd underestimated Leanna it seemed, and shouldn't have drunk so much wine before attempting to claim her. She'd been cowering against the wall as he explored her lithe body, and then she'd kneed him in the cods—twice.

The wee bitch had put every ounce of her strength into the attack too. In the days that followed, Duncan had wondered if he'd ever father another child; although Dunan's healer had assured him there had been no lasting damage.

He'd been curled up on the floor, retching from the pain, when Campbell burst into the bed-chamber. He'd trussed Duncan up like a capon, and then the pair of them had fled, locking him inside the room.

"I repeat," MacKinnon growled, shoving aside the memories that made him break out in a cold sweat. "Until I see my bastard brother's body, I'll not believe he's dead." He leaned back in his carven chair then, drawing a deep breath as he sought to master the rage that made his pulse thunder in his ears.

Wisely, Drew didn't argue the point with him. Dismissing her, he pinned Broderick with a hard stare. "Ye have already failed me once ... if ye let Craeg slip through the net, I won't give ye another chance to redeem yerself."

The threat fell heavily in the silence. Everyone in the hall had stopped eating now and was watching their clan-chief.

Broderick stared back at him, and although his expression was still inscrutable, Duncan saw his gaze narrow slightly. The hardening of his jaw also betrayed him; like Ross Campbell before him, Carr Broderick was a proud man. He didn't like being threatened.

MacKinnon didn't care—he was done with being thwarted.

Raising a hand, he dismissed the Captain of the Dunan Guard before clicking his fingers, holding his goblet aloft to be refilled.

A young woman appeared at his elbow. She was a shy, dark-haired lass—one of his cousins—of plain face and with a figure so slender that MacKinnon found her sexless. A pity really, for he was in the mood for some bed sport.

The lass filled his goblet and scurried away, gaze averted. Duncan ignored her. Leaning back in his chair, he took a large gulp of sloe wine and retreated into his own thoughts.

And as often when he withdrew from others, his mind went to Lady Leanna MacDonald.

The pounding in his ears increased. How he'd wanted the woman—ever since he'd first set eyes upon her at a gathering between the MacKinnon and MacDonald clans. Her father had thwarted him, but after his sudden death in a hunting accident, Duncan had wasted no time in tearing Leanna from Kilbride Abbey, where she'd been living as a novice nun.

Things should have gone his way then. Campbell and Broderick delivered her to Dunan, but fate had turned against him. MacKinnon couldn't believe she'd managed to escape, or that Ross Campbell had betrayed him. Where had Campbell taken her? He'd even dispatched men to the mainland to look for her, when his search upon Skye was fruitless. He'd sent word to all the clan-chiefs and chieftains upon the isle, along with thinly veiled threats of what he'd do to any who dared harbor her, but none had responded to him.

Over a month on, Leanna still dominated his thoughts, as did fantasies of what he'd do if he ever caught her.

Duncan took another gulp of wine, welcoming its heat as the rich liquid slid down his throat. He was drinking too much these days, yet he found that it was the only thing that took the edge off his rage. He hadn't lain with a woman since that disastrous attempt with Leanna. It was time to break the curse she'd cast upon him.

Setting down his goblet, the clan-chief shoved back his chair and rose to his feet. Next to him, Drew stopped eating, her gaze swiveling to his untouched platter and then to his face.

"Does the food displease ye?" she asked.

"I'm not hungry."

"I thought blood sausage was yer favorite?" Drew continued, her dark brows drawing together. "Ye hardly eat at all these days ... ye will be nothing but skin and bone soon if ye don't take care."

Heat flushed across Duncan's face as irritation surged. "Stop nagging, sister," he snarled. However, as he stepped off the dais and strode across the floor of the hall, past long tables where his retainers still ate and drank, he reflected that, indeed, his clothing was starting to hang on him these days. His need for vengeance had become an obsession; it had narrowed his world. He'd lost his taste for food.

He was having trouble accepting that Leanna was lost to him, but he wouldn't give up on seeing his brother swing from a gibbet. Once Craeg was caught, the world would return to normal.

Bran, his faithful wolfhound, leaped down from where he'd been sitting under the table upon the dais and fell in behind Duncan. The dog loped at his heel as the clan-chief strode across the broch's wide entrance hall and descended the steep steps to the bailey below.

The wolfhound was the only occupant of the broch who didn't irritate Duncan on a daily basis. But of late he hadn't paid the dog the attention he usually did. Bran didn't appear to care though—he merely trotted after his master, his ever-present shadow.

MacKinnon left the bailey through a high stone arch and made his way into the streets below. Without even thinking about his direction, his feet carried him toward 'The Warren', a squalid tangle of alleyways in the lower village.

Duncan hadn't walked this way in a while. Of late, what with the threat of pestilence, and everything else, he'd been preoccupied. After Leanna's brutal attack, his cods had taken a while to heal. Yet the ache in his bollocks now had to be satisfied. It would also relieve the tension within him, distract him from his own thoughts for a short while.

The Goat and Goose was a high, narrow building made of pitted grey stone that loomed over a shadowy lane. The air outside the brothel reeked of stale piss, but Duncan paid it no mind. *The Goat and Goose* had the best whores on the isle, and Old Maude always did her best to ensure the clan-chief left satisfied.

Stepping inside the common room, Duncan left behind the squalor of 'The Warren' and entered a softly lit space. Pine and herbs scented the air, from the soft mattress of sawdust underfoot, and flickering cressets of oil perfumed with rosemary and lavender lined the walls. Yet underneath it all the faint odor of stale sweat pervaded—it always did here. There weren't many customers present at this hour, and as such, the whores who lolled on chairs near the glowing hearth all snapped to attention at the clan-chief's arrival.

"MacKinnon!" Maude, blowsy and busty with a mane of greying blonde hair pinned up into an elaborate tangle upon her head, swept in from nowhere. The woman brought with her a wake of rose perfume—a scent MacKinnon would always associate with this brothel. "We have missed ye."

"I've been busy," he replied, his tone deliberately cold. Duncan wasn't here to indulge in idle chatter.

Maude favored him with a sly smile. The woman was sharper than most, and she'd sensed his mood. "Would ye like the usual?"

"Aye." Duncan lowered himself down into a chair one of the whores had just vacated and took the goblet of wine the serving lass passed him. "But give me a different girl this time ... the last one didn't please me."

A shadow passed over Maude's face. This was ill news indeed, for she lived to please the clan-chief. "Of course," she replied hastily. "If ye would give me a few moments to organize things for ye?"

Duncan nodded curtly. He didn't mind waiting, just as long as he got the whore he wanted. Indeed, the last time he'd visited *The Goat and Goose*, he'd ended up with a lusty, over-eager whore who'd tried to wrench his braies off him and suck his rod. He preferred women who let him take control—and if he glimpsed fear in their eyes all the better.

That last thought brought another woman to mind—one he'd thought of often over the years.

Coira.

Every time he stepped into this brothel, he felt a pang of longing for her. His obsession with Lady Leanna had distracted him over the last few years, but Coira was always there, a shadow from his past. And Duncan's recent visit to Kilbride Abbey had brought her back into his thoughts.

He was sure he'd seen her there.

It was true that the black habits and veils the nuns wore made them difficult to tell apart, yet he'd never seen anyone with eyes the color of Coira's—violet. And that nun, long-limbed and broad-shouldered, who'd stood at the back of the group while he'd confronted the abbess about Leanna's whereabouts, had violet eyes.

She'd also watched him with contempt and fear upon her lovely face.

It could be her.

One day, MacKinnon intended to go back to Kilbride Abbey—and when he did, he'd investigate.

A whore shouldn't be hiding in the guise of a nun anyway. A smile curved Duncan's mouth then as he remembered the games he used to play with Coira. If that woman had, indeed, been her, it was a real irony.

"More wine?" The serving lass drew near him once again, and with a jolt, Duncan realized that he'd drained his drink without even realizing it.

He nodded and held out the goblet for her to fill. As he did so, he noticed that the lass didn't look well. A light sheen of sweat covered her thin face, and the hand that poured the wine trembled slightly. When she moved away, the girl hunched, as if her belly was in pain.

She was a plain-looking wench, Duncan observed, and on the brink of womanhood. He certainly wouldn't be asking for her to warm his bed.

"MacKinnon ... if ye are ready?" Maude descended the stairwell from the upper levels. "Yer woman awaits ... upon the top floor ... last room on the right."

Duncan nodded before draining his new goblet of wine in a few gulps. He then rose to his feet and shoved it at the pale-faced serving lass. Without a word, he strode past Maude and climbed the stairs to the upper levels. As he went, he heard Maude's voice, harsh now that the customer was out of sight. "Stand up straight, Fiona ... what's wrong with ye today!"

Reaching the top floor, Duncan strode toward his destination. His belly tightened in anticipation, the ache in his groin intensifying as he imagined what awaited him.

He strode along the narrow hallway, the wooden floor creaking underfoot, till he was before the last room on the right. Then, he tore the door open and stepped through the threshold.

A small lass, barely old enough to be called a woman, sat perched upon the bed. She watched him, blue eyes huge upon a winsome, heart-shaped face. A black habit and veil swathed her slender form.

Duncan halted, his gaze drinking her in. A moment later, a delighted smile stretched his face. Maude had done well indeed; he could smell this lass's fear.

Still grinning, he kicked the door shut behind him.

5

Happy Endings

"I TOLD YE I would return." Father Camron picked up his spoon and viewed the bowl of stew before him with thinly veiled distaste. "I warned ye that yer behavior would be investigated, Mother."

Heat rose in the pit of Coira's belly as she listened to these words, and her fingers clenched around her own spoon. She couldn't believe this man's arrogance, his presumption.

However, at the head of the table, Mother Shona appeared unruffled by the abbot's inflammatory words. "Ye are always welcome here, Father," she said, meeting his eye. "We have nothing to hide."

Coira's pulse accelerated, and she quelled the urge to exchange glances with the other nuns at the table.

They all knew that statement was a lie.

There was much Father Camron didn't know—much he couldn't know. If there was anyone in the outside world they had to protect themselves against, it was this man. The abbess had confided in Coira that Gavin MacNichol had offended the abbot's pride when he'd gone to Scorrybreac to corner Ella about leaving the order. To compound matters, when Father Camron had arrived at Kilbride, he'd not gotten the welcome he'd expected. Mother Shona had let her temper get the better of her for once, and had given him further offence.

She would be regretting those rash words now.

Father Camron was a man who nursed grievances like a bruise. He never forgot a slight.

"I have informed the Pope about the goings-on here," the abbot continued, undaunted by the abbess's sanguine reaction. "MacKinnon sent word to me that yet another of yer nuns has left the order ... this is highly irregular."

Mother Shona inclined her head, favoring the abbot with a long-suffering look. "Did he also tell ye the reason for Sister Leanna's departure?"

The abbot's blank look told them all that the clan-chief had not.

"Sister Leanna's father died, and she was going to his burial when MacKinnon's men abducted her." The abbot's face tensed at this, his dark gaze narrowing, yet Mother Shona pressed on. "He took a novice nun against her will back to Dunan, where he planned to wed her. Sister Leanna managed to escape, and we haven't heard from her since." The abbess paused there, letting her words sink in. "I can assure ye, we had nothing to do with her disappearance. It saddens me greatly that we have lost such a devoted sister."

Father Camron watched the abbess, high spots of color appearing upon his already florid cheeks. "MacKinnon said none of this to me."

Mother Shona's expression grew grave. "That doesn't surprise me. He wouldn't wish to cast himself in a poor light."

Coira watched the abbot's heavy jaw tighten, although he held his tongue this time. This news clearly shocked him, and she could see he was debating whether to believe the abbess or not.

With a suppressed sigh, Coira dropped her gaze to her half-full bowl of stew.

The man's company was tiresome at best.

A few years ago, Father Camron had spent three months at the abbey. But during that stay, he'd been a guest, not an inquisitor. And at that time, the relationship between the abbey and the MacKinnon clan-chief hadn't deteriorated to this level. A heavy sensation settled in the pit of Coira's belly, dulling her appetite.

She'd joined the order to embrace a life of peace, stability, and order—but the chaos of the outside world was always clawing at the door, seeking a way in.

Craeg watched the nun climb up onto a stool and peg a heavy woolen curtain to the rafters. The thick material blocked out the pale light filtering in from the infirmary's tiny windows and the glow of the hearth. His stuffy corner of the building was now illuminated only by a guttering candle.

"What are ye doing, Sister?" he asked. The weakness of his voice both shocked and irritated him. It didn't sound like it belonged to him. He wasn't used to feeling this physically feeble either.

Finishing her task, Sister Coira stepped down from the stool and turned to him. Her expression was carefully composed, those startling eyes shuttered. "There's a price on yer head," she said, her voice low. "And as such, I'm taking precautions."

"Surely, no one is likely to see me in here," he pointed out.

"The abbey has visitors at the moment," the nun informed him coolly, "and we don't know how long they'll stay."

A fluttery sensation rose in Craeg's gut. The way she'd said the word 'visitors' immediately made his hackles rise; years of living as a fugitive had honed his instincts. Craeg attempted to push himself up off his nest of pillows. "I should go," he grunted. "My band will be wondering what's become of me, and I don't want to put ye and the others here at risk." An instant later a wave of sickly pain crashed over him. Sweating, Craeg sank back down onto the pillows. "Maybe not ... just ... yet. Looks like ye might have to put up with me a bit longer."

Sister Coira's mouth compressed as she eyed him. "Aye, ye are in no fit state to be going anywhere."

"These visitors," he wheezed. "Who are they?"

The nun's gaze met his. "The Abbot of Crossraguel Abbey ... he's here to investigate the abbess's conduct."

Craeg frowned as he struggled to focus on her words. The pain in his side was starting to subside although his body still quivered in its memory. "Really? What has she done to warrant that?"

Sister Coira let out a slow exhale, and he sensed her wariness around him. However, he wasn't about to push her. If she didn't want to speak openly, he understood. "There have been a few ... incidents ... here over the past year," Sister Coira admitted finally. She folded her arms across her chest then, an unconscious defensive gesture. "Two nuns have left the order in ... questionable circumstances."

Craeg cocked his head. "Now I'm curious."

"Aye, well some things are best not discussed."

The clipped tone of her voice didn't put him off. Instead, it merely intrigued him further. "Ye can't just leave it there."

Her gaze narrowed. "Can't I?"

They watched each other for a long moment, and Craeg suddenly became acutely aware of every detail of the woman standing before him. The voluminous black habit she wore, along with the veil and wimple that shrouded everything except her face, did their best to cancel out her femininity. And yet he saw beyond the austerity of her clothing. She was tall, which he liked, and the generous swell of her breasts was evident despite the heavy material of the habit.

But it was her face that drew him in. The blend of strength, vulnerability, and sensuality in her features.

What a pity she's a nun, he mused. Life had been a fight for a survival of late, and there had been no time for women. Yet he'd never met one that intrigued him like this Sister of Kilbride did.

"Around a month ago, I met a young woman who claimed she'd been a nun here at Kilbride," he said finally, shattering his silent appreciation. "Her name was Leanna."

Sister Coira's lips parted, her gaze widening. "Where did ye see her?"

"She was fleeing Dunan ... with the aid of Ross Campbell," Craeg replied, his gaze steady as it continued to hold hers. "They entered the valley not far from where my band camped, and we hosted them for a night." He paused there, aware that her expression had turned stern. Craeg made a face. "Worry not, I didn't take them prisoner ... although I made an error of judgement during their stay that cost me dearly." His chest constricted then as he remembered the mess Brochan had made. He should have seen that coming. "One of my men tried to use Leanna and Ross to blackmail my brother ... and everything went to hell."

Sister Coira didn't answer him, although her face now wore a wintry expression. Craeg knew he wasn't giving a good account of his band, yet he forced himself on. Nonetheless, it was an effort to keep eye contact. His throat thickened as he continued. "The man, Brochan, under-estimated my brother—we all did. Before he killed Brochan, MacKinnon tortured him ... and discovered where we were hiding."

Craeg dragged a shaky hand through his hair and sank back into the nest of pillows behind him. "Ross and Leanna helped us defend our camp when MacKinnon's men attacked, but it wasn't enough to save us. Many of my band fell that day, and I took the arrow that landed me here."

Sister Coira was watching him, her gaze shuttered. Craeg thought she might comment, but when she didn't, he pushed on, concluding his tale. "When the fight turned against us, I told Ross and Leanna to run. I hope they managed to elude MacKinnon."

He stopped speaking then, his eyes flickering shut. Their conversation, short though it was, had drained him, the weight of guilt settling over him. Brochan had been one of his closest friends. Aye, he'd acted foolishly, but that didn't make Craeg feel any less to blame for his end.

"They're safe," Sister Coira said finally. "Mother Shona received a letter around two weeks ago. We don't know where they are now ... but they've left Skye and made a new life together."

Craeg's eyes snapped open, and a little of the heaviness lifted. "That's good," he replied, his mouth rising at the corners into a half-smile. "Ye could see Campbell was in love with the lass. At least life has happy endings for some of us."

It was her turn to incline her head then, her gaze questioning. "Aye," the nun murmured, favoring him with a rare smile that was tinged with sadness. "Leanna wasn't suited to be a nun. Her father sent her to Kilbride only in order to protect her from yer brother; her heart was never in it. I miss her all the same though."

Again, Craeg felt a pull toward the woman before him. What a contradiction she was: at once strong and capable, yet with a softness, a vulnerability, just beneath the surface.

"What about ye, Sister Coira?" he asked finally. "Why did ye take the veil?"

The moment he asked the question, Craeg realized he'd overstepped. It was like watching a door slam shut between them. Sister Coira took an abrupt step back, her jaw tightening and a shadow passing over her eyes.

"I came here for a better life," she replied, her tone clipped. With that, the nun turned, pushed aside the curtain, and departed the alcove, leaving Craeg with his own company.

6

Sickness

DREW MACKINNON STEPPED out of her bed-chamber and closed the door firmly behind her. Leaning up against it, she inhaled deeply, a chill seeping through her. Behind her, she could hear the rumble of the healer's voice and the weak sounds of his patient's reply.

Mother Mary, save us.

Drew clenched her eyes shut and wished she was a pious woman. Her mother had tried to instill religious fervor within her years earlier, but the hours spent kneeling on the stone floor of the kirk, praying for forgiveness for her numerous sins, hadn't made the slightest difference. If anything, it had made Drew rebel further.

But a strong faith would be welcome now.

"Lady Drew?" A gruff male voice intruded. Drew's eyes snapped open, and she glanced left to where Carr Broderick had halted. He was watching her, his grey-blue eyes clouded with concern. "Are ye unwell?"

Swallowing, Drew shook her head. "No ... but my handmaid, Tyra, is." She paused there before forcing the words out. "The healer thinks she has the plague."

Plague. The word hung between them like a death sentence.

Broderick's features tightened. "Is he sure?"

"The signs are there." Bile stung the back of Drew's throat. "Her fingertips have blackened, and she has swellings under her arms and at her groin."

Did she imagine it, or did Broderick's face pale at this description? The symptoms of the sickness that was now sweeping across Scotland were clear enough.

There could be no doubt.

"How is he treating her?" he asked, the rough edge to the warrior's voice betraying his alarm.

Drew screwed up her face. "In the usual fashion ... not that it seems to do much good. Blood-letting and a tonic of vinegar and heather honey. He's rubbed raw onion over the swellings on her skin ... the chamber reeks of it."

Their gazes fused then and held for a long moment. It was unusual for Drew to interact with her brother's right-hand in such a fashion. She and Carr Broderick had lived under the same roof for over fifteen years now, but until recently their paths rarely crossed. However, with Ross Campbell's disappearance, Broderick had taken on his role as Captain of the Dunan Guard. These days, the warrior was never far from her brother's side.

"I should go and inform Duncan," she said, breaking the tense silence between them. "It's the first sickness inside the broch ... he will want to know."

"I will tell him, milady," Broderick replied with a brusque nod.

The tension that had turned Drew's shoulders to stone eased just a little. She'd been avoiding her brother recently, and had taken to having most of her meals alone in her solar. It wasn't like her to shrink from confrontation—but she needed time to think, to plan.

Of late, Duncan had become not only a danger to himself, but to the MacKinnon clan. Ross Campbell had been her only ally here—and just hours before she'd helped him flee Dunan, he'd agreed to support her if she ever made a move against her brother.

Campbell was no good to her now though. She didn't even know if he still lived. And with his absence, she was truly alone here.

She could ask Carr Broderick for help, but the man was an unknown quantity. It appeared his loyalty to her brother was unshakable. She couldn't confide in him.

"I shall go and inform the servants then," Drew said, injecting a brisk note into her voice. She needed to get ahold of herself. Fear of the sickness wouldn't help any of them. The number of cases inside Dunan village was rising sharply with each passing day—it had only been a matter of time before someone within the broch fell ill.

And now that it had happened, they'd have to deal with it.

"Very good, milady," Broderick replied. The usual impassive mask the man wore had slipped back into place. You would never have thought the news about the sickness had alarmed him. Drew admired the man's self-control, his strength.

Watching him turn and stride off down the hallway in search of her brother, Drew inhaled slowly and wiped her damp palms upon the skirts of her kirtle.

Aye, they'd all have to be strong in the face of what lay ahead.

Carr Broderick was sweating as he stood before MacKinnon—a chill sweat that made his skin crawl. Dread ran its cold fingertip down his spine, causing his pulse to slow. Yet he kept his reaction to Lady Drew's news hidden under a mask it had taken him years to master.

He wasn't the only one shaken by news that the sickness had entered the broch. In all the time he'd served the MacKinnons, he'd never seen Lady Drew scared. Yet, the pallor upon her lovely face, the alarm in those iron-grey eyes, had made him want to reach for her, enfold her in his arms.

Something he would never do.

Lady Drew was likely to scratch his eyes out if he ever attempted such a thing.

Nonetheless, he'd noted the slight tremor of her body, the way her throat had bobbed as she swallowed. She was alarmed, and she was right to be. The devil had entered their home. How many of them would survive his visit?

A scowl split Duncan MacKinnon's forehead once Broderick had delivered his news. The clan-chief sat before the hearth, a goblet of wine in hand, his wolfhound, Bran, curled at his feet.

"If the maid is ill, I don't want her in my broch," he growled, his voice slurring slightly. It was still an hour or two till the noon meal, yet MacKinnon was clearly not on his first sup of wine. Ever since Lady Leanna's disappearance, MacKinnon seemed always to have a goblet of wine in hand—a habit that had turned his already mercurial temper into something even more dangerous.

Carr chose his words very carefully around the clan-chief these days.

"But the healer is attending her," he ventured. "Surely, it's dangerous to move the lass?"

"Get her out of my broch," MacKinnon ground out. He rose unsteadily to his feet, stepped over his sleeping hound, and stumbled to the sideboard, where he helped himself to another goblet of wine. "And burn her bedding … that is my final word. Don't argue with me, Broderick."

Silence filled the clan-chief's solar. The window was open, revealing a monochrome sky beyond. A breeze, chill for this time of year, blew inside causing the lump of peat in the hearth to glow bright red. However, the draft couldn't mask the stale odor of wine and sweat that emanated from the clan-chief.

Carr studied MacKinnon as he returned to his place by the hearth and sank back down in his chair. Of late, his master's state-of-mind had started to concern him. MacKinnon had always liked to drink, but there was a recklessness to his behavior in the past days, a bleakness in his gaze that worried Carr.

Ross was the clever one, he mused. *He got out while he could.*

No one here knew that he'd caught up with Ross Campbell and Lady Leanna in Knock, a fishing village on Skye's south coast, where they'd been about to board a merchant's birlinn. He'd confronted Ross, but had let him leave all the same.

Today, he wished he'd gone with him.

He wondered what MacKinnon would do if he knew. Most likely lunge for his dirk before plunging it into Carr's belly. If the clan-chief ever discovered what he had done, his life would be forfeit.

"How long are ye going to stand there, gawping at me?" MacKinnon eventually growled. "Instead of bothering me with ill news, how about some good tidings instead?" He swirled the wine in his goblet, his grey eyes narrowing as he fixed Carr with a glare. "How goes the search for Craeg the Bastard?"

Carr returned the clan-chief's stare. "I have half the Dunan Guard out searching for him now, MacKinnon," he replied. "We have redoubled our efforts, especially along the borders and coast. He may be trying to leave Skye."

A muscle ticked on MacKinnon's jaw at this admission. Of course, as much as his half-brother had caused him trouble over the years, the clan-chief didn't want him to move on. Instead, he wanted the man caught.

A heavy sensation settled upon Carr then, like two large hands had just fastened over his shoulders and were pushing him into the floor. He would never admit as much to MacKinnon, but he held out little hope of finding the outlaw leader, or his band of followers. In all the years they had caused strife here, MacKinnon had only been able to get close to them a couple of times.

They were ghosts, appearing and disappearing at will.

Some of the folk of this land actually believed that the outlaws were Fair Folk who disappeared into fairy mounds at dusk. However, Carr knew better. He'd seen the village hidden deep within that lost valley. After the skirmish with the band a month earlier, he'd searched the ruins of the camp, and had been surprised to see how settled they'd been there. He'd discovered a forge, store huts full of food, and fields full of crops on the southern slopes of the valley.

They weren't supernatural beings; they were just very good at hiding.

"The Bastard mustn't slip through our net," MacKinnon said, his voice rough now. "I want ye to bring him to me in chains."

Duncan MacKinnon shifted in his chair and stared moodily down at his goblet of wine. The rich liquid gleamed darkly up at him, but after Carr's visit, he'd lost his taste for it. He'd sent his right-hand on his way and was grateful to be left alone in the solar once more.

But, of course, that left him alone with his thoughts. And they were bleak these days.

Muttering a curse, Duncan ran a tired hand over his face. Fatigue pulled him down, making his limbs feel leaden and his body ache. He was only forty winters old, so why did he suddenly feel like an old man?

With a sigh, he set his goblet aside on the stone edge of the hearth, and leaned down, ruffling Bran's ears. The charcoal grey brindled wolfhound stirred from its sleep and sat up, pushing against his leg.

Warmth rushed through Duncan, and he let the hound lick his hand.

No matter what happened in his life, despite his many disappointments and betrayals, he could always rely on Bran. Dogs were uncomplicated. No matter what he did, Bran would remain at his side.

Heaving himself up out of his chair, Duncan walked unsteadily to the open window of the solar. There, he braced himself against the stone ledge, closing his eyes for a few moments as his head spun. He'd consumed too much wine on an empty stomach. A foolish thing to do.

I must stop drinking so much. With everything he had to deal with at the moment, he needed a clear head. He needed to be strong. And that also meant that he had to start eating properly again.

Duncan opened his eyes. He would make sure he cleared his platter at the noon meal today. He would also resume his afternoon swordplay sessions with Carr. At his age, he couldn't afford to let his physical condition slip.

The clan-chief's gaze swiveled then to the view beyond his window. He spied industry in the bailey below: men shoeing horses, and servants carrying barrels of ale and sacks of grain into the broch. Beyond, the roofs of Dunan village itself rose. Outside the walls, stark against the jade pinewood, he saw smoke rising in a dark column.

A lump rose in Duncan's throat at the sight of it.

Funeral pyres.

Just after daybreak, he'd been returning from a ride out with his hounds when he'd seen the folk of Dunan carrying the dead out of the fortress.

There had been a dozen of them, and he'd heard that at least another dozen were gravely ill in 'The Warren'. The sickness now had Dunan in its grip, and he was powerless to stop it.

The pressure in Duncan's throat increased, clamping down and making it hard to breathe. This stronghold belonged to him, and the lives within it were his responsibility.

Yet for the first time since he had assumed the role as clan-chief of the MacKinnons, Duncan wished the charge had fallen to someone else.

7

Unnatural Behavior

ONE DAY SLID into the next, and Coira grew
increasingly jittery and on edge.

Kilbride felt overrun with men.

Coira didn't like it. Her past had left her with a
distrust of males. The best thing about coming to live at
Kilbride had been the ability to thrive in a female
environment. She didn't need to be wary of her
companions here, or drop her gaze in fear of
inadvertently enticing a man. She didn't need to lock her
door at night, scared that some drunken letch might
stumble in and collapse on top of her. It had happened
once at *The Goat and Goose*. But here, Mother Shona
ruled. And she was a woman who taught others to be
strong. She'd given Coira skills that made her feel as if
she was taking back just a little control over a world that
had nearly destroyed her.

One evening, as the shadows lengthened and a chill
breeze blew in from the sea, Coira decided that she
needed to relieve some tension, to forget about the
worries that plagued her.

It was bad enough that they were harboring a
fugitive—although Coira had slowly relaxed in Craeg's
presence over the past days—but they now had Father

Camron and his flock to contend with. The mere sight of the abbot's self-righteous face put her teeth on edge.

She'd deliberately avoided practicing with her quarter-staff since Father Camron's arrival. However, this evening Coira decided to take a calculated risk and find a private spot away from prying eyes.

Retrieving the stave from her cell, she made her way to the eastern edge of the abbey grounds, to a secluded area where a small orchard of apple and pear trees grew on the far side of the vegetable plots.

The trees were in full leaf now, the first tiny bulbs of fruit just making an appearance.

Carrying her staff loosely at her side, Coira entered the orchard. A little of the strain within her unknotted, and she deepened her breathing, letting the stress of the past few days release.

In the midst of the orchard, in a small clearing, she halted. There, she began to go through her drills. Immediately, as the staff whistled through the air, Coira started to feel better. The physical exertion eased the tightness in her chest and loosened the rigid muscles in her neck, back, and shoulders. She hadn't realized she'd been so tense.

Sweat trickled down Coira's back between her shoulder blades as she went through her drills again and again—thrusting, spinning, and blocking with her staff. Her blood pulsed in her ears, her breathing now coming in gasps. She had almost reached the limits of her endurance, and was about to stop, when she heard stifled gasps behind her.

Whipping around, Coira's gaze settled upon two black-robed figures standing but a handful of yards away.

Ice slithered down her sweaty back, and her fingers clenched around the staff.

Two young monks, their smooth faces slack with shock, gaped at her. It was almost comical, for the pair stared as if they'd just seen her sprout horns and a forked tail. A heartbeat passed, and then another—and a sickening sensation clawed up Coira's throat from her belly.

How was she going to explain this to Father Camron?

"This is unnatural behavior."

The abbot's voice boomed through the chapter house, making the stained glass windows that lined one side of the small building vibrate.

Eyes downcast, her gaze fixed upon the flagstone floor, Coira wondered how Mother Shona was going to respond. She'd barely been able to meet the woman's gaze since being called in here. Guilt compressed Coira's chest, and she started to sweat. Not from exertion this time but from dread.

"Sister Coira has a different background to most of the nuns here," the abbess finally replied. To Coira's surprise, the woman's voice was serene. Raising her chin, she shifted her attention to where Mother Shona stood, facing the abbot. Hands clasped before her, the crucifix about her neck glinting in the light of the surrounding banks of tallow candles, the abbess appeared unruffled. "Before coming to live with us, she had to fend for herself. She developed skills that most women do not."

The abbess's attention shifted then to Coira. "I have told ye, child. Ye are safe here. There is no need to keep up such ungodly skills."

"I am sorry, Mother." Coira dropped to one knee before the abbess, allowing her to make the sign of the cross above her. "With all the talk of pestilence and outlaws, I grew fearful for our safety here. I wish only to protect the abbey should evil men attack us."

Coira's contrition wasn't feigned. She was truly sorry for putting Mother Shona in this position. She would apologize properly later though, when the abbot wasn't present.

"Foolish, presumptuous woman." Father Camron's harsh voice slammed into her. It grated like a rusty saw. "How dare ye take matters into yer own hands? Have ye not learned to trust in God? Ye have no need to take up arms ... not if yer faith is strong enough." His face twisted then. "Ye are no better than that *witch*, Annella MacNichol. I saw how she wielded knives. Such skill is unnatural in a woman!"

Tearing her gaze from the abbess, and remaining upon one knee, Coira forced herself to look at the abbot. His high colored face had gone the shade of a boiled beet. His dark eyes blazed, and his heavy jaw was locked in rage. Wisely, she did not contradict him. Instead, she swallowed what little pride she had left, clasped her hands before her, and bent her head. "I am sorry, Father. I should know better. Please forgive me for my sin. Please forgive me for my lack of trust."

A brittle silence settled in the chapter house. The three of them were alone in here. A small mercy at least; Coira was spared an audience to witness her humiliation. Even so, her belly clenched and indignation pulsed like an ember under her breastbone. Her faith was strong these days. Mother Shona had taught them that a nun could do the Lord's work while learning how to defend herself. There was no shame in it, and it galled her to apologize to the abbot.

It had been years since she'd knelt before a man, and she hated the feeling.

When the abbot spoke again, his voice hadn't softened. "It is not entirely yer fault, Sister. Mother Shona has clearly been too lenient with ye over the years." His attention shifted to the abbess, his gaze narrowing. "This transgression should never have happened. Ye should take a rod to this nun for her behavior."

Coira's breathing hitched. The heat that pulsed within her now threatened to ignite into a raging furnace. She couldn't believe the abbot would suggest such a thing, and yet she shouldn't have been surprised. Just the night before, she'd seen him smack one of his monks around the ear for accidentally spilling some ale during supper.

Shifting her attention back to the abbess, Coira saw, for the first time, Mother Shona's calm splinter. Her jaw tensed, and she frowned. "There will be no violence here,

Father. I have never lifted a hand to any of the nuns here. And I never will."

Father Camron snorted. "Well, I have no such qualms, Mother. Find me a good stick, a rod of willow will do nicely, and I will see to this nun for ye. He glanced back at Coira, his dark eyes gleaming. "I'll teach her a lesson she won't forget."

"I repeat, Father, there will be no violence at Kilbride." The steel in Mother Shona's voice was evident now. She was done holding back her irritation with this man. Coira tensed at this realization. The last thing she wanted was for Mother Shona to lose her temper with the abbot. He could make life very difficult for them all if he so chose.

Witnessing the stand-off between the pair, a hollow sensation lodged itself in the pit of Coira's belly. Mother Shona wasn't going to back down—and from the look on the abbot's face, neither was he.

"Sister Coira knew harsh treatment before coming to live here." Mother Shona's voice was low and firm, although the hard edge was still there. "I vowed that she would only ever know kindness within these walls."

Coira's throat thickened at these words. It was true; the abbess had always treated her with respect.

However, Mother Shona hadn't yet finished. "The Sisters of Kilbride entrust me with their well-being. I will not betray that trust," she continued, her gaze never wavering from the abbot. "Sister Coira will spend the night praying before the altar in the kirk for her transgression. That will be sufficient punishment."

"That's not enough," Father Camron countered, a vein now pulsing in his temple. "Ye need to set an example!"

Mother Shona folded her arms across her chest, her chin lifting as she eyeballed her adversary. "And I am," she said, her tone hardening. "If one of my flock strays, they will be guided back to the fold. My methods differ from yers, Father, but in the end we both serve our Lord the best we can. That's all that matters."

Coira welcomed the solitude and peace inside the kirk. A night here was supposed to be her penance, yet part of her actually looked forward to it.

After supper and Compline, the abbey entered the Great Silence. Usually, she'd have gone to the infirmary to tend to her patient, but the abbess had insisted that she was to go to the kirk immediately to begin her prayers. As such, Coira had sent Sister Mina to attend to Craeg in her stead. The nun would bring the man some gruel and bread, and check that his fever hadn't returned.

Coira would visit him again in the morning.

A frown marred her brow when she thought about her patient. With each passing day, his presence here grew riskier for them all. Craeg kept insisting he should leave, and yet he still wasn't well enough to do so. Coira hoped Sister Mina would be careful when she went to the infirmary.

Strangely, she felt a little envious that the novice would get to spend time with Craeg this evening, would hear of his escapades with his band of outlaws. She liked hearing his stories, but tonight she'd do penance instead.

Kneeling upon the stone floor of the kirk, Coira winced. The flagstones were ice-cold. Despite that the warmer months were now upon them, the air inside the kirk was chill, and it remained so even on the hottest days in summer.

It was going to be a cold, uncomfortable night.

She had no cushion to protect her knees from the cold stone, and after a short while, her kneecaps began to ache, numbness creeping up her thighs. But, hands clasped before her, Coira didn't move. Head bowed, she murmured prayers of penance, asking the Lord for forgiveness for her sins.

However, she didn't ask forgiveness for practicing with her quarter-staff—only that she'd let selfishness blind her to the risk she was taking.

She was truly sorry about that. Sorry too that she'd compromised Mother Shona.

Slowly, the tension ebbed out of her. As always, when she prayed in the kirk, Coira felt God's presence settle upon her like a warm, comforting blanket. She hadn't been devout before entering the abbey, but the kindness she'd found here had made her change her views.

The evening stretched on, and eventually the witching hour approached. Twice Coira heard someone enter the kirk. The first time, it was a gentle presence, and although Coira didn't look up from her prayers, she sensed that it was Mother Shona, checking in on her. The second visitor arrived much later, at the time of night when the world seemed to hold its breath. The heavy scuff of sandaled feet on stone approaching from behind warned her that it was not the abbess or any of the other nuns.

A man approached.

Coira's spine stiffened, her body growing taut. Even after all these years, her instincts were honed around men. After over a decade now, she still didn't trust them. It couldn't be Craeg, for the man was barely able to rise from his sickbed. No, she knew, without even glancing up, who her visitor was.

Father Camron.

The footsteps halted behind her, and she heard the rasp of a man's breathing. When he spoke, his voice was barely above a whisper. "Ye are a wicked woman, Sister Coira. Don't think yer averted gaze, and yer feeble apologies, have fooled me. I see through it all."

Coira's mouth went dry, her heart hammering against her ribs. Wisely, she kept her gaze downcast, her hands clasped tightly in prayer. She squeezed her eyes shut and continued to murmur her prayer. "Please, Lord, forgive us our trespasses, as we forgive those who trespass against us, and lead us not into temptation, but deliver us from evil."

"Empty words," the abbot murmured. "But lucky for ye, the abbess guards ye all with the fierceness of a mother hen." She heard the whisper of his feet on stone as he moved closer still. Coira's skin prickled, her breathing accelerating.

If he touches me, I'll defend myself.

"But be warned." His voice lowered further still. "I'm watching ye."

8

Until My Last Breath

"I WAS HOPING to see ye, Sister," Craeg greeted Coira with a smile when she pulled aside the hanging and stepped inside the alcove. However, an instant later, his expression grew serious. "Ye look as if ye haven't slept?"

Coira huffed and let the hanging fall behind her. "I haven't."

The air was close in here. She didn't like it. Coira believed that the sick should have free-flowing air around them, for it chased away ill humors. But it was too risky to set this patient up near the window. One of Father Camron's monks could peek into the infirmary at any time. The hanging wouldn't keep prying eyes at bay forever, but it was the best she could do in the meantime.

Stiffly, for her knees ached with each step, Coira made her way toward the sleeping pallet. In one hand she carried a bowl of warm water, in the other her basket of healing herbs.

Observing her patient, Coira was pleased to see that color had returned to Craeg's cheeks. A sheen of sweat no longer covered his skin, and his eyes weren't fever bright as they had been. He sat, propped up on a nest of pillows.

The man exuded an impatient energy—Coira could see he wasn't the type used to being forced to stay still.

"I sometimes have trouble sleeping too," he admitted with a boyish grin. "Maybe it's the result of a guilty conscience."

"I sleep like a bairn," Coira replied, arching an eyebrow. "It wasn't restlessness that caused my sleepless night. I transgressed yesterday, and so had to spend the night praying as penance."

Hs gaze widened. "A nun who doesn't follow the rules ... I'm intrigued."

"The abbot wasn't," Coira answered, breaking eye contact as she set the basket down on the end of the bed. "How are ye feeling?"

Craeg didn't answer right away, and Coira eventually glanced up, frustrated that he wasn't letting her change the subject. She was tired and irritable. She didn't want to discuss herself. Their gazes held for a long moment, before his smile faded. "Much better, I guess. My side doesn't hurt as much as it did. Can I go now?" She caught the restlessness in his voice.

Coira frowned. "It depends on how yer wound is faring."

"Take a look at it then." Craeg sank back against the pillows and pushed down the coverlet covering his bare torso.

After a moment's hesitation, Coira moved close to him. Even injured and weakened, this man had a strong physical presence. His chest was broad and heavily muscled, with a light dusting of dark hair across it that narrowed to a thin strip at his belly. And that strip then disappeared under the waist band of his breeches.

Coira hurriedly averted her gaze. It wouldn't do for a nun to stare at a man's groin, even if it was clothed.

Stepping forward, she removed Craeg's bandage with deft, practiced ease. Observing the wound to his flank, Coira relaxed a little. She had packed the arrow hole with a poultice of woundwort, and it had done its work beautifully, withdrawing the evil humors from the flesh.

The wound no longer festered, and it was beginning to heal.

Coira glanced up, catching Craeg's eye once more. "It looks like it is mending well."

Craeg's mouth lifted at the corners. "Thanks to ye."

Coira smiled. This man had a warmth and charisma that was hard to resist. No wonder he had inspired a band of loyal followers—men and women who lived as fugitives simply because they believed in him.

I'd believe in him too.

Catching herself, Coira straightened up.

Mother Mary, what a foolish thought.

Coira set her jaw and began to clean the wound. Fatigue had clearly turned her witless this morning. She then reached for her basket and extracted a small wooden pestle and mortar. "I need to mix up some more woundwort," she murmured. "Just to make sure the injury doesn't sour again."

"I should leave," Craeg said after a pause. "My band is waiting for me ... if I don't reappear soon, they will think I have died here."

Coira glanced up to find him watching her, his expression shuttered. "Ye are gaining strength," she replied, holding his gaze, "but ideally ye should rest for another day or two before moving on."

A muscle bunched in his jaw. "I don't have a day or two. My brother still hunts me ... I can't stay here."

"I'm aware of that ... but if ye leave before ye are ready, all my work will be undone."

Silence fell between them for a long moment, before Coira moved to the small table next to the bed and lowered herself onto a stool; it was hard not to groan as she did so. Her knees felt as if they belonged to a crone this morning. Trying to ignore her aching back and legs, she transferred a handful of fresh herbs to her mortar. She then began to mash them.

"The hatred between ye and MacKinnon," she said finally, as the hush drew out between them. "It runs deep?"

He huffed a bitter laugh. "Aye … deeper than most realize."

"Clan-chiefs sire bastard bairns all the time," Coira pointed out as she continued to mash the woundwort into a paste.

"Aye, but few threaten the order of things," Craeg replied, his voice lowering. Coira could tell from his tone that he didn't want to continue this conversation. But, glancing up at him, Coira's interest blossomed further.

"How so?" she asked.

Craeg's face tensed, and Coira instantly regretted the question. What was she doing interrogating the man anyway? It was best she knew as little about him as possible, best that she healed him and then got rid of him.

"I see ye know of my origins," he said, a wry tone creeping into his voice.

Coira nodded. These days, there were few folk in this territory who didn't know that Craeg was the result of Jock MacKinnon plowing a whore. The story had often been told at *The Goat and Goose* during Coira's time in the brothel. Years earlier, Craeg's mother was said to have worked there before succumbing to consumption.

"I grew up in a brothel," he said, glancing away. Did she imagine it, or did he seem embarrassed by this admission. "While Ma worked, it was my job to clear tables, empty hearths, and run errands for the woman who ran the place."

Coira tensed. *Maude*. "Were ye ill-treated there?" she asked softly.

Craeg's mouth twisted, although he shook his head. "Not particularly … I was seen more like an annoying hound that gets under everyone's feet. Although as I grew into a strapping lad, I had my uses. It became my role to throw out any patrons who became violent or mouthy. Maude—the woman in charge—kept me on, even after Ma died … and that's how I met my brother."

Coira stopped mashing the woundwort, her breathing slowing. She hadn't heard this part of the story.

"Our father continued to visit *The Goat and Goose*, even after Ma died," Craeg continued. His gaze looked past her now, as if he was no longer seeing his surroundings, but his old life. "And one day he brought Duncan along ... so that his son might bed his first woman." Craeg paused there, his gaze snapping back to the present. He favored Coira with a harsh smile. "It was hate at first sight."

"He knew who ye were?"

"Aye ... everyone in Dunan did."

Coira swallowed hard before picking up the mortar and carrying it over to Craeg. Perched on the edge of the straw-stuffed mattress, she began packing his cleaned wound with the paste. She wished now that she hadn't been so curious about Craeg's past. Even the mention of Duncan MacKinnon made a chill shiver down her spine.

"Our father didn't help matters," Craeg continued, a bitter note in his voice. "He acknowledged who I was ... in front of Duncan ... deliberately provoking him."

Coira's chin raised, her gaze narrowing. "Why would he do that?"

"He wanted his son—his *legitimate* son—to prove himself, I guess. He wished to see if Duncan would be threatened by me ... and he was." Craeg paused there, his eyelids fluttering closed, his face going into spasm. Coira knew that although she was trying to be gentle, she was hurting him as she applied the salve.

"It's alright, I'm almost done here," she murmured.

Craeg nodded, and she saw that sweat had beaded upon his forehead. She didn't know how the man thought he was going to get up and walk out of here today. His injury, and the sickness that had followed, had seriously weakened him.

"We fought once, in the brothel," Craeg said finally, his voice rough with pain. He continued to keep his eyes shut, his big body tense while Coira completed her ministrations. "He was rough with one of the lasses, and she was in tears. I confronted him downstairs, and he attacked me." A smile curved Craeg's mouth then, unexpectedly. "I split his lip, blackened his eye, and sent him away." The mirth faded as quickly as it had appeared. "And that was when the tide turned against me.

"Until then, I'd been liked in Dunan ... but as the months passed, the mood changed. Vendors refused to serve me at market, women spat at me when I passed them on the street, and when business slowed at *The Goat and Goose*, I was blamed. I'd just passed my sixteenth winter when I found myself living rough, sleeping in alleyways and begging for crumbs. No one in Dunan would give me a job."

Coira sucked in a breath. She knew what hardship was, what it was like to look hunger in the eye. The outlaw didn't realize how much she understood what he'd gone through. "Why didn't ye leave?" she asked finally.

Craeg's eyes opened, and for a moment their gazes fused. "I eventually decided that I would," he replied softly, "on the day my father died, I realized that there was no future for me in Dunan. Duncan, who was eighteen at the time, would become clan-chief, and what little protection I'd had from him would be gone. But that last night, as I scrabbled for scraps of bread to feed me on the journey I planned to take north into MacLeod lands, Duncan and a group of his friends found me."

Craeg paused there, scrubbing his face with his fist. Coira realized then that this was a tale he rarely shared with anyone. Even though it had happened a long time ago, it clearly still pained him to dredge up the memories.

"One against six isn't good odds," Craeg said, his tone wry now. "They beat me bloody, and then Duncan drew his dirk and slashed me across the face with it." Craeg reached up, a fingertip tracing the fine white scar that ran from his temple to his cheek, skirting his left eye. "They then dumped me in the river outside Dunan and left me for dead."

"But ye didn't die," Coira finished the story for him. "And ye have plagued Duncan MacKinnon ever since."

Craeg flashed her a hard smile, his gaze gleaming. "Aye ... and I will continue to do so until I draw my last breath."

Craeg watched the nun pack up her supplies. Her movements were deft and purposeful, matching the resolute expression upon her face.

He drank her in.

He'd missed her last night. When one of the other nuns had tended to him, he'd been disappointed. As much as he hated to admit it, Sister Coira had gotten under his skin.

Why else would he have been so candid with her?

He rarely spoke of his past. Telling the tale of how his half-brother had nearly killed him still left a sting of humiliation in its wake. That humiliation had fueled his need for vengeance, and he felt it again now.

He liked the way Sister Coira listened to him, the understanding and compassion in those lovely eyes. She lived a sheltered existence here behind the walls of Kilbride, yet he'd sensed that she grasped exactly how difficult his upbringing had been. There had been no shock in her eyes when he'd spoken of his quest for revenge.

Somehow, she understood.

Ye shouldn't be lusting after a nun, his conscience needled him as he continued to observe Sister Coira. She had almost finished tidying up and would soon leave him alone. *Ye shall go straight to hell.*

A grim smile stretched Craeg's lips then. Luckily for him, he wasn't a pious man. As a lad, he'd regularly gone to the kirk to pray. Father Athol had been good to him, had given him soup and bread when his mother was too busy to feed him. Yet despite the priest's best efforts, Craeg had never embraced God. Maybe he'd seen too much ugliness already, even as a lad.

"Sister Coira," he said finally when she picked up her basket and moved toward the hanging that separated his dark space from the rest of the infirmary. "Would ye stay with me a while longer?"

She halted and turned to him, her eyes widening. "I shouldn't really," she murmured, favoring him with a half-smile. "I have chores to do."

"Just for a wee while?" he replied, returning her smile. He knew he could be charming when he wanted, although Sister Coira seemed immune. "I've spent too much time alone of late ... it sends my thoughts to dark places."

Her expression softened at this, and her gaze shadowed. Once again, he got the feeling that she understood him better than anyone ever had. How was that possible?

"Very well," Sister Coira said softly, setting the basket down on the end of the bed and moving toward the stool. "I suppose I can spare a little time."

9

Ships in the Fog

"CRAEG CAN'T REMAIN here."

The tension in Mother Shona's voice made Coira glance up from the psalm she'd been reading. The abbess closed the leather-bound history volume perched upon her knee. She then fixed Coira with a level look.

"It's been over a week … he has to go."

Coira let out a soft sigh. "He's still weak, Mother."

"That may be, but the abbot is showing no signs of leaving. Just this morning he informed me that he wishes to inspect all the buildings within the abbey to ensure 'good practices' are being upheld.

Coira's belly tightened at this news. "How long before he or his monks venture into the infirmary?"

"Exactly." The abbess's small frame bristled with indignation, her brown eyes hard, and her jaw tight. Her outrage at Father Camron's interference was palpable. The two women sat in the abbess's hall. It was a cool, grey afternoon, and Vespers was approaching. Often, Mother Shona spent this time alone, but over the past few days, she'd asked Coira to join her.

Coira wondered if it was to keep her out of trouble, and out of the abbot's way.

"I'm sorry about that incident ... with the quarter-staff," Coira said after a pause. She hadn't properly apologized to the abbess about that, although she'd meant to. "It was a foolish thing to do. I wasn't thinking."

The abbess sighed, leaning back in her chair. Her gaze shifted to where a single lump of peat glowed in the hearth. It was proving to be a cool summer, and without a fire burning, the air inside the hall would have been unpleasantly chill and damp. "I don't blame ye, Sister ... it's hard to break a routine ye are used to. But unfortunately, Camron is sniffing around like a hound on the scent, looking for anything that will damn me." Her gaze shadowed. "And sooner or later, he shall find it."

Alarm fluttered up under Coira's ribcage. It was unlike the abbess to sound so defeated. "No, he won't," she said firmly. "He will stay on a few months, like he did last time, and leave Kilbride empty-handed." She shut the book of psalms with a 'snap'. "Ye are right ... even if he still has some healing to do, the outlaw has to leave. I will see to it this evening."

Mother Shona fixed her with a wary look. "Be careful, Sister. The abbot's monks hide in shadows and listen at open windows and doorways. If ye will take Craeg out of here tonight, ye must wait until well after the witching hour."

"Make sure to leave the gates ajar," Coira replied with a nod, her pulse accelerating as she contemplated just how careful they'd have to be. There was only one way in or out of the abbey. "We will have to leave quickly."

"I will ask Sisters Mina and Firtha to keep watch on the gates tonight," the abbess replied, her brown eyes narrowing. "They will let ye know when it is safe."

The two women watched each other for a long moment, and Coira noted the lines of strain on the abbess's face—lines that hadn't been there a year earlier. The troubles with Ella and Leanna had taken their toll upon her.

A chill settled in the pit of Coira's belly then, a foreboding. For years, Mother Shona had managed to keep the rest of the world at bay. Kilbride had grown strong and prosperous under her guidance, and they'd been able to help the folk of this corner of the isle as a result.

But now, the defenses that the abbess had built were starting to crumble. Mother Shona knew it, and Coira felt it too—the sensation that control was slowly slipping through their fingers.

The future of this abbey now teetered upon the edge of a blade, and it would take very little to topple them all off it.

The wind moaned and sighed against the stone walls of the infirmary, and made the roof creak. The noise was reassuring, for Coira had worried that it would be a still evening, one of those nights when the slightest noise traveled. Even so, the waiting was stretching her nerves to breaking point.

Restless, Coira shifted upon the uncomfortable stool and spared a glance at the man who sat upon the edge of the sleeping pallet.

Clad in the cleaned vest and braies he'd arrived in, but with a new woolen cloak about his broad shoulders, Craeg was dressed and ready to go.

He looked as on edge as Coira felt, his hands clenching and unclenching, his jaw tense.

"How much longer?" he asked finally, his voice a harsh whisper.

"Sister Mina will arrive soon," she replied, hoping that would be the case. "We wanted to wait until we were sure *everyone* was abed."

"But surely no one is awake at this hour?"

Coira huffed. "Ye would be surprised … the abbot and his monks like to keep us all on our toes."

Craeg frowned at this news. "He's determined to find something to discredit the abbess, I take it?"

"Aye … and that's why ye must go tonight."

They fell silent again while the wind continued to whine and rattle. Over the past days, the silences between Coira and Craeg had often been companionable. After he'd told her the brutal story of exactly why he hated his half-brother, Coira had felt an odd kinship toward the outlaw.

He had no idea of her own history with MacKinnon, or of her past at all, but knowing that they'd once lived under the same roof—albeit during different timeframes—made her feel as if this man understood her a little.

His mother had been a whore, after all.

A lump rose in Coira's throat, her body flushing hot and then cold. Even after a decade away from the brothel, a sickly sensation still swept over her whenever she thought about her previous life.

Will I ever outrun the memories?

Coira's breathing started to come in short, fast breaths as her chest tightened. She wanted to run right now. It was torture to sit and wait like this. Time inched forward, and just when Coira decided she would have to get up and start pacing the cramped space of the alcove, she heard a gentle thud of the door.

"Sister Coira?" Sister Mina's voice reached them, low and urgent. "It is time."

Wordlessly, Coira rose to her feet, took the quarter-staff that she'd rested against the wall, and motioned to Craeg. He stood up, his attention shifting to the weapon she held loosely at her side. His gaze widened questioningly, for he hadn't noticed it till now, but Coira ignored him.

It was best he didn't know Kilbride's secrets.

Pushing aside the hanging, Coira led the way into the main space of the infirmary. Sister Mina awaited them by the door, a small figure outlined against the shadows. They followed her outside into a blustery night, shutting the door quietly behind them.

The wind had a bite to it, cold for mid-summer, and clouds raced across a mottled sky. A waxing half-moon hung above, casting the world below in a silvery light.

Coira pulled her cloak close and followed Sister Mina's slender silhouette around the back of the kirk. They hugged the shadows, the sound of their footfalls masked by the whistling wind. Although Coira didn't glance behind her, she sensed that Craeg was following at her heel, no more than three paces behind.

She didn't need to worry about him being careless or noisy. The man was used to making himself one with the darkness, to traveling unseen.

Skirting the edge of the complex of buildings that spread out around the kirk, the three of them avoided the shortest route to the gates, which would have taken them into the open across a wide dirt yard. Instead, Sister Mina took them the long way, past the graveyard and the fowl coop, before they edged along, under the shadow of the high stone wall that encircled the abbey.

Sister Firtha, a lanky young woman who'd just recently taken her vows of perpetuity, awaited them at the gates. Swathed in a slate-grey cloak, the nun blended in perfectly with the darkness. When she stepped forward to greet them, Coira's step faltered, her heart leaping in her chest.

Placing a hand over her thudding heart, Coira nodded to Sister Firtha. Without a word, Sisters Firtha and Mina both went to the gates—high slabs of oak and iron. From a distance the gates appeared closed, yet this close, and now that her eyes had adjusted to the darkness, Coira realized that they were indeed ajar. The two nuns hauled them open, creating a gap of around two feet.

Coira and Craeg squeezed through it. As she crept away and scanned her surroundings, Coira heard a soft creak as the nuns pushed the gates closed once more. They'd leave them ajar ready for her return, hopefully sooner rather than later.

Still not speaking, she led Craeg east, into the hazel wood that flanked the abbey. Earlier that evening he'd told her that direction was the closest to where he was headed. Craeg had been careful not to reveal any detail about the location of the new outlaw camp.

She supposed he was being tightlipped for her benefit, not just for his. If she didn't know where he and his band were hiding, she couldn't betray them, even under duress.

As soon as they entered the woods, a little of the tension that had coiled tight within Coira eased. They were outside the abbey walls now at least, and she was confident that no one had seen them leave. Father Camron would now be none the wiser that they'd been harboring a wanted criminal inside the walls.

It was beautiful amongst the trees, with the moonlight frosting them. Coira rarely walked in the woodland after dark, and despite the roar of the wind through the branches, the peace settled over her, soothing her jangled nerves.

Behind her, she heard Craeg's heavy tread and the whisper of his breathing. He walked close now, so she slowed her stride, mindful that he'd been bed-ridden for the past week.

"How are ye feeling?" she murmured, slowing further so that he drew up alongside.

"A bit weak, but well enough," he replied in a voice that warned her from inquiring further. Of course, his injury would be paining him, but he was stubborn and he wouldn't tell her that.

Ye need to stop fussing, Coira reminded herself. *He's no longer yer patient.*

No, he wasn't, but she worried for him nonetheless. An odd sort of friendship had struck up between them in the past days, and she'd found herself looking forward to her trips to the infirmary. Despite that he couldn't linger at Kilbride, she knew Craeg shouldn't be up and about this soon, not after being so ill.

They continued walking, side-by-side now, the wind tugging at their cloaks, until they reached a small glade. They were around ten furlongs east of the abbey, and here the land sloped upwards. If they were to keep walking in the same direction, the trees would soon give way to foothills. And then shortly after that, they would stand under the shadow of great mountains.

Craeg halted in the midst of the glade and turned to Coira.

Moonlight filtered in, highlighting his face in sharp angles. However, his eyes were dark as his gaze settled upon hers. "This is where our paths diverge," he said softly. "It's not safe for ye to travel any farther, Coira."

The intimacy in the way he spoke her name made Coira catch her breath. She'd never thought her name a beautiful one, but it was when *he* said it. Warmth spread across her chest, and she was glad the darkness hid the blush she was sure now stained her cheeks. "It's *Sister* Coira," she managed finally, her voice higher than usual.

"Aye ... it is." He stepped closer to her, dipping his chin just a little so that he could continue to hold her gaze. "Ye saved my life ... and I will never forget it. Ye are an angel."

An angel.

Coira's breathing quickened, as if she'd just been running. The low timbre of his voice, the sensuality of it, made her struggle to catch her breath. For the first time, his nearness, the heat of his body, caused her to feel light-headed.

What was the man doing? It almost seemed as if he was trying to seduce her.

"I am a healer," she finally managed, cursing the sudden huskiness in her voice. "I wasn't going to let ye die, was I?"

"No." There was a smile in his voice now, a masculine self-confidence that was both attractive and irritating. And yet she wasn't cowed by him. For years, she'd been afraid of men—any man. The first few farmers from Torrin she'd tended had terrified her; big men with rough voices and hot stares. She'd been sure they'd take liberties, and yet they hadn't.

Craeg was taller and stronger than her. He was a warrior used to living rough, and he shared the same blood as a man who'd used and tormented her. But he wasn't Duncan MacKinnon. The past days had made that evident.

He stepped even closer to her then, and suddenly she realized that they were standing little more than a hand-span apart. Coira lifted her chin, holding his eye.

She heaved in a steadying breath. The air seemed to have been sucked out of the clearing, and her surroundings disappeared. The roar of the wind, the chill of the night air, the rich smell of damp earth and vegetation—all of it faded. Craeg dominated her senses.

"Ye and I are but ships passing each other in the fog," Craeg said softly, his voice husky now, "but know this, Sister Coira ... if things were different. If I wasn't a fugitive, and if ye weren't a Bride of Christ, I would do all I could to make ye mine." His hand reached up and, gently, his knuckles brushed her cheek. Coira stopped breathing, stopped thinking. "I've never met a woman like ye," he concluded softly, "and I doubt I will again."

10

Unrepentant

I WOULD DO all I could to make ye mine.

Craeg's words whispered to Coira, mocked her, all the way back to Kilbride. She strode out briskly, cheeks burning, yet his voice, rough with longing, still followed her.

I've never met a woman like ye, and I doubt I will again.

They were bold words, charming words, and yet they had drawn a web around Coira. And she'd been ensnared by them. Once he'd finished speaking, they'd stared at each other for a long, drawn-out moment—and then he'd stepped back from her, dropping his hand and breaking the spell.

Clutching her staff so hard her knuckles ached, Coira had spun on her heel and taken off back the way she'd come.

They're just words. Aye, but words had power. Hadn't Coira been her most frightened when Duncan MacKinnon loomed over her, whispering cruel, hateful things?

Why hadn't she seen this coming? All these days Craeg had been her patient and she hadn't realized that he'd developed feelings for her. Coira hadn't encouraged him. She'd treated him as she did all those who needed her help—but that hadn't prevented him from seeing her as a woman.

Looking back, she now saw the signs. The way his gaze often lingered upon her face, the intense way he watched her, and the warmth of his smiles.

How could I have been so blind?

It was improper, both she and Craeg knew it. A man didn't say things like that to a nun, and a nun wouldn't tolerate it. She should have reviled him, should have made the sign of the cross and warded him off like the devil. But instead, she'd turned tail and fled.

Coira's breathing came in ragged gasps. Despite the cool wind whipping against her face, the blush that had started in her cheeks had now spread over her entire torso, pooling in her lower belly.

"Dear Lord," she murmured, horrified by her body's betrayal, "please forgive me." She couldn't believe how swiftly she'd responded to Craeg, how she'd leaned into him as he spoke. For an instant she'd longed for him to dip his head and capture her lips with his. She'd wanted to tangle her fingers in his wild, dark hair, to plunge her tongue into his mouth and—

Stop it!

Coira clenched her jaw so fiercely that pain darted through her left ear. This was wrong, all of it. When she returned to the abbey, she'd spend the night praying on the floor of her cell. She'd do anything to send these lustful thoughts back to whence they'd come.

She hurriedly retraced her steps back to the abbey, and when the high walls of Kilbride loomed before her, Coira sucked in a deep, relieved breath. Despite all the dangers around them, the abbey was still her refuge, still the place where she could shut out the rest of the world.

Pushing the gates open wide enough so that she could slip through, Coira re-entered the abbey. As she'd expected, both Sisters Firtha and Mina had retired to the dormitory for the night. The yard before the kirk was empty, and no cloaked figures waited in the shadows around it.

Coira pushed the gates shut, but didn't risk bolting them. She didn't like leaving the abbey gates unlocked, but even in the wind, the noise would travel. She would just have to hope that no one slipped in.

Heaving a deep breath, Coira edged her way right, past the stables and the guest lodgings—where the abbot and his monks would be slumbering—toward the low-slung complex of buildings that were the dormitories, and the cells belonging to the more senior nuns. And since Coira had lived at Kilbride for many years now, she was considered one of them.

Coira's chest tightened in anticipation at being able to close the door on the world for a few short hours, to be able to put herself back together again and make sense of her jumbled thoughts and emotions.

She'd almost reached the entrance to the lodgings when a man's voice, rough and accusing, cut through the chill night air. "Stop right there."

Light blazed behind her, and Coira abruptly came to a halt. Her heart then started pounding. Without turning, she knew that Father Camron stood at her back and that he was carrying a torch.

"Turn around," he ordered sharply. "Let me see yer face."

"The nun is unrepentant. This time, she must be punished."

Father Camron's voice boomed through the abbess's hall, echoing off the stone walls. Standing a few feet back, her gaze bleary, for she'd just been torn from sleep, Mother Shona winced. "There's no need to bellow, Father," she said wearily. "None of us are hard of hearing."

"I caught her, Mother," the abbot continued, barely lowering his tone. "With that staff of hers. And look at her ... she's wearing a cloak. The nun has clearly been outside the abbey walls!"

Coira said nothing, although she didn't take her gaze off the abbot's face. His dark eyes gleamed, and his cheeks were flushed. He could barely contain his glee at catching her.

"Was she practicing with the quarter-staff again, Father?" Mother Shona asked with a long-suffering tone that Coira knew well. It was one she used with the likes of Sister Elspeth, when the nun came to her telling tales about the 'misconduct' of other sisters.

"No." A little of the abbot's glee ebbed from his face. "But that matters not ... the point is, Sister Coira has no godly reason to leave the abbey at night." His attention swiveled to Coira then, his gaze pinning her to the spot. "What were ye doing?"

"I have trouble sleeping, Father," Coira replied, her voice frosty as she fought anger. It was rising within her like a springtide, and it took all her effort to choke it down. "So I took a walk in the hazel wood. I didn't go far ... and I took my staff with me, for the ground is uneven and I didn't want to trip in the dark."

The abbot gave a loud snort, his broad chest expanding with the force of his disbelief. The large iron crucifix he wore gleamed in the light of the cressets burning upon the surrounding walls. "Ye must take us both for fools, Sister Coira. Ye were out consorting with men, weren't ye? Ye were *fornicating*!"

"Father!" Mother Shona gasped. "How dare ye suggest such a thing?"

"I dare because it is the truth!"

"But ye have no proof."

"I don't need any ... not when I caught her returning from outside the walls." Father Camron rounded on Coira before taking a menacing step toward her. "This time, ye will be flogged ... and I shall wield the rod."

"No, she won't—and *ye* won't." The abbess's voice cut in, flint-hard now. Glancing Mother Shona's way, Coira saw that the last vestiges of sleepiness had disappeared from her face. The abbess's eyes had turned dark and hard, and her nostrils flared.

Coira's belly dropped in response. In all the years she'd lived at Kilbride, she'd never seen Mother Shona look so angry.

"If ye dare take a rod to anyone here, I shall rip it from yer hands and use it upon ye," the abbess said, her voice tight with the force of the rage she was barely keeping in check. "Ye are a guest here, Father. Remember that."

The abbot pulled himself up short, his broad chest expanding even further. His eyes bulged, and he began to breathe noisily, in short, rasping breaths. "I am an *inquisitor*, Mother," he growled. "I can do what I wish."

Mother Shona drew herself up, eyeballing him without the slightest trace of fear. "No ... ye can't." Her voice had turned icy now. Watching her, Coira's breathing caught. How she admired the abbess. Although small in stature, she wasn't afraid to stand up to men. That day Mother Shona had stood her ground against MacKinnon, Coira had been frightened for her. But now watching her face-off against the abbot, her small hands balling into fists at her sides, Coira felt nothing but respect for the woman.

How she wished she was that brave.

It hurt to kneel upon the hard stone floor of the kirk—especially since the bruising upon Coira's knees had only just healed. But it was preferable to a flogging so she bore the pain in silence.

Dawn wasn't far off; she sensed its approach. The interior of the kirk was beginning to lighten as the sky outside the high narrow windows turned from black to indigo.

Closing her eyes, Coira swayed. Fatigue pressed down upon her. She was so tired she could have happily stretched out upon these icy flagstones and gone to sleep.

But instead, she was praying to atone for her misbehavior.

The words of the prayers blurred into each other now, for tiredness had muddled her thoughts. Instead, the abbot's words intruded.

Ye were fornicating!

If the accusation hadn't been so serious, she'd have laughed at its ridiculousness. After what she'd suffered at the hands of men in the past, sneaking out to copulate with one was the last thing she desired.

However, the abbot didn't know of her past—and if he had, he'd likely have just used it against her.

The argument had escalated after Mother Shona had thwarted the abbot. He'd bellowed and threatened, yet the abbess had stood firm.

In the end, he'd turned and stormed from the abbess's hall, leaving a hollow silence in his wake.

Coira's legs had weakened with relief at the sound of the door slamming shut, yet she knew it was but a brief reprieve. Father Camron would be out for her blood now.

At least Craeg got away.

Coira's fingers, clasped together in prayer, curled into each other. Since returning to the abbey, she'd done her best not to think about the outlaw. Having to deal with the abbot had been a distraction, as had her cold and discomfort as she knelt on the floor of the kirk.

But with this last thought, her shields came down.

Suddenly, she was back there in that dark, windy glade, staring up into his eyes. His face had been beautiful in the moonlight, had seemed carven from marble, yet his touch—feather light and reverent—had been warm.

His touch had lit a fire within her. Coira's return to the abbey had banked it momentarily, but now that Craeg crept back into her thoughts, it flared once more.

How she'd wanted him to kiss her. How her fingertips had ached to touch him, to trace that thin silver scar on his face.

A lump rose in Coira's throat, and it hurt to swallow. The abbot would have her flayed for such thoughts. Maybe he wasn't that wrong about her after all.

A nun shouldn't desire a man's touch.

A burning sensation rose behind Coira's closed eyelids, and she squeezed them even tighter shut, forcing back tears. She hadn't wept in years, had thought she'd forgotten how.

This wasn't any good. She couldn't continue like this—as soon as she could, Coira would seek the abbess's counsel. Mother Shona would teach her how to overcome this weakness.

She has to.

11

A Fiery Dawn

IT TOOK CRAEG longer than he'd expected to reach his camp.

His injury had weakened him on a deeper level than he'd realized. Aye, he could walk, yet he seemed to have lost his stamina. It was as if the soured wound and the terrible fever that followed had both sapped him of strength.

As such, he found himself needing to rest numerous times during the journey inland, especially once the land steepened. The woods gave way to scrub-covered hills, and then stony slopes.

The wind whipped against Craeg as he climbed, cooling his heated cheeks. Yet it wasn't enough to keep exhaustion at bay.

Panting, he stopped halfway up the mountainside and lowered himself onto a rock to rest. He reached inside the small leather pack the nuns had given him and withdrew a bladder of beer before taking a few gulps. The liquid revived him, yet his limbs felt as if they were weighted down with boulders.

Once he got to safety, he'd have to spend a few days resting up. He was no use to his people in this state—as weak as a newborn lamb.

Seated there upon the mountainside, staring up at the windy sky, where the clouds chased each other over the glowing face of the moon, Craeg enjoyed a rare moment of solitude. A lot of responsibility had rested upon his shoulders of late. Despite the attack on their old camp earlier in the summer, his followers had swollen in number once more.

Folk throughout MacKinnon territory had heard about the skirmish, and many men—farmers and shepherds mostly—had left their families to join his cause.

Craeg's jaw tensed as he dwelled upon just how much these men trusted him.

He wouldn't let them down. Until now, he'd been content to make his half-brother's life difficult. It had been enough to rob from him, to inconvenience him. But the situation had shifted. MacKinnon had tortured and murdered Craeg's friend. His guard had killed a number of Craeg's followers.

It had been personal before, a grudge that followed Craeg like his shadow. But now the need for vengeance burned like an ulcer in his gut.

I'm going to bring him down.

An idea formed in his mind then—one that would require a huge risk. He'd never be able to get to his half-brother behind Dunan's high walls. Instead, he needed to draw him out.

Craeg's mouth thinned. This time, when Duncan MacKinnon went looking for the outlaws, he'd be ready for him.

Heaving himself up off the rock, Craeg stifled a groan. Sister Coira had bound his side tightly for the journey, and had given him instructions on how to look after the healing wound once he returned to camp. However, he now realized why she'd looked concerned as she'd secured the bandage one last time. It was too early for him to be exerting himself like this.

It didn't matter though. Sometimes circumstance was against you. Every day he lingered at Kilbride increased the risk of his discovery by that visiting abbot.

Craeg moved off, gingerly picking his way up the slope. The going was harder now, and his boots slipped on loose shale. Nonetheless, he pushed himself forward. He needed to reach the camp by dawn.

Yet as he walked, his thoughts returned to the woman who'd saved his life. The nun who'd risked much on his behalf.

Coira.

How lovely her face had been in that clearing, her proud features bathed in the soft glow of the moon. For a few instants, he'd forgotten that she wore a habit under that cloak, that a veil and wimple framed her face.

He'd forgotten she was a nun.

He wasn't sure where his declaration had come from. He certainly hadn't planned to say anything so inappropriate. The past days, he felt as if he'd strayed into a strange dream.

He and Sister Coira had spent many hours together, and during that time a connection between them had been forged. Those expressive eyes were filled with wisdom and understanding, and often shadowed by a sadness that only served to intrigue him further.

Lord, how he'd wanted to kiss her in that glade.

He couldn't believe he'd had the audacity to touch her face. A man didn't *touch* a nun.

And yet, he wanted to do much more than that.

Reaching up, Craeg scrubbed his hand across his face. He needed to stop these thoughts. It was hard enough scaling this mountainside as it was, without a pole in his breeches.

Ye don't make life easy for yerself, do ye? Craeg's mouth twisted. All the women living upon this isle, and the only one he wanted was a Sister of Kilbride. A foolish wish indeed. It was just as well he had other, more urgent, matters to draw his attention now.

The sooner he forgot about Sister Coira, the better.

Dawn was breaking behind the dark bulk of the mountains, when Craeg reached his destination. It was a fiery daybreak, a foreboding one.

Climbing the last slope, this one so steep that he had to virtually claw his way up on his hands and knees, Craeg's mouth thinned.

A Blood Dawn.

The ancient people of this isle had believed such a dawn was an ill-omen, a harbinger of death and destruction. These days, folk were just as superstitious of such a red sky.

Misgiving feathered in the pit of Craeg's belly. Over the last few months, all his neatly laid plans had unraveled. MacKinnon had closed in on him. He couldn't hide forever, and neither could the men and women who followed him. It was definitely time to meet his half-brother in battle.

Breathing hard, Craeg reached the top of the slope and paused. A group of men, leather-clad and bearing drawn swords, awaited him. He wagered the scouts had been observing his journey up the mountainside. Two of them broke away from the group and approached him.

"I knew it was ye." One of the men, a huge warrior with wild red hair, stepped forward, sheathing his claidheamh-mor. "Although ye climb like a woman ... we started to take bets on whether ye would make it by sun up."

Craeg snorted. It was hard not to pant like a winded carthorse. Holding his flank, he favored his friend with a tight smile. "Ye try climbing a mountain with a hole in yer side."

Gunn's gaze narrowed. "How's the wound?"

"Healing. The nuns at Kilbride managed to stop the festering ... and the fever lifted."

"Ye have been away for days." The second man also put away his broadsword. Tall and rangy, with a lean, sharp-featured face, Farlan was at least a decade younger than Gunn and Craeg. "We were beginning to think we'd lost ye."

"Ye almost did," Craeg grunted. "Come on. Leave the others to keep watch and follow me. We'll continue this back at camp. I need to eat something, or I'm going to keel over."

The three men left the mountainside and slithered down a pebbly slope into a narrow ravine. The rock walls of the gorge were so steep that Craeg had to crane his head to see the sky. The heavens looked ablaze now, and Craeg's mouth thinned.

Blood Dawn indeed.

It had been a while since Craeg had left this place, and the ravine was busier than he remembered. It seemed that even more folk had joined them. Word of mouth traveled fast, even among the sparsely populated villages of Skye. Men, with a few women and children among them, were shaking out their bedding and breaking their fast.

A smile stretched Craeg's face as he remembered Sister Coira questioning him about the loyalty of those following him. He took great risks letting the folk of this territory learn of his hiding places. He had to if he wanted to rally more fighters to his side. And yet, till now, none but Brochan had betrayed him. As he'd pointed out to Coira, he wasn't the only one who bore a deep hatred for Duncan MacKinnon.

The rise and fall of voices broke the morning hush, echoing off the surrounding stone, as did the clang of metal. Men sharpened blades as they waited for their bannocks to fry upon iron griddles, and a forge had been built against the valley wall. Craeg passed the smithy hard at work, hammering out glowing splinters of iron that would be fashioned into arrow-tips.

Craeg's smile widened at the sight of such industry. It pleased him to know that his people hadn't been idle in his absence. Although he hadn't announced his plan to face MacKinnon in battle, they had anticipated him.

The folk of this land wanted rid of the oppressive clan-chief as much as he did.

Breathing in the scent of frying bannock, Craeg's empty belly let out a loud growl. There were few things he liked better in the morning than a freshly baked bannock smothered in butter and honey.

At the heart of the ravine, he came upon a large fire pit. A tall woman with curling blonde hair stood over an iron griddle and was flipping a circular cake over. Her attention focused upon her task, she didn't see the three men approach.

"Morning, Fen," Craeg greeted her with a tired smile. He lowered himself down onto a boulder, suppressing a groan as he did so.

God's bones, he felt eighty winters old this morning.

Fen—Fenella—glanced up, her blue eyes widening as her gaze settled upon him. "Craeg! We thought ye were dead."

"I didn't," Gunn interrupted, before seating himself next to Craeg.

Fenella ignored her man, her attention remaining on Craeg. "How are ye feeling?"

"Hungry," Craeg grunted. "How about some bannock?"

"Healed, I see," she replied not bothering to hide a wry tone. "Thinking of yer stomach, as usual?"

Craeg ignored the jibe and instead waited while she cut the bannock into hearty wedges, before smearing it with yellow butter and heather honey.

Watching her, Craeg's mouth filled with saliva. If she didn't hand over a slice of bannock soon, he'd have to beg.

When she did, Craeg flashed Fenella a wide smile.

The first bite nearly made him groan in pleasure. The wedge of bannock was gone moments later, and Craeg had his platter out for another.

"Didn't they feed ye at the abbey?" Fenella asked, dishing Craeg up another two slices.

"Aye ... but no one makes bannocks like ye, Fen," he replied.

"Still haven't lost yer charming tongue I see." Fenella's voice was stern although she was smiling.

"No ... I'd have to be extremely under the weather for that to happen."

Next to Craeg, Gunn snorted. "Stop flattering my woman and tell us what happened ... I take it the nuns won't tell anyone ye were at the abbey?"

The question sobered Craeg. Finishing his third wedge of bannock, he brushed crumbs off his braies. He then met Gunn's eye.

"They kept me hidden ... although things got difficult when the abbey had visitors."

Gunn inclined his head. "MacKinnon?"

"No ... a meddling abbot sent to investigate the abbess."

"Ye know, I've heard rumors about the Sisters of Kilbride," Gunn said, his expression turning thoughtful. "Three men from Torrin arrived yesterday. One of them said that he once spied the nuns sparring with blunted swords. One of his companions added that he'd seen them bring down deer with longbows in the woods."

Craeg went still at this news. He remembered then the iron-tipped quarter-staff that Coira carried. He also recalled how skillfully Lady Leanna had wielded a longbow when she and Ross Campbell had helped defend the outlaw camp earlier in the summer.

"After everything I've seen of late, I'd believe such tales," he murmured. "There's something odd about that abbey."

His companions digested this news, before Farlan spoke up. "Ye will note that our numbers have swelled in yer absence, Craeg."

Craeg nodded, meeting the warrior's eye. "The tide is turning against MacKinnon now ... fear of the sickness has made folk take action. Life was hard enough here as it was, thanks to him."

"We hear that things are getting worse in Dunan," Fenella said quietly. "A man arriving from there yesterday said that they're burning the dead outside the walls."

A chill settled over Craeg at this news. The Grim Reaper had indeed come to Skye. Things were looking bleak for them all, and yet in times like these, folk looked for a savior.

He turned to Gunn then. "How are our coffers looking?"

His friend smiled. "Healthy ... we still have a bag of silver left over from the last raid at Kyleakin."

"Good," Craeg grunted. "See that it's distributed in as many villages as possible in the coming days ... make sure everyone knows the silver came from MacKinnon's purse." He paused then, his gaze sweeping over the faces of his companions. "That raid was our last though. I've had plenty of time to think while I was laid up. I'm done hiding in the shadows. The men who've joined us don't want to rob MacKinnon ... they want to fight him. The hour has arrived for us to bring my brother down."

12

Distracting Thoughts

"FOLK ARE STARTING to flee Dunan, brother," Drew's voice, tense and sharp-edged this morning, made Duncan MacKinnon glance up from buttering a wedge of bannock. "They are saying ye have abandoned them."

The challenge in his sister's tone was evident, and the clan-chief heaved in a slow, steadying breath. He hadn't seen much of Drew lately, although this morning she'd honored him with her presence in his solar while he broke his fast.

"I haven't," he sneered. "But the good Lord has."

"A group of flagellants have taken up residence in the market square," Drew continued. "Did ye realize?"

MacKinnon scowled. His sister's acerbic tone was starting to grate upon him, although her news came as a surprise. "No," he admitted.

Across the table, Drew put down her knife. Those storm-grey eyes narrowed. "They've taken to beating each other with long leather straps studded with sharp pieces of iron … they do it three times a day as a display of penance and punishment for our sins."

Duncan snorted. "Best of luck to them."

"They are saying that our clan-chief is depraved and immoral … that God is punishing Dunan for his wickedness."

A heavy sensation settled across Duncan's chest then, and his belly closed. He'd been enjoying his morning bannocks until this conversation. To cover up the chill of dread that now crawled up his spine, he reached for a cup of milk and took a measured sip.

Nonsense, all of it.

His mother had turned him against religion many years earlier. Every time she'd beaten him, she'd shrieked that he was full of sin and that God would one day punish him for it.

A sudden dropping sensation in his belly made Duncan's fingers tighten around his cup. "And what do ye think, Drew?" he asked finally, meeting her eye. "Do ye blame me as well?"

The woman's boldness made him itch to take his fist to her face. He'd done so before when she'd overstepped, and she'd minded her tongue for a while afterward. However, now that nearly two months had passed since that incident, Drew had grown viper-tongued and critical once more.

His sister's mouth pursed, and he watched her slender shoulders tense as danger crackled between them. "Of course not, Duncan," she replied, her voice as cold as her gaze. "But I thought it worth bringing to yer attention … this outbreak could well put yer position here in danger."

MacKinnon peered down at the horse's hoof, a scowl marring his brow. "Damn the beast … it's got an abscess."

Carr leaned forward, at where the clan-chief still held his stallion's fetlock between his knees. Pus oozed from the horn of the sole. "Aye," he muttered. "That's why he's been favoring his near forequarter."

"Favoring?" MacKinnon replied with a snort. "Curaidh is as lame as a club footed peasant."

As if hearing his master's appraisal, the huge bay courser snorted. Curaidh—Warrior—had been the clan-chief's mount for the past five years. True to its name, the horse was tough. It hadn't foundered once, but this morning it had limped its way out into the yard.

MacKinnon would have to take another horse out hunting.

The clan-chief released Curaidh's fetlock and straightened up. He then gave the stallion an affectionate slap on the shoulder. Watching him, Carr marveled how the clan-chief was always gentler with animals than with his own kind.

Bran sat a few feet away. The wolfhound waited expectantly, ears pricked. MacKinnon always took the dog out hunting.

"See to this, would ye, Broderick," MacKinnon said, meeting Carr's eye. "I'll saddle another horse and ride out."

Carr nodded. He wouldn't be joining MacKinnon and the others on the hunt. Not that he cared. With half of Dunan ill at the present, he found it difficult to relax and enjoy such pursuits. Tyra, Lady Drew's hand-maid, had died two days earlier, and the situation was so bad in the village now that folk were starting to panic.

MacKinnon continued to watch him, his gaze narrowing, as if he had somehow read his right-hand's thoughts. "Have any of the other servants within the broch sickened?" he asked.

Carr's spine stiffened. He hadn't been looking forward to this question—although he'd known MacKinnon would ask it eventually. There was only so long the clan-chief could ignore the worsening situation. "Aye," he admitted softly. "Two of the scullery maids and a stable hand."

MacKinnon broke eye contact then, his gaze swinging around the yard, at where two lads were cleaning tack in the misty morning light. "Get all of them out of the broch," he said, his voice tight. "And if anyone else falls ill, ye are to tell me immediately. Is that clear?"

Carr nodded, heaviness settling in his gut. Lady Drew wouldn't be pleased—she'd told Carr not to bring up the sickness with her brother. She'd known about the three servants who'd fallen ill over the last day, and she'd called Dunan's healer to tend to them.

However, Carr had just let her secret slip.

The clan-chief's gaze settled upon one of the stable lads. "Brice ... saddle me another horse."

"Aye, MacKinnon." The youth dropped the stirrup he'd been polishing and darted back into the stables.

MacKinnon swung around to Carr, a deep frown marring his brow now, his lips parting. Drawing in a deep breath, Carr readied himself for the sharp edge of his master's tongue once more.

However, the arrival of a man on horseback, clattering into the bailey under the stone arch that led down into the village and the North Gate, forestalled the clan-chief.

Both men watched the newcomer approach. He was a heavyset man of around forty winters, clad in a sweat-stained, dusty léine and braies. Red faced, the man rode upon a swaybacked beast that was lathered from the journey, its thin sides heaving.

"MacKinnon?" The stranger greeted them, his gaze settling upon the clan-chief.

"Aye, who are ye?" MacKinnon barked.

"My name is Gowan," the man replied, his voice rough with fatigue. "I'm a smithy from Torrin." He paused there, his throat bobbing. "Ye have sent out word that anyone with news of Craeg the Bastard will be paid ten silver pennies?"

"Aye," MacKinnon growled, "and any man delivering him to me will be paid out his weight in silver."

Gowan's rugged face tensed. "I don't have the outlaw ... but I have news of him. Yesterday afternoon, I spied the Bastard and a group of his men in the woods east of Kilbride."

Silence settled upon the yard.

"How many of them?" MacKinnon asked, his voice sharp now.

"It was hard to tell ... their numbers were many though."

Something dark and feral moved in Duncan MacKinnon's eyes. Slowly, he turned to Carr, his face taut, eager. "Ready the guard ... we ride out within the hour."

Carr nodded and stepped back, preparing himself to do the clan-chief's bidding. However, MacKinnon hadn't finished yet. "Ye will remain here, as steward of Dunan, until my return."

Carr halted, tensing. "Why?"

"My sister's been meddling in my affairs too much of late," MacKinnon growled. "I don't want her in charge of the broch while I'm gone."

Carr's breathing slowed. "MacKinnon," he began, making sure to keep his tone low and respectful. "I'm captain of yer guard ... ye will need me if ye are to face yer brother."

"My *bastard* brother," MacKinnon snarled. "How many times must I correct ye, man?" He paused there, his mouth thinning into a hard line. "I can captain my own warriors, Broderick. Ye are more use to me here. Get the sick out of my broch and keep an eye on my sister. I expect a full report on her behavior when I get back ... ye had better not keep anything else from me."

A dog's soft whine behind them drew the clan-chief's attention then. Bran stood, tail wagging, impatient to ride out.

Favoring his hound with a tight smile, MacKinnon shook his head. "Not this time, lad," he murmured, his tone gentling. "Best ye remain here too. Keep my seat warm while I'm gone."

"Mother Shona ... may I speak with ye for a few moments?" Coira halted before the abbess and lowered herself onto one knee. She'd found Mother Shona in the tiny herb garden behind the kitchens, a rambling space filled with profusions of rosemary, sage, mint, and parsley—as well as a number of healing herbs that Coira used in her poultices and salves.

"Of course, Sister Coira," the abbess replied with a smile. The tension in Mother Shona's expression betrayed her. She made the sign of the cross above Coira and waited while she rose to her feet.

"Lavender?" Coira asked, peering into the basket.

The abbess's smile turned rueful. "I've had trouble sleeping of late ... I thought the scent of lavender might help."

Coira's own mouth curved. "Aye ... it should. My mother always said lavender soothed the soul."

Mother Shona huffed a brittle laugh. "Mine could do with some soothing. The abbot's presence here grates upon my nerves, I'm afraid ... no amount of prayer lessens my desire to slap his impudent face."

Coira's mouth quirked at the abbess's frankness. It was reassuring that Mother Shona also struggled with her baser instincts. It would make it easier to tell her what was on her mind.

"Mother," she began hesitantly. "May I be frank?"

The abbess inclined her head. "Always."

"I too have been a little on edge of late, although I must confess that the abbot's presence here only plays a small part." Coira paused, suddenly unsure how to phrase the rest. It felt strange, frightening, to expose her thoughts to anyone, even the abbess. Coira was used to keeping all her feelings under lock and key. "Craeg ... the outlaw's ... stay here unbalanced me."

Mother Shona's eyes narrowed, her expression sharpening. "We've all been worried that MacKinnon might somehow track him here," she replied softly.

Coira shook her head. "It's not that ... I mean ... I don't want MacKinnon here ... and I'd never turn

someone who needed my help away. It's just that ..."
Coira broke off there once more. The Lord give her
strength, this was harder than she'd anticipated. "Since
Craeg left, I have found myself plagued by ... distracting
thoughts."

The abbess went still at this admission, her brown
eyes widening. Moments passed, and with each one,
Coira's throat tightened further.

I've made a mistake in being so open. Maybe she
shouldn't have confided in Mother Shona.

However, when the abbess spoke, her voice was
gentle. "Ye are attracted to him?"

Coira nodded, feeling even more wretched than
before.

Mother Shona let out a soft sigh. "Come, Sister Coira.
Let us sit together for a few moments."

The abbess led Coira over to the low wooden bench
on the far side of the herb garden. Nestled up against a
wall festooned with flowering honeysuckle, it was a
sheltered, welcoming spot bathed in sunlight. Even so,
Coira started to sweat as she took a seat. Inhaling the
sweet scent, Coira waited for the interrogation to begin.

"Please don't look so grim, Sister," the abbess said
with a sigh. "I'm not going to condemn ye."

Coira, who had been staring down at her folded hands
upon her lap, glanced up. "Ye should," she replied, her
voice rising. "A Bride of Christ mustn't fall prey to lust."

A soft smile curved the abbess's mouth. "The vow of
chastity is perhaps the hardest one for many nuns," she
replied.

Coira's jaw clenched. "But it shouldn't be for me," she
countered, hating the bitterness she heard in her own
voice. "Ye alone know I spent years in a brothel, being
used and abused by men. I should hate them."

"So ye mean to say that ye have never before felt
desire?" Mother Shona asked, surprise lacing her voice.

Coira shook her head, her gaze dropping once more.
She twisted her fingers together, a sour taste flooding her
mouth. "Would ye, in such circumstances?"

It was an impertinent question, but tension had given Coira a sharper tongue than usual. Moments passed, and she braced herself for a chastisement from the abbess. However, none came.

"I imagine some ... who have been in the same position as ye ... do feel desire," Mother Shona said. She spoke slowly, as if choosing each word with care. "There will be women who will never leave the brothel ... even if they have the opportunity to do so. Few would take the risk ye did in order to make a new start."

Coira continued to stare down at her entwined fingers, her throat thickening. The abbess was right. There were a number of women she knew would always remain at *The Goat and Goose*. Some didn't appear to dislike the life, and one or two actually seemed to enjoy servicing patrons. Others grew insensitive to the life over the years. These women had frightened Coira, for when she'd looked into their eyes, they'd been empty. She suppressed a shudder at the memory. She'd feared that she too would end up like that if she stayed.

"Aye, a nun should cast off all earthly desires ... and that includes carnal sin," the abbess continued when the silence between them drew out. "But that does not mean that most of us don't struggle with the vow from time to time."

Coira's chin snapped up. She twisted around so that she faced the abbess squarely. "Have ye?"

Mother Shona smiled. "Ye know that my life hasn't always been as sheltered as it is now."

Of course, the abbess had barely escaped being raped and murdered when her convent on the mainland had been set upon by brigands. But there had always been a gap in her story. Mother Shona was always vague about the time she'd spent with outlaws before her arrival on the Isle of Skye. All Coira knew was that they'd taught her how to wield weapons.

"I have known carnal pleasure," Mother Shona said finally, her words so bald that Coira resisted the urge to flinch. "I have known what it is to love a man ... and to lose him."

Coira stared at her, taking in the abbess's finely boned face. The older woman looked sad.

Mother Shona's gaze shadowed, and she sighed. "As ye know … after I fled from those brigands, I would have surely starved if a group of outlaws hadn't found me," she continued. "They became my family for a time." The abbess's mouth lifted at the corners then. "A man named Aaron led the band. He was charismatic, strong, and so arrogant that just being near him robbed me of coherent thought. The moment he took me in, I knew that I was in trouble."

Coira made a surprised sound at this, but Mother Shona pushed on. "During my time with the outlaws, I simply became Shona, a wild young woman who ran with the wolves. And after the first summer had passed, Aaron and I became lovers." The abbess halted there. She met Coira's eye once more, her gaze gleaming. "I was never happier than when I was with him. We had a hard life, but an exciting one. I never lost my faith though … my prayers were always sacred to me … and he knew what I'd given up to remain with him."

The abbess paused then, her expression changing. Her eyes developed a faraway look, as she lost herself in memories. "Scotland was immersed in dangerous times during those years; we were engaged in a violent struggle against the English. Soon enough, there was an uprising, and our band got dragged into it." Mother Shona's eyes fluttered shut then. "I lost him in the battle that crushed Scottish hope. A few of us survived, but sadly Aaron didn't."

Mother Shona inhaled sharply, her shoulders squaring. "Without Aaron, living as a fugitive lost its appeal. I decided that I would take the veil once more. But this time I traveled to a far-flung corner of Scotland where I could leave my past safely behind me." The abbess shifted her attention back to Coira then, and she gave a wry smile. "Ye see, Sister. Ye are not the only one with a weakness for handsome rogues."

For a few moments, Coira was at a loss as to how to respond. When she did, her voice was subdued. "It must have been hard to go back to a nun's life after all that."

"It was ... at first," the abbess admitted. "But then I realized that it's much easier to take a vow of chastity when ye know exactly what it is ye are giving up. I felt very lucky with Aaron. We had four years together ... years that I will forever cherish. But because of that, I was able to give myself wholeheartedly to serving God." Mother Shona's gaze grew intense then. "What I'm trying to say ... is that what ye felt for Craeg was natural. Ye are a woman, and he is a man ... and men like him are difficult to resist. Take what ye felt for him, cherish it, and put it somewhere safe within yer heart. It is part of who ye are now, but don't use it as a stick to beat yerself with. Such self-blame will only make ye miserable ... and how can ye do the Lord's work then?"

Coira gazed back at Mother Shona. Once again, she had no idea how to respond. The abbess had completely floored her. This woman's wisdom had always been an anchoring force in the abbey, and it was no different now.

A little of the guilt that had formed a hard knot in Coira's chest unraveled. Mother Shona was right; she needed to find a way to make peace with her conscience.

Silence stretched between the two women, and when Coira eventually broke it, her voice was subdued. "There's something else, Mother ... something I have never told ye."

The abbess frowned, and Coira dropped her gaze to her lap, nervousness fluttering in her belly. There was a good reason why she'd never spoken of this to a soul. However, she might never have the opportunity to confide in Mother Shona like this again. She had to tell her everything.

Clearing her throat, Coira forced herself to look up and met the abbess's eye. "Ye know of my past," she murmured. "But I've never told ye about the man who is the real reason I fled to Kilbride ... the man who nearly broke me."

13

The Odds are Against Them

"CRAEG, WAKE UP."

Gunn's rough voice jerked Craeg from a fitful slumber. Sprawled out upon a fur in his tent—a lean-to that had been built up against the rocky side of the ravine—he'd been dreaming. It had been a pleasant dream. He'd been back at Kilbride again, and Sister Coira had been leaning over him, her cool fingertips tracing lines across his naked chest.

However, Gunn brought him rudely back to the present, and the vision of lovely Coira evaporated like morning mist.

"Satan's cods, Gunn. What is it?" Craeg pushed himself up into a sitting position and scrubbed a hand over his face. His heart was racing after being torn from a deep sleep. He felt disoriented in the aftermath.

"Sorry to wake ye," Gunn replied, not sounding sorry in the least. "But we've got a problem, and I thought ye would want to know."

The last of sleep sloughed away, and suddenly Craeg was alert. "What's wrong?"

"The two men from Dunan who joined our ranks a few days ago are both unwell," he replied, his voice flattening. "I'm no healer, but I think it's the sickness."

A chill settled in the pit of Craeg's gut at this news, seeping outward. It was as if he'd just stepped, waist-deep, into a freezing loch. "Where are they?"

"We've isolated them from the rest of the camp in a tent at the end of the ravine," Gunn replied. "Ye had best come and see for yerself."

Craeg walked through the camp, aware of the anxious gazes that tracked his progress. Unlike when he'd returned here from Kilbride, there were no cheery waves and relieved smiles. News of the two sick men had spread through the ravine—faster than any illness could.

If he was honest, Craeg didn't want to go anywhere near the men from Dunan.

He'd been awaiting the arrival of the pestilence for a while now, and the chill the news had given him had not yet abated. But he couldn't show fear or weakness in front of his people. Every man, woman, and child here was his responsibility. They had all come here to aid him, and he wouldn't turn his back on them.

Until this morning, things had been progressing well for the outlaws. Craeg had deliberately been taking his men out on patrols and letting locals catch glimpses of him. One of them was sure to bring word to MacKinnon.

The pungent, woody aroma of burning sage greeted Craeg as he approached the long tent pitched in the shadow of an overhang. Someone had lit burning pots of herbs outside the door. Sage was said to chase away the dark humors that caused sickness. However, right at that moment, Craeg didn't set much store in its ability to ward off the pestilence.

Fenella stood outside, waiting for him, and when Craeg halted before the entrance to the tent, he met her eye. "How bad is it?"

"They both have terrible pains to the belly, and are racked with chills. I'm told these are the first signs," she murmured, her blue eyes shadowed.

Craeg set his jaw. *Great.* "I should speak to them," he said, hoping the reluctance didn't show in his voice.

"Don't get too close," Fenella warned. "They've developed coughs as well."

Craeg set his jaw. Fenella's words weren't making him feel any better—yet he'd never been one to shy away from unpleasant tasks, and so he ducked his head and entered the tent.

A single brazier lit the cramped interior, although the fug of peat-smoke couldn't mask the sour odor of illness.

Two figures lay either side of the brazier, their bodies covered with blankets.

Craeg's gaze swept from the face of one man to the other. They were both awake, both staring at him with fever-bright eyes, their faces taut with fear and pain.

"I'm sorry, Craeg," one of them, the youngest of the two, croaked. "We didn't mean to ... but I fear we've brought the sickness here."

"Ye have had contact with it at Dunan?" Craeg asked, fighting the urge to retreat from the tent.

"Aye," the man rasped. "I served in the Dunan Guard ... but when some of the other warriors fell ill, I panicked."

Craeg went still. "Ye served MacKinnon?"

The man nodded. "Long have I wanted to join ye ... to help the folk of this land rise up against him. With the sickness rife in Dunan, I took my chance."

Craeg held the man's desperate gaze, not sure whether to be angry, flattered, or exasperated. Right now, he felt all three emotions. After a pause, he shifted his attention to the second man in the tent. He was a hulking fellow, the sort that would have been useful in a fight, if he hadn't been so ill.

"Are ye from the Dunan Guard as well?" he asked.

The man shook his head. "I'm a weaponsmith," he said, his weak voice at odds with his powerful frame. "I lost my family to the sickness ... and when it didn't touch me, I thought that perhaps God had spared me." The man halted before taking in a labored breath. "It seems I was wrong."

Stepping out of the tent, Craeg sucked in a deep breath. He was grateful for the steadying aroma of burning sage, and that Fenella and Gunn were both waiting outside for him. Gunn had an arm around Fenella's shoulders, and the pair of them wore somber expressions. Craeg's breathing slowed. God knew how much contact these two had already had with the sick men.

They might be infected ... and so might I now.

A prickly feeling rose up within Craeg then. Gunn and Fenella had been with him from the beginning. They were family to him.

"Does anyone recover from the plague?" Craeg finally asked, dreading the answer.

Gunn shrugged, his expression unusually helpless. Next to him, Fenella's full lips flattened. "From what I hear, it spares some folk," she replied, a husky edge to her voice ... but few who develop the sickness appear to live through it."

Bile stung the back of Craeg's throat. *Not what I was hoping to hear.*

Inhaling deeply once more, Craeg shoved the slithering chill of fear aside; it was the last thing he needed now. Instead, he had to look for a solution. Perhaps there was some way these men could be cured. They needed a healer—a skilled one.

Coira. He didn't like the idea of putting her at risk, yet without her skills, these men would most certainly die.

Craeg raked a hand through his hair and met Gunn's eye. "Get Farlan ... he's the fastest rider amongst us. I need him to deliver a message to Kilbride."

Coira straightened up, her gaze traveling over the girl's slender form, to her flushed face. Lying upon a stuffed straw pallet, the girl wore nothing but a sleeveless shift. "My belly hurts terribly," the lass groaned. "Make the pain go away, Sister."

Coira's breathing grew shallow, her chest tightening as she met the girl's panicked gaze. She was only eight winters old; she didn't understand what was happening to her. "I shall give ye some hemlock juice," Coira murmured. "Hopefully, it will ease yer pain a little."

The lass favored her with a tremulous, grateful smile, and Coira's throat started to ache in response. Hemlock juice would only dull the pain, but it would not provide a cure.

It had only taken Coira a few moments alone with this girl and her mother, who was also poorly, to ascertain that the scourge had reached them. Both mother and daughter were at early stages, for there were no signs of swellings at the armpit or groin—the 'plague boils' that were said to form on the skin as the illness progressed. However, they both had a hacking cough, stomach pains and chills, and they were both horribly weak.

Also, Coira had noted that they had inflamed flea bites upon their arms, a sign that both mystified and confused her.

A few feet away, the mother started to cough, the sound muffled by the bundle of cloth she now pressed against her mouth. Coira had insisted they both did that, the moment she entered the dwelling.

She knew little about this illness, although she realized that most healers would try to fight it by bleeding the patient and rubbing certain herbs upon the skin. Coira—like her mother before her—wasn't an advocate of bleeding. In her view, it merely weakened the patient.

With little news of the plague to aid her, she was forced to use her intuition now. Her mother had been a gifted herb-wife. She'd once told Coira that many illnesses were passed from one person to another by bodily fluid, or by breathing in the same tainted air as the afflicted.

It made sense then that if a patient had a cough, one should keep their distance. These were the first cases in Torrin, and Coira wanted to stop the illness from spreading.

Emerging from the cottage, Coira found Sister Mina waiting with a heavyset man. The farmer was pale and wild-eyed, and he didn't look at Coira, but past her, toward the open doorway.

"Where have yer kin been of late?" Coira asked, pulling the door shut behind her.

"My wife went to visit her sister a few days ago," the farmer answered. "She lives in a village near Dunan."

Coira frowned. This was what she'd been afraid of. Of course, folk traveled, and when they did, they inadvertently brought the sickness home with them.

"Can ye do anything for them, Sister?" The farmer asked, desperation in his voice now.

"I've made them as comfortable as I can," she replied softly. But I'm afraid I can do nothing more for the moment."

The farmer's gaze guttered, his jaw clenching. "I feel so useless," he ground the words out.

"Attend to yer wife and daughter," Coira answered, "but do not venture into the village or have contact with the other folk here. Ye must ensure the sickness doesn't spread. I will make sure food is brought to ye."

The farmer stared at her, his gaze hardening. He didn't want such advice. It didn't help his plight; it only prevented others from falling ill. But that wouldn't aid his wife and daughter, nor him if he was to sicken.

Coira swallowed. How she wanted to give assurances—to tell him she had all the answers. Her throat aching, she nodded to Sister Mina, indicating that they should go. She then glanced back at the farmer. "I will visit again tomorrow," she promised.

Heart heavy, Coira started back in the direction of the abbey. The farmer's cottage lay on the southern outskirts of Torrin, apart from the other houses. That was a good thing, for if they could isolate the sickness, perhaps they could halt its spread.

The weight in her chest only increased, however, as she followed the path through fields of kale. Coira had taken precautions when entering the cottage and been careful not to touch her patients directly. When she returned to the abbey, she would scrub her hands with lye soap, but there was still a chance she could fall sick too.

Coira set her jaw. *I can't ... the people here need me.*

Ironically, that was often the fate of healers—dying from the same illness as those they sought to heal.

Forcing herself not to dwell on that possibility, Coira glanced up at the darkening mackerel sky. It was growing late in the day. The afternoon was odd, without the slightest breath of a breeze to stir the humid air. She didn't like this kind of weather; it put her on edge.

"Will they die?" Sister Mina asked finally, breaking the silence between them. They were halfway back to the abbey now, the high walls outlined against the sky.

"The odds are against them," Coira admitted. "I will not lie to ye. And I fear that this is just the beginning of things."

She glanced left at the novice, expecting to see fear upon her face. Yet Sister Mina's gaze was steady, and although she was a little pale, she looked resolute. Not for the first time, Coira was pleased that she had Sister Mina to assist her. Panic wouldn't do them any good now. She needed someone with a cool head at her side.

However, Sister Mina didn't speak again, and Coira withdrew into her own thoughts. They continued in silence and, a short while later, re-entered the abbey.

To Coira's surprise, she found the yard in front of the kirk filled with men and horses. Rough male voices and laughter echoed over the grounds, shattering Kilbride's tranquility.

And then Coira saw that the warriors—for they carried claidheamh-mors at their sides—wore sashes of a familiar green and red plaid.

MacKinnon.

14

Breaking Bread

"THIS IS POOR man's fare, Mother Shona."
MacKinnon's voice rumbled across the table where the
abbess and her senior nuns—Coira among them—ate
quietly.

"I apologize for the frugality, MacKinnon," the abbess
replied, her voice toneless. "But we live simply at
Kilbride ... as the Lord would wish."

"Aye ... but ye have important guests."

"If ye had sent word that ye were planning to stay at
Kilbride, we would have made preparations," Mother
Shona replied gently.

MacKinnon snorted, and Coira started to sweat.

Years had passed since she'd been this physically near
him, but the man could still instill terror in her.

It wasn't Coira the clan-chief sat next to this evening,
but Sister Magda, at the far end of the dais. The sisters
and their guests—the clan-chief and the abbot—lined the
long table upon the raised platform at the end of
refectory. Yet, even so, MacKinnon's presence
dominated the space. Coira had deliberately avoided
looking in his direction since taking her seat.

The devil is sitting at my table.

Bile bit at the back of Coira's throat. Gaze downcast, she tried to ignore the crawling sensation that now covered her arms and chest, and the horror that made it hard to breathe.

MacKinnon is breaking bread with me.

As guests at the abbey, the abbess had been obliged to invite MacKinnon to eat with them, while extra tables and benches for his men had been dragged into the refectory. The warriors' voices echoed loudly in what was usually a tranquil space. The other nuns and the monks were seated a few feet away, hunched over their bowls of stew, faces pale and pinched.

Coira didn't blame them. MacKinnon and his men brought an atmosphere of aggression into what was usually a silent, peaceful time of day.

This evening the odious company had killed Coira's appetite for her supper of mutton, leek, and carrot stew served with coarse oaten bread.

Opposite Coira, Sister Elspeth wore a sour expression as she helped herself to some bread. She disapproved of any man setting foot inside the abbey—yet now there were so many of them that they far outnumbered the women here. The abbot was forced to share the guest lodgings with the clan-chief, while the monks had shifted over to the dormitories with the nuns—something that Sister Elspeth was still fuming over. Meanwhile, MacKinnon's men would sleep in the byre and stable complex.

You couldn't go three paces without spying a man inside the abbey now. It had put all the sisters, including Coira, on edge.

"How long do ye plan to remain at Kilbride, MacKinnon?" Sister Elspeth's sharp voice lashed across the table. Coira, who'd just taken a tentative mouthful of stew, nearly choked. The nun had drawn herself up and was staring down the table at the clan-chief. Her thin body vibrated with outrage—an emotion that she clearly could no longer suppress.

Long moments passed, and when MacKinnon didn't answer, Coira chanced a look in his direction.

She immediately wished she hadn't.

Heavens preserve her, he and Craeg looked so alike. They had the same arrogant bearing, chiseled jaw, and brooding good-looks. The shape of their mouths and noses were identical.

A hard knot clenched in Coira's breast, her pulse speeding up, as she stared at him. Fortunately, he wasn't looking in her direction. Instead, he watched Sister Elspeth, his expression shuttered.

However, those eyes—iron-grey—weren't Craeg's. MacKinnon was thinner than she remembered, his shoulders lacking the outlaw's breadth, his face bordering on gaunt. His dark hair, although the same peat-brown as Craeg's, was cut much shorter.

And no scar disfigured his face.

Coira's heart calmed just a little. No, they weren't identical. And when MacKinnon spoke once more, the gulf between the two brothers widened further.

"As long as it takes, Sister." His mouth twisted into a sneer. "Why ... do ye disapprove of our presence here?"

"I'm sure Sister Elspeth is merely curious," Mother Shona cut in smoothly. "We aren't used to having so many visitors, and do wonder at the reason for yer arrival ... especially with so many of yer guard."

MacKinnon shifted his attention from Sister Elspeth, who was now scowling, to the abbess. "Word has reached me that Craeg the Bastard and his band are sheltering near Kilbride," he replied. "I'm here to find him."

Coira flushed hot and then cold. She lowered her spoon, her heart now hammering against her ribs.

No one at the table spoke. However, Father Camron wore a shrewd expression, his gaze flicking from MacKinnon to the abbess.

"Have ye seen any of the outlaws?" MacKinnon asked after a pause, his attention never leaving the abbess. His voice had lowered, and Coira shivered. It was a tone she knew well, one that screamed 'danger'.

Mother Shona didn't react. Her face remained a mask of serenity, her eyes guileless. "No, we have not."

"Are ye sure?"

"We live sheltered lives inside these walls," the abbess replied, her voice as steady as her gaze. "The outlaws could well be nearby, and we wouldn't know. However, none of the sisters have reported seeing anyone suspicious."

"And yet a man from Torrin tells me that he has seen them ... in the woods no more than ten furlongs from Kilbride's walls."

"As I said ... we are sheltered here."

Silence fell once more at the table, tension vibrating through the air. MacKinnon still stared the abbess down although Coira noted how the muscles in his jaw flexed. He was angry, and suspected that Mother Shona was hiding something.

The knot in Coira's breast clenched tighter. He suspected right—and if he ever discovered the truth, it would be over for all of them.

Long moments passed, and then MacKinnon's attention shifted to the abbot. "Father Camron ... how long have ye been visiting the abbey?"

"Nearly two weeks now," the abbot replied, helping himself to a cup of ale.

"And ye have not seen anything to arouse yer suspicions?"

Coira's breathing hitched, her heart now racing so fast she started to feel dizzy. Suddenly, she wanted to dive under the table and cower there like a beaten dog. She felt exposed seated at the same table as MacKinnon—and was grateful that he hadn't yet noticed her presence at the far end of the dais.

But the abbot had long been looking for an opportunity to cause trouble—and now it had arrived.

Father Camron's mouth curved into a small, wintry smile, an expression that did not warm his dark eyes. "I'm here in the role of inquisitor ... did ye not know, MacKinnon?"

The clan-chief raised a dark eyebrow. "And why's that?"

The abbot raised his cup to his lips and took a leisurely sip, aware that all eyes were now upon him. For the first time since the meal had begun, the abbess's serene mask was slipping. Tension now bracketed her mouth, and her gaze had narrowed.

"Of course, ye know about the two nuns who have *mysteriously* left the order of late," the abbot continued.

"Aye ... ye know I do." The words were uttered roughly, a sign that MacKinnon's patience was thinning.

Coira wondered then whether the abbot would dare raise the issue of MacKinnon's own part in Leanna's disappearance.

Her fingers clenched around her spoon. Father Camron was playing a game, and from the glint in his eyes, she knew he was enjoying it. For the first time since arriving at Kilbride, he felt in control.

"The Pope takes a dim view of such things," he said after a pause, clearly deciding to steer clear of the clan-chief's poor behavior. "I have written to him, and he has given me permission to investigate Mother Shona."

MacKinnon inclined his head. "And have ye found any condemning evidence?"

Feeling a gaze upon her, Coira glanced over to where Sister Elspeth was watching her. Of course, all of the nuns knew about her run-ins with the abbot. And the warning glint in the older nun's eye told Coira that Sister Elspeth knew Camron was going to drop her right in it.

Coira's spine tensed. There was nothing she could say or do; she was trapped.

"The abbess is far too lenient with her nuns," the abbot drawled, favoring Mother Shona with a quick, nasty smile. "She allows them to practice with weapons ... to take witching hour walks outside the abbey walls with no explanation."

And then, Father Camron looked straight at Coira.

The world stopped, and it felt as if, for an instant, so did Coira's heart.

All gazes at the table swiveled to her—including MacKinnon's.

And when he looked at Coira, his expression froze. Until this moment he'd been so intent on his conversation with the abbot and abbess that he'd barely paid any attention to the senior nuns seated around the table.

But he did now.

MacKinnon and Coira's gazes fused. The years rolled back, and suddenly Coira was cringing upon a soiled bed at *The Goat and Goose*, watching as MacKinnon loomed over her.

Despite that the air was close inside the refectory, Coira's limbs started to tremble as if she'd just caught a chill.

"How many of the nuns have behaved this way?" MacKinnon asked. His voice was soft now, barely above a whisper.

"Just this one." Father Camron's tone was jubilant. "Sister Coira." He paused a moment before adding. "Although I suspect there are others who are just as *deviant*."

MacKinnon ignored the abbot's last comment, his attention never wavering. "Sister Coira."

"Aye ... two of my monks found her practicing with a quarter-staff in the orchard over a week ago. She wields it like a man." The disgust in the abbot's voice was evident, yet MacKinnon continued to ignore him. "And I suspect her of *fornication*."

An unpleasant smile twisted the clan-chief's lips. His gaze then shifted to Mother Shona. "I need to question this nun," he drawled. "Alone."

Coira's breathing choked off, sweat now trickling down between her breasts. *Mother Mary, No*.

The abbess scowled, her face growing taut as she cast a worried look at Coira. "Why?"

MacKinnon inclined his head, his gaze narrowing. "If she has been outside the abbey walls at night, she may have had contact with the outlaws."

Mother Shona drew herself up. "If ye have any questions for Sister Coira, ye can ask her here."

A heavy beat of silence passed, and then MacKinnon leaned forward, his gaze snaring the abbess's. "I think ye misunderstand, Mother Shona," he said coldly. "That wasn't a request ... but a command."

15

No Way Back

COIRA WALKED INTO the chapter house on trembling legs.

She couldn't believe Mother Shona was allowing this meeting to take place, that she was letting MacKinnon bully her. The abbess knew the full story about Coira's past—of her history with the clan-chief.

But, unlike the abbot, MacKinnon wasn't a man you defied.

MacKinnon's threat had hung over the air, like the heavy pause between a lightning flash and a thunderclap. They'd all sensed the danger, and when Mother Shona had dropped her gaze, giving her silent assent, Coira had felt as if the walls of the refectory were suddenly closing in on her.

The same sensation assaulted her now, as she walked into the chapter house. Deliberately, she left the door open behind her, but even so, the usually lofty ceiling and large windows seemed oppressive this evening. Outside, it was still light—for night fell very late this time of year—and as such the banks of candles that lined the walls hadn't been lit.

In the center of the space, MacKinnon awaited her.

He stood still, legs akimbo, hands hanging loosely at his sides. Yet his gaze tracked her every step across the floor.

Pulse throbbing in her ears, Coira halted a few feet back from him. She was relieved that her long skirts hid her shaking legs, and she clasped her hands together in front of her so that he wouldn't see how they trembled.

"My last visit ... I knew it was ye," he greeted her, his voice a low rumble.

Coira forced herself to meet his eye. "I wasn't sure ye recognized me," she admitted. The steadiness of her voice surprised her. One thing her experiences over the years had taught her was self-control, it seemed.

MacKinnon favored her with a sharp smile. "I wasn't sure, I admit ... for one nun looks much like another ... but few women have eyes like yers. Ye are a difficult woman to forget, Coira."

The intimacy in his voice made her skin crawl. Acid stung the back of her throat, yet Coira swallowed it down. She needed to keep a leash on her fear; if he saw it, things would only go worse for her.

MacKinnon took a step closer, his gaze raking over her. "Aye ... ye are still comely ... especially in that habit ye wear." His smile widened to a grin then. "And all the 'Hail Marys' in the world can't cancel out who ye were ... *what* ye still are."

Coira remained silent, even if his words made her nostrils flare. Lord, this man knew how to wield words like blades; he always had. Deliberately, she didn't answer him, didn't deny his comment.

MacKinnon's gaze hooded. "So ye go for walks at night, do ye Coira?" He stepped closer still. They now stood little more than three feet apart, and it took all Coira's will not to shrink back from him.

"Sometimes," she admitted. "I'm the healer here at Kilbride ... some woodland herbs have to be collected at night."

He snorted. "That's a weak excuse ... I thought ye were cleverer than that. Ye are still a whore at heart, aren't ye? I'd wager ye sneak out at the witching hour to spread yer legs for outlaws."

His words were a slap across the face, and Coira started to sweat with the effort it was taking her not to react. Unfortunately though, Duncan MacKinnon wasn't yet done. "Have ye serviced my bastard brother yet?"

Nausea swamped Coira. She'd not done anything to be ashamed of with Craeg, and yet MacKinnon's words made her feel dirty.

"I haven't seen any of the outlaws," she lied, her voice husky with the effort it was taking not to turn tail and bolt from the chapter house. "And if that's all ye want to know, our conversation is at an end."

"No, it isn't." MacKinnon closed the gap between them, and suddenly he was looming over her, invading her space.

Coira went rigid. Her arms dropped to her sides, and her fingers curled into her palms, the nails digging in. Her heart was pounding so fast that she was sure he'd be able to hear it.

"I've missed ye, Coira," he murmured, his voice lowering. It was an intimate tone, a lover's voice. "And seeing ye again has reminded me how much I enjoyed our time together."

"I didn't," she bit out the words. "I hated every moment."

His eyebrows raised, and then he gave her a slow smile. "Good."

Coira backed away from him. Once again, the walls were closing in on her. His closeness was a stranglehold. However, his hand shot out, his fingers closing roughly over her upper arm and halting her.

"When I'm done with the outlaws, I'm coming for ye, Coira," he growled, "and if ye give me any trouble, I will have my men butcher every last nun within these walls. Is that clear?"

Coira's breathing came in short, rasping gasps, her body now shaking uncontrollably. "Ye are a beast, MacKinnon," she replied, choking out the words. "Curse yer soul to eternal damnation."

He grinned at her, his gaze gleaming. "It's too late for that." His grip tightened, his fingers biting into her flesh. "I'm done being thwarted. Ready yerself to leave Kilbride ... prepare for a life as my whore at Dunan."

MacKinnon let go of her then and stepped back, his chest heaving. The lust on his face made Coira's belly roil. Clamping her jaw shut, she staggered back from him. Her hands fisted at her sides.

Enough. If he dared reach for her again, she'd break his jaw.

But MacKinnon didn't. Having delivered his terms, he favored her with one last lingering look before turning on his heel and striding from the chapter house.

A hollow silence, broken only by the rasp of Coira's breathing, settled over the space. For a few moments, she merely stood there, body coiled. She'd almost wanted him to grab her, so that she could unleash the fury she'd smothered for over a decade. But he hadn't given her the chance.

Once again, MacKinnon had bested her.

A sob splintered the air. Had she just made that wretched sound? Trembling, Coira wrapped her arms about her torso and staggered over to the narrow bench-seat that ran around the perimeter of the floor. She sank down onto it and squeezed her eyes shut as terror pulsed through her.

He won't have me again. The vow was a silent scream inside her head.

The abbey had become a prison.

It seemed that everywhere Coira turned there was a man wearing MacKinnon plaid, leering at her. She was sure she was imagining the lecherous looks, and yet she couldn't help fear that the clan-chief had told his men about her past, of who she'd been before taking the veil.

The morning following the clan-chief's arrival was misty and cool. Coira and Sister Mina escaped the confines of the abbey with a trip to Torrin to tend on the sick farmer's wife and daughter. Although it was a relief to be free of Kilbride, the visit didn't provide Coira any solace. Her patients' conditions had worsened—they both had swellings under their armpits and their bodies were wracked with fever—and the farmer had grown more agitated.

"Ye must be able to do something?" His voice rose as he loomed over Coira when she emerged from the dwelling. "They're going to die."

Coira faced the farmer down, her belly twisting when she saw the grief in his eyes. "I've done all I can I think of ... but they're not responding to the herbs that usually bring down fever. I'm sorry. I can do nothing but pray for them."

Her words were heartfelt, and yet they felt hollow. The farmer didn't want them. The man's face grew hard. "Useless," he rasped, as he turned away from her. "What good is yer God to me now?"

"It's not yer fault," Sister Mina murmured as they left the cottage behind and stepped onto the path that would take them back to Kilbride. "Deep down, Bred knows that."

Coira heaved a sigh, putting away the scarf she'd tied around her mouth and nose when dealing with the patients. Her mother had often covered her face when tending those she thought infectious, although it hadn't stopped her from succumbing to a terrible fever sickness that had swept through Dunan and the outlying settlements one winter. It likely wasn't going to protect Coira much either, yet she had to do what she could to keep herself healthy.

"I know," she replied, her heart heavy. "I wish I could have given him hope ... but it would be a false one."

"So they really will die?"

"Aye."

Sister Mina's grey eyes clouded, but she didn't comment further. There wasn't really anything one could say to that.

The two nuns had walked another few yards when a man suddenly stepped out onto the path before them. Tall and lean, with a sharp-featured face, the stranger wore dusty leathers and carried a longbow and quiver over his back.

Sister Mina cried out, fumbling at her belt for the knife she always carried. Meanwhile, Coira dropped her healer's basket and brought up her quarter-staff; she gripped it two-handed, barring him from approaching further.

The man halted. His gaze widened, flicking between Coira and Sister Mina, even as his mouth quirked. "Fighting nuns ... now I've seen it all."

Coira gritted her teeth. She'd had enough of the arrogance of men. One more jibe and she'd jab him in the cods with the pointed iron end of her staff.

As if reading the fierce expression on her face, the stranger's face grew serious and he raised his hands, palms faced outward above him. "I mean ye no harm." His attention flicked from where Sister Mina now held her knife at hip level, blade pointed toward him, back to her companion.

"Are ye Sister Coira?"

Coira scowled. A long moment passed, before she nodded.

The man let out a gusting breath that she guessed was relief. "Just as well ... I've not been able to get near the abbey gates to ask for ye."

"MacKinnon's here," Sister Mina spoke up.

"So I've gleaned," the stranger replied, his gaze never leaving Coira.

"Who are ye?" Coira demanded, her temper fraying.

"My name's Farlan ... I'm part of Craeg's band. He sent me here." The outlaw paused, his lean face tensing. "Two of our men are sick ... we think it's the plague but have no healer to attend them. Craeg asks that ye visit them."

Coira stiffened. "The sickness is here now too ... I've just come from a mother and daughter afflicted with it. They'll likely die ... as will yer men." The words were harsh, and yet Coira's nerves had been stretched to breaking point of late. She didn't have it in her to soften her answer.

However, Farlan didn't appear offended. He continued to hold her gaze, his own steady. "All the same, Craeg has asked for ye ... will ye come?"

It was on the tip of her tongue to refuse, to send the outlaw away with a sharp reprimand.

But then a strange sensation settled over Coira—one that made her pause.

She looked away from him, her gaze settling upon the grey stone walls of Kilbride in the distance.

For years, the abbey had been her refuge from the world, but not anymore. Her past had finally caught up with her. If she returned to her life amongst the sisters, it would only be a matter of time before MacKinnon made her choose: her life or theirs.

Coira glanced over at Sister Mina. The nun still had her knife raised, her young face screwed up in consternation as she glared at the outlaw. "Ye go on ahead, Sister," Coira said softly.

Sister Mina's attention snapped to her. "Ye are going?"

Coira nodded, her belly fluttering as she did so. *If ye do this, there's no way back.*

But did she actually want to go back? For years she'd lived contentedly as a nun, yet in the past days something had shifted within her. A restlessness had surfaced, a yearning that would not be quietened.

Craeg had been the catalyst. The hours she'd spent in his company while he'd been recovering, and then that intense exchange in the moonlit clearing, had ignited something inside her. She wasn't sure what the future held, but the urge to go to him grew with each passing moment.

She wouldn't ignore it.

"But ye can't go alone ... I'm coming with ye."

"Ye can't, Sister," Coira replied with a shake of her head. "I've gotten myself into trouble with both the abbot and MacKinnon now. This will be one step too far. If I go to the outlaws, I won't be able to return to the abbey ... and so neither will ye."

Sister Mina stared at her, realization dawning. "Ye are leaving the order?"

Coira favored the young woman with a soft smile. There was so much she wanted to say to Sister Mina; her chest felt tight with the need to unburden herself. Yet she held herself back. "It seems that way, doesn't it?"

Silence fell, and then Farlan cleared his throat. "Sorry to interrupt, but if we linger out here in the open much longer, someone's going to see me. We need to go now."

Still holding Sister Mina's eye, Coira gave a curt nod. "I'm ready."

The novice's eyes gleamed, and she started to blink rapidly. "This isn't right. Ye mustn't leave."

"I'm afraid, I must," Coira replied, her throat tensing. The determination in her voice surprised her, as did an overwhelming sense of relief. She didn't actually want to return to Kilbride. "Peace be with ye, Sister Mina. Please tell the others I've gone to collect herbs and will be back later."

Sister Mina's throat bobbed. She lowered her blade and resheathed it at her waist. "Peace be with ye, Sister. Worry not, I will not betray ye," she murmured.

Coira forced a smile. "Thank ye."

She then lowered her quarter-staff, picked up her basket and looped it over one arm, and followed Farlan into the trees without a backward glance.

Hidden in a clump of bracken, the watcher observed the two nuns part ways.

He saw Sister Coira follow the man into the woods, while Sister Mina continued on her way along the path leading down the hillside toward the abbey.

Heart racing, Brother Ian rose to his feet and dusted off his habit. He'd shadowed the healer for days now, watching and waiting for her to transgress once more.

Following someone without being spotted was a challenging task, but the monk was small and slight, and could easily make himself invisible if he so wished.

Secretly, he'd begun to question Father Camron's fixation with this nun—until now.

Excitement fluttered in Brother Ian's belly. The abbot was right. The nun did fraternize with outlaws. He'd seen it with his own eyes.

Drawing his robes close, the young monk crept away through the bracken.

16

Yer Luck Has Run Out

COIRA FOLLOWED THE outlaw and wondered if she
had taken leave of her senses. The heady rush of resolve
that had made her turn her back on Kilbride was now
ebbing, and she was starting to doubt her decision.

*There's still time. Ye can turn around and flee back
to the abbey.*

Back to MacKinnon.

The thought made her keep walking, although her
heart leaped with each step. The people she was traveling
to help were those who'd risen up against the clan-chief,
those who would one day bring him down.

She wanted to be part of that. She'd gladly help those
who rebelled against a clan-chief who over-taxed his
people, who controlled these lands by terrifying folk into
submission. His time was coming to an end, and she
would join the rebellion against him.

Heat spread across Coira's chest, recklessness
catching fire in her veins. Suddenly, she knew in her
bones that she'd made the right decision.

The time had come to act.

Reaching into the small leather pouch upon her belt,
Coira's fingers curled around a silver ring. After arriving
at Kilbride, she'd been forced to remove the ring from

her right hand, and had instead donned a fine gold band when she'd taken her vows—a new ring that marked her as a Bride of Christ. But she had always kept her mother's ring close, even though she knew she really shouldn't. It was the only thing she had left from her past—the only link to her parents.

And although she still donned her habit, the desire to wear the old ring once more swept over Coira.

Removing the gold band, she put it away in the pouch and slipped her mother's ring onto her right hand. A smile spread across her face.

Once again, instinct had taken over, and she would follow where it led.

Farlan took her to a glade where a saddled horse awaited them. Wordlessly, he untied the gelding and tightened its girth, before he sprang up onto the saddle. Reaching down, he helped Coira up behind him.

To keep her seat, she squeezed with her thighs as the outlaw urged the horse into a bouncing trot and then a jolting canter.

Moments later they were flying through the trees, heading east.

Duncan MacKinnon stirred the turnip and kale pottage around the earthen bowl before him.

Stew ... again.

Maybe that was why his appetite was poor today. Did these nuns eat anything else but stew and coarse bread?

Putting down his spoon, Duncan reached for his cup of ale and took a sip. He didn't feel himself. He'd awoken feeling listless and hadn't broken his fast with a plate of bannocks as he usually did. Now the sight of food made him feel queasy, and his belly had developed a faint ache.

He hoped the mutton stew he'd eaten the day before hadn't made him sick.

Next to him, Father Camron spooned great mouthfuls of stew into his mouth. Heavyset with an appetite of three men, the abbot certainly hadn't complained of the fare at Kilbride. However, he was obviously used to eating this way.

Gaze drifting around the table, Duncan searched for Sister Coira. He knew that she took her meals with the senior nuns at the abbess's table, yet he hadn't seen her enter the refectory.

And there was an empty space at the table.

He glanced over at the abbess to find Mother Shona watching him. Duncan frowned at her. "Where's Sister Coira?"

"There are sick villagers in Torrin," the abbess replied, her voice cool. "Sister Coira has gone to attend them."

Across from Mother Shona, Father Camron stopped shoveling stew into his mouth. Straightening up, he wiped his lips with the back of his hand. "Ye should forbid her to do so, Mother." His dark brows knotted together as he frowned. "Do ye want the plague entering the abbey?"

The abbess glanced over at the abbot, her mouth pursing. In the day he'd been here, Duncan had seen the woman grow increasingly tense. "The abbey has an important role," she replied, her tone sharpening. "We will not abandon the folk of these lands."

MacKinnon snorted, drawing her gaze once more. "From what I hear, there is no cure for the sickness ... Sister Coira is wasting her time."

His belly tightened then as he considered that the nun might fall ill and die. He had plans for the lovely Coira—the last thing he wanted was to lose her again.

Ye don't want to catch the pestilence off her either, he reminded himself.

"MacKinnon is right," Father Camron added with a cold smile. "A nun's place is here ... serving the Lord in prayer."

"A nun's place is helping others ... as Christ taught us," Mother Shona replied crisply. "Sister Coira is a gifted healer. Even if she can't cure folk, she can ensure their last hours are as comfortable as possible ... and bring comfort to their families."

The abbot's smile twisted. "A lot of good that'll do."

Mother Shona's brown eyes glinted, and she inhaled sharply. Her lips parted as she readied herself to reply to the abbot. However, the arrival of a monk at their table forestalled her.

The monk was young—small and slender as a lass. His dark hair was cropped short, the crown tonsured. And even though heavy dark robes swathed his small body, MacKinnon could see that the monk was quivering with excitement.

"Father Camron!" The monk dropped to one knee next to the abbot, his voice high and breathless. "I have news."

The abbot swiveled, his face creasing into a scowl. "Not *here*, Brother Ian," he snapped. "Come ... we'll talk outside."

Father Camron made to rise from the table, but MacKinnon reached out and caught the sleeve of his robe, restraining him.

"Yer friend looks excited," he murmured. "I think we'd all like to hear his news."

The abbot's throat bobbed, his gaze darting from Duncan to the abbess. Mother Shona was watching him with a furrowed brow. "This is private," he muttered.

"Ye are on my land, Father," MacKinnon warned him with a tight smile. "And as such, I will hear what this man has to say." The clan-chief shifted his attention to the monk. The excitement had ebbed from his lean face, and he now wore a hunted expression. No doubt, this transgression would earn him a beating from the abbot later.

Father Camron sank back down onto the bench-seat, defeated. "Very well," he growled. "Tell us then, Brother Ian."

"The nun ... Sister Coira ... I saw her on the path back from Torrin, Father. She was talking with a man. And then she left with him."

Duncan went still, his tender belly clenching further. "Describe him."

The monk's gaze flicked between the abbot and clan-chief, before he swallowed hard. "Tall and lanky with dark hair … he was clad in hunting leathers and carried a longbow."

MacKinnon sucked in a breath. *An outlaw*. "Why didn't ye follow them?"

The monk's gaze widened. "Father Camron told me to return to him if Sister Coira did anything suspicious."

Heat exploded in Duncan's chest, creeping up his neck in a sensation he knew well; he was having trouble keeping a leash on his temper. "Lackwit," he growled. "What good is this news, if we don't know where they went?"

Brother Ian licked his lips, his gaze darting now. The abbot hadn't uttered a word, although his face had turned red. Indeed, the monk was going to get a thrashing the moment he got him alone. "Maybe the other nun knows," he finally replied, his voice strangled.

Duncan scowled, his hands fisting as he prepared himself to lash out at this clod-head. "*Other* nun?"

"Aye … she was with Sister Coira at the time, but she returned to the abbey afterward." The monk's thin cheeks flushed while the words poured from him. He then swiveled around, his gaze searching the sea of faces beneath the dais. The nuns, monks, and warriors seated there had all stopped eating and were watching the scene unfold. "There!" he gasped, pointing. "There she is!"

MacKinnon's gaze followed his and settled upon a young nun seated at the far side of the refectory. Large grey eyes stared back at him, and the lass cringed under the weight of his stare. The clan-chief pushed himself up from his seat and slowly beckoned to the nun. "Come here," he growled.

"We've picked up their trail … they're heading east."

The warrior panted the words, pulling his horse up in the yard before MacKinnon.

Duncan nodded, his jaw clenching. Frustration pulsed through him. It had taken much longer than he'd have liked to get the information out of that novice. She'd looked young and easily cowed, yet the wee bitch had kept her mouth shut initially. It was only when Duncan twisted her arm to breaking point behind her back that she'd gasped out the details he needed, tears of pain streaming down her face.

Two of his bastard brother's men were sick—the outlaw was taking Coira to their camp.

"Track them as far as ye can," Duncan growled. "I want to know the location of their hide-out."

"And then?" The warrior asked. Tall and blond with a broad face, the man's name was Keith MacKinnon—a distant cousin to the clan-chief. In Carr's absence, he was now MacKinnon's second. However, unlike Carr Broderick, Keith lacked initiative. He didn't do anything unless Duncan barked an order at him.

"Get back here, and we'll pay them a visit," Duncan snarled back. "Go!"

He watched Keith ride out of the yard, dust boiling up under his horse's hooves, and listened as his second cousin bawled orders at the other members of the Dunan Guard waiting outside the walls.

Reaching up, Duncan raked both hands through his hair. He was aware then that the listlessness that had afflicted him since rising that morning had grown. His limbs felt heavy and achy, and despite the cool, cloudy afternoon, he was sweating.

It's the strain of all of this, he told himself. *It's getting to me.*

Tension coiled within him, longing for release. For years he'd hunted his half-brother, and for years Craeg had eluded him. However, the game of cat and mouse was coming to an end.

"Not long now, Bastard," he muttered. "Yer luck has run out."

17

I Will Do What I Can

FEET SLIPPING ON the loose shale, Coira made her way down the bank into the ravine. Below her lay a narrow valley floor, shadowed either side with high stone walls. The smoke from numerous cook fires drifted up to greet her, as did the aroma of roasting venison. The murmur of voices and the wail of a bairn somewhere in the ravine echoed off the damp rock.

Coira's breath caught. Just how many people were packed in here? She'd heard that over the past month many folk had rallied to the outlaws' side, but she hadn't expected to see such a crowd.

Farlan walked ahead, booted feet slithering on the steep bank. They'd both dismounted his horse, and he now led the beast.

"How long have ye been camped here?" she called out.

"Nearly a moon now," he replied, not looking her way.

They continued down the ravine. Curious gazes settled upon her, and Coira knew she must cut an unusual figure: a tall nun with a basket of herbs in one hand and a quarter-staff in the other. Many of the faces of the men, women, and children watching her were strained, their gazes worried.

News of the sick men was clearly common-knowledge throughout the camp.

Farlan led her down the length of the valley, past clumps of hide tents and fires where MacKinnon's deer spit-roasted over embers. Coira's mouth watered at the aroma, reminding her that she hadn't eaten since dawn.

Eventually, as the ravine narrowed to a point and the rocky sides, studded with clinging outcrops of pine, reared overhead, Coira spied this band's leader.

A man she'd never expected to set eyes upon again.

Coira's breathing quickened, and her heart started to drum against her ribs. It was hard not to remember the intensity of the last words he'd said to her, and how she'd fled like a frightened deer into the night afterward. She'd never thought it was possible to be both frightened and captivated at the same time.

Seeing him again brought it all back.

Craeg stood before a single large tent, muscular arms folded across his broad chest. He wore a sleeveless leather vest and leather breeches that molded to his body. His wild dark hair was unbound, stirring gently in the light breeze that whispered through the gorge. His moss-green eyes were fixed upon her, tracking her steps as she drew near.

Mother Mary, give me strength. Coira needed to keep her composure. She was here to help the sick, not for a reunion with Craeg. Awkwardness warred with the urge to rush to him.

With a jolt, she realized just how much she'd missed the outlaw in the past days. He'd only been in her life a short while, but she already felt a bond with him that went beyond the friendship they'd forged as patient and healer.

Craeg stepped forward to greet her. Behind him stood a huge man with a mane of red hair—he was a striking individual, yet Coira had been so focused on Craeg, she hadn't even noticed him. Another figure, an older woman with greying dark hair and a careworn face, ventured forth.

The grim look on the red-haired outlaw's face made her belly tighten.

"Thank ye for coming, Sister Coira." The formality in Craeg's voice caused Coira to tense. His face was a study in composure. Had he forgotten the things he'd said to her in that clearing? Of course, he'd called for her help, not for any other reason.

"Peace be with ye, Craeg," Coira answered, dipping her gaze. Once again, shyness was getting the better of her.

"It's good to see ye," he said, breaking the awkward silence between them. "I—"

"MacKinnon's at Kilbride, Craeg," Farlan interrupted from behind Coira.

She glanced back up to see that Craeg had gone still, his expression suddenly hawkish.

"It's true," Coira murmured. "He's brought the Dunan Guard with him ... someone in Torrin has betrayed ye after all, it seems."

Craeg's mouth stretched into a humorless smile. "Aye ... I was hoping they would."

Coira frowned. "Excuse me? Ye told me the folk of this land were loyal to ye. Why would ye want one of them to inform on ye?"

"I wanted to draw MacKinnon out," Craeg replied, his smile widening. "So we can face each other at last."

"But didn't ye already do that ... earlier in the summer?"

Craeg snorted. "That was an ambush, not a fair fight. This time we're ready for him."

Judging from the gleam in Craeg's eye, he couldn't wait to face his half-brother.

"Victory in battle will feel hollow indeed, if yer band sickens and dies," she said crisply, her attention shifting to the tent behind him. "Are yer men in there?"

Craeg nodded, his expression sobering.

"One of them is in a bad way." The older woman added softly. "I don't think he's got much time left."

"My woman, Fenella, has taken ill too." The red-haired outlaw spoke up behind Craeg. "Will ye take a look at her as well?"

Coira met the man's gaze. "Of course, I will."

Setting down her staff, she withdrew her scarf from her basket and began to tie it around her mouth and nose.

"What are ye doing?" Farlan asked, suspicion edging his voice as he watched her preparations.

"Just taking precautions," Coira replied. She glanced Craeg's way then. "Ye must keep folk away from those who have taken sick."

He nodded, his handsome face taut with concern now. "Fenella has been looking after the sick men." He motioned to the man and woman behind him. "As have Gunn, Flora, and I."

Coira drew in a deep, steadying breath. "Then all three of ye are at risk as well." She shifted her attention to where Farlan stood a few yards behind her. "Keep back from this area ... and warn the others to do the same."

The young man nodded, his brow furrowing. He then glanced over at Craeg, awaiting his confirmation.

"Do as she says," Craeg said. His voice was cool, calm. She was grateful that he wasn't letting fear of the sickness, which could turn folk witless, dominate his decision-making. "Let the others know that MacKinnon is at Kilbride ... and that we'll be riding out to meet him first thing tomorrow."

Coira caught her breath and turned back to Craeg, to find him observing her. His mouth then lifted at the corners. "Aye, that's tomorrow's plan ... but tonight we focus on other matters," he said quietly. "Since we're already at risk of getting sick, consider me and Flora yer assistants."

Coira's own mouth curved, although he wouldn't see that under the scarf that protected her face. "There's no point in ye taking risks though ... keep yer distance from those afflicted unless absolutely necessary."

He nodded, stepping aside to let Coira past. "Is there anything ye need?"

"A bowl of steaming hot water and a cake of lye soap would help."

"I'll see to it," Flora spoke up. She shot Coira a quick, grateful smile, before hurrying off to fetch the water.

Heaving a deep breath, Coira walked forward and ducked through the entrance into the tent.

One glance at the two men within and Coira knew they were both past her help.

The man lying to the left of the brazier certainly was—he was dead, eyes staring up at the roof of the tent, his mouth twisted in a grimace of pain.

Coira swallowed hard as dread trailed its icy fingers down her spine.

I don't know how to stop this.

She'd always felt confident in her skills, yet she was seriously out of her depth here. Nothing she'd learned from her mother, or from the last decade working as a healer, could prepare her for this moment. She had no idea how to proceed.

"Sister." A weak, raspy voice interrupted her.

The man lying to the right of the brazier was still alive, although barely so. He stared up at Coira, his gaze glassy. "Help me."

Coira swallowed hard. "Aye," she whispered, reaching with shaking hands for a small clay bottle of hemlock juice inside her basket. "I will do what I can."

Night fell over the ravine, a misty day giving way to a damp, cool night.

Craeg crouched before the fire pit and nudged the embers with a stick before adding a gorse branch. A moment later, a shower of bright sparks and tongues of flame shot up into the darkness.

Shifting his attention from the fire, Craeg's gaze settled upon Gunn. His friend sat cross-legged opposite him. The warrior's eyes were desolate, his face seeming carven from stone.

Fenella was his life, his soul. And now she was gravely ill.

Sister Coira was still with her.

Craeg studied Gunn a moment, his chest tightening. They'd spoken little as the last rays of daylight had seeped from the world—there wasn't much either of them could say. Both of them risked falling sick too. It was just a matter of waiting to see.

Strangely, Craeg wasn't worried for himself. He'd long ago overcome a fear of death. He'd been reckless with his own life too many times to be afraid of losing it. Instead, the thought of losing Fenella and Gunn filled him with a sense of despair so powerful that it hurt to breathe.

And underneath it all, guilt plagued him over Coira. He shouldn't have called her here. In doing so, he'd put her life at risk as well.

Fate was a cruel bitch. They were so close to bringing MacKinnon down. But if this pestilence dug its claws in and ripped through his band of followers, it would be a hollow victory indeed. It was poor timing, and yet the moment had been coming for a long while now. He wouldn't turn away from it, and neither would those who followed him.

Gunn glanced up then, his eyes hollowed in the firelight. He seemed to have aged a decade in the past few hours. "Dawn can't come soon enough," he said roughly. "I'm looking forward to giving MacKinnon's men a taste of my blade."

"Ye don't have to join us," Craeg replied. "If ye wish to remain here with Fen, I'll understand."

Gunn shook his head, his expression turning vehement. "Fen wants me to fight tomorrow. I'll not stay behind."

Craeg nodded. He certainly wasn't going to argue with Gunn when he was in this mood.

He was aware then of a dark robed figure appearing from the small tent where Fenella was laid up. Coira had finally joined them.

Both men turned to her, watching as she approached the fire and pulled off the scarf that covered the lower half of her face. Her expression was tense, her lovely eyes hollowed with fatigue.

Once again, guilt arrowed through Craeg's gut. When he'd seen her earlier, for the first time since she'd helped him escape, his pulse had quickened. Heat had then flowered across his chest, obliterating the gnawing worry the sickness had brought.

He'd devoured the sight of her, and for just a few moments, had forgotten why he'd called her to his side. All that mattered was that Coira was with him.

He hadn't lied. He was happy to see her again—happier than Coira realized.

"How is she?" Gunn asked, his voice hoarse with worry.

Coira met his gaze steadily. "She's worsening ... I'm sorry."

Gunn's face went taut. "Do none of yer herbs and potions work?"

Coira's expression shadowed. "I've given her something for the fever, which should slow the sickness's progress," she replied softly.

"Join us at the fire," Craeg spoke up, motioning to the hunk of bread and cheese that sat on an oiled cloth beside him. "I've kept some food back for ye."

Coira nodded, relief suffusing her face. She crossed to him and lowered herself to the ground with a stifled groan.

Craeg looked at her sharply, concern knotting his belly. "Are ye unwell?"

She shook her head. "No ... just exhausted." She paused there, looking about her. "Do ye have some water and soap. I need to wash my hands."

"The water's cold," Craeg said, rising to his feet. "Will that do?"

"Aye, well enough. Thank ye."

Craeg brought the bowl and soap to the fireside, handing them to her. He watched as Coira washed her hands and then devoured her supper.

"Are yer men ready to face MacKinnon tomorrow in battle?" Coira asked finally, brushing the crumbs off her habit. Her tone was guarded, and she avoided his eye. He wondered if she thought him rash.

"Aye ... they've been ready for weeks now," he replied. "And with the sickness in the camp, it will give them something else to think about."

"The men are eager to fight." Gunn spoke up, his jaw set, his gaze gleaming. "As am I. If the pestilence is going to take us ... we want to see MacKinnon go down first."

Coira glanced up, before her gaze flicked between the two men. Her mouth compressed. Craeg sensed she wanted to say something but was holding herself back. Moments passed, and then her attention settled upon him. "How is yer wound?"

Craeg smiled. "Healing well ... thanks to ye."

Coira stared back at him, her cheeks growing pink. The nun's blush intrigued Craeg. Everything about Coira fascinated him.

She cleared her throat. "If ye are set on going into battle tomorrow ... I should take a look at it."

"What ... now?"

"Can we go to yer tent?" she asked, the blush upon her cheeks deepening. "I have something to ask of ye."

18

Broken

COIRA FOLLOWED CRAEG into his tent, her heart hammering. Wiping damp palms on the skirts of her habit, she attempted to steady her nerves.

Calm down.

She hadn't expected to be this anxious, but the thing she needed to ask Craeg made her feel as if she were climbing the steps to the gallows.

What if he denies me?

She hoped he wouldn't, for her hopes rested upon his consent. If she never intended to return to Kilbride, she needed to carve another role for herself among these people.

It was a conversation that couldn't wait.

Craeg's tent was a lean-to built against the ravine wall. It was small and furnished only with a single fur on the floor and a brazier in the center, where a lump of peat glowed.

The outlaw leader turned to Coira, and suddenly the tent felt cramped and airless. His presence sucked the air out of the smoky interior. Craeg's height and breadth made her feel tiny in comparison. Her thoughts suddenly scattered.

Concentrate, she chided herself. *Ye must focus.*

"What did ye want to speak to me of?" he asked with a slow smile. It was a purely masculine expression and a reminder that Craeg hadn't forgotten what he'd said to her back in that moonlit glade.

Neither had Coira, but that wasn't why she'd asked for a moment alone with him.

She swallowed. "I will get to that in a moment," she replied. "First ... let me take a look at yer side."

Craeg hesitated, as he continued to watch her intently. He was probably wondering what was amiss with her. However, he didn't argue. Not shifting his focus from her, he began to unlace his vest. He then shrugged it off.

The sight of his naked chest was distracting. She'd seen his nude torso before, yet this time it made Coira's breathing grow shallow, an ache forming just under her breast bone.

Forcing herself to focus, she stepped toward him, set down her basket, and deftly unwrapped the light bandage he wore. Then, bending close, she examined the injury to his left flank.

It was healing beautifully—better than she'd expected. The scab that had formed was dry, and there was no unpleasant smell issuing from it.

"Ye are tough," she admitted, drawing back from him. "Such a wound would have killed many men."

Craeg's mouth curved, his eyes gleaming. "Aye ... so I'm healthy enough to swing a sword tomorrow?"

Coira nodded. His proximity was making it hard for her to keep her thoughts netted. The heat of his body was like a furnace, and the warm, spicy scent of his skin made a strange yearning rise within her belly. "Make sure ye bind the injury well first though ... or ye risk splitting it open again."

Reaching for a clean bandage, she wrapped it around his torso, and as she did so, she became increasingly aware of his nearness and the gentle whisper of both their breathing.

The words that he'd said that night returned to her, taunting her. She'd not remind him of that incident. Yet she knew he was watching her, waiting for her to speak.

Coira finished her task and stepped back from him. "Ye can put yer vest back on now," she said, cursing the huskiness in her voice. She couldn't let herself get distracted. He looked like he wanted to kiss her, and although part of her yearned for it, her heart suddenly shrank at the thought.

She'd made this journey partly because of him, but the situation was starting to feel too real, too intense. Coira realized then that she wasn't ready to take the next step, whatever that was.

Craeg did as bid, but as he laced up the vest, his mouth quirked. His eyes darkened as he gazed upon her. "Out with it then … what do ye wish to ask?"

Coira heaved in a deep breath. When he looked at her like that, it was nearly impossible to form a coherent thought. Yet now he'd given her an opening, she wasn't going to waste the opportunity. "Would ye let me remain here?" she asked, the words rushing out of her. "With yer band?"

Craeg's eyes widened, a smile creasing his face. "Of course, Coira." He reached forward then, clasping her hands with his. "So ye have left the order?"

Coira nodded. "I must," she whispered. She was tempted to leave it at that, but her thudding heart warned her that she couldn't. Craeg needed to hear this story—even if the truth repelled him. She was tired of carrying around her dark secrets. The urge to bare her soul to him was too great.

Coira's breathing caught. "It's MacKinnon," she gasped the hated name. "He's after me."

Craeg went still, dangerously so. The joy in his eyes faded, as did his smile. All trace of good humor leached from his face. "Why?"

Dear Lord, please have mercy on me. This was her chance to lie, to cover up a past that she wished belonged to someone else. But she wouldn't. She'd tell the truth.

"Do ye remember when ye told me about yer upbringing in Dunan?" she asked finally, forcing herself to keep looking at him.

"Aye," he replied, his tone wary.

"Well." She cleared her throat then. Lord, this was harder than she'd expected. "I didn't tell ye at the time, but I know *The Goat and Goose* well ... for I ... I worked there for a time."

His green eyes grew wide at this admission, before they shadowed. In their depths she saw sympathy, and a hard knot formed in her belly in response. She doubted he'd look so compassionate when he heard the next part of her story.

"I arrived around a year after ye left," Coira pressed on. She lifted her chin then as she continued. "I was yer brother's favorite whore."

Craeg's sharply indrawn breath filled the tent. He drew back, as if she'd just struck him, although he didn't release her hands. Coira swallowed hard. It was as she'd feared, and yet she forced herself to continue. He might as well know everything.

"My parents were cottars who worked the land near Dunan. They died suddenly, and then I fell on hard times. I was still young when Maude took me on as a serving lass ... but when I entered womanhood, I was expected to service the men who visited the brothel—or be cast out onto the street again." Coira sucked in a deep breath, noting that Craeg's face had gone taut. "MacKinnon took a liking to me ... and then started asking for me each visit."

Coira broke off there. Saying the words aloud made her feel ill. Surely, Craeg would be revolted by her once he heard it all.

"He liked me to dress up as a nun ... and then he'd rip off my habit and use me." Her voice, raw now, choked off. Suddenly, it was too difficult to continue.

"Coira," Craeg breathed her name, his voice raw. "Mo chridhe ... did he hurt ye?"

My heart. How could he even call her that? Didn't the truth disgust him?

"Aye … he used his fists on me … did vile things to me," she whispered. "And finally, one day, I couldn't stand it any longer. I fled Dunan to Kilbride … and started a new life." She halted, sucking in a deep breath. "But MacKinnon knows where I am now, and he has given me an ultimatum: return with him to Dunan or he'll slaughter everyone at the abbey."

A hollow silence filled the tent as her voice died away. Coira's belly twisted. It occurred her then that she might have already put the sisters' lives in danger. Had her act in running away made MacKinnon turn on Mother Shona and the other nuns? Had he already taken his revenge?

Coira clenched her jaw, her gaze remaining upon the fur beneath her feet. She couldn't bear the thought.

Craeg didn't answer immediately, yet when he did his voice was barely above a whisper. "No one should have to endure what ye did," he said, his grip upon her hands tightening as he spoke. "*No one.*"

Coira lifted her chin and forced herself to meet his eye. She expected to see disgust written upon his face, yet she didn't. His face was taut, and a turmoil of emotions in his eyes had changed them from moss-green to dark jade. But there was no revulsion.

Suddenly, Coira felt as if she were standing naked before him. "Will ye still let me stay with yer band?" she asked softly. She needed to bring the conversation back to safer ground. "As ye can see … I can't go back to the abbey."

Silence stretched between them, and finally Craeg broke it. "Do ye remember what I said to ye that night … the night I left Kilbride?"

Coira's pulse started to gallop. *Dear Lord.* This wasn't the time to bring that up. However, when she didn't answer, he continued.

"I said that if things were different, I'd do everything in my power to make ye mine."

"Stop, Craeg," Coira gasped. She tried to pull her hands free, yet he held her fast. "Things aren't different

... they're *worse*. How can ye even say that ... after what I've just told ye?"

He scowled. "None of what happened to ye was yer fault. I care not about yer past. My own isn't a rosy tale as ye well know."

Coira shook her head. Her belly now churned. Her eyes burned, and it felt as if an iron band was squeezing her throat. "But I'm broken," she whispered.

His eyes shadowed, and he stepped closer to her. He then lifted one of her hands to his lips. The kiss he bestowed upon the back of her hand was feather-light, reverent. "So am I, Coira," he said, a rasp to his voice. "Why don't we heal together?"

19

Let Me Have Mine

I'M GOING TO enjoy killing him.

Cold, splintering rage pounded through Craeg as he watched Coira leave the tent. Whispering a curse, he raked his hands through his hair. The urge to storm out of this ravine, go straight to Kilbride, and rip Duncan MacKinnon's heart out almost overwhelmed him. The look on her face as she'd recounted that tale, the shadows in those beautiful eyes, would haunt him forever.

Cursing once more, Craeg scrubbed his face with his fist. An edgy, twitchy sensation swept through him. His hands clenched and unclenched as he imagined them around Duncan MacKinnon's throat—as he squeezed the life out of him.

The man had to die, and he would enjoy ending his cruel, perverted life. MacKinnon scorched anyone he came in contact with. Tomorrow couldn't come soon enough.

Heart hammering, Craeg left his tent and made his way back to the far end of the ravine.

Gunn still sat by the fire, staring sightlessly into the dancing flames, whereas Coira was nowhere to be seen.

"Have ye seen Coira?" he asked his friend.

Gunn glanced up, his gaze struggling to focus. "She's gone back in to attend Fen."

At that moment a slight figure emerged from the larger of the two tents, where the two men had been tended. Flora—a woman who'd lost her husband earlier that summer when MacKinnon raided their camp—was pale and tense.

"They're both dead now," she announced, her voice flat. "There was nothing to be done."

Craeg nodded, his already racing pulse quickening further. The lives of all the souls in this ravine were his responsibility. If the sickness took more of them, he'd feel to blame.

The bodies of the dead men would have to be burned, but there would be no time for that tomorrow. They would have to wait.

Craeg's hands fisted. Battle had to come first. He had to have his reckoning against his brother—especially now that he'd discovered what Coira had suffered at MacKinnon's hands. He'd make him suffer before the end, and how he'd enjoy doing so.

Events were set in motion now; they couldn't have turned back even if they'd wanted to. MacKinnon was after him too.

Craeg knew his brother wouldn't have wasted any time in sending out scouts; it was likely he'd discovered their hiding place by now. Craeg would need to leave a group of warriors behind to protect the camp, and he'd make sure the war party left a little earlier than planned, just in case MacKinnon decided to launch a dawn raid.

A few feet away, Gunn's face twisted. "It will take Fen too," he said, his voice hoarse with grief. "My bonny love."

Flora's chin trembled at these heart-wrenching words, while Craeg swallowed hard.

He wanted to reassure his friend, to tell him that maybe Coira would find a way to save her. Yet he wouldn't lie to Gunn. He wouldn't lie to himself either.

"Dear Lord of Mercy, send out yer words to heal."

Coira's whispered words blended with the rasp of Fenella's breathing in the tent. Kneeling before the fur on which the sick woman lay, her hands clasped in prayer, Coira squeezed her eyes shut. "Please send yer healing words to yer servant. In the name of Jesus, drive out all infirmity and sickness from this woman's body."

The words, murmured in desperation, poured out of Coira. She'd donned her scarf over her lower face to re-enter the tent, but noted immediately that Fenella's condition had worsened.

The lumps that had formed under her armpits had grown. They were now red and angry-looking. Her skin had gone a pasty color, highlighting a strange rash upon her lower arms. Just like the farmer's wife and daughter in Torrin, it looked as if Fenella had been bitten by fleas. The woman's breathing had become labored.

If she continues this way, she won't last the night.

Coira squeezed her eyes shut. She couldn't let despair in; she couldn't lose hope. "Dear Lord," she continued with dogged determination. "I ask ye to turn this weakness into strength, this suffering into compassion, sorrow into joy, and pain into comfort. Let this woman be filled with patience and joy in yer presence as she waits for yer healing touch."

Drawing in a ragged breath, Coira opened her eyes. The prayer had calmed her, focused her. She'd been close to tears when she left Craeg's tent, and the urge to find a shadowed corner where she could seek refuge and weep had almost been overwhelming. His gentle words had nearly unraveled her.

However, she couldn't indulge in tears—not when she had the sick to attend.

Fenella needed her.

Coira lowered her clasped hands, her gaze sweeping over the woman's body. She was clad in a sweat-soaked linen tunic, and although she'd been conscious when Coira entered the tent, she appeared to have entered a strange delirium now. Her limbs twitched and shivered, and she uttered soft, piteous groans.

Watching her, Coira searched her mind for every last bit of healing knowledge her mother had imparted upon her.

How I wish ye were here, Ma, she thought. *I could do with yer wisdom right now.*

Indeed, her mother had been bold and fearless in her skills; never afraid to go against common wisdom if she thought it would save a patient.

Coira's gaze settled upon those horrid swellings under Fenella's armpits. The two men from Dunan had shown the same symptoms. She'd heard about these 'plague boils' and how they appeared during the latter stages of the illness. However, no one had said how a healer dealt with them.

Shifting closer, Coira peered at one of the boils. It reminded her of a large abscess.

How would she treat such a thing usually?

I'd lance it.

Coira's belly twisted at the thought of touching the vile swellings. However, as she continued to stare at the swelling, an idea took form in her mind.

Her pulse quickened then, and she rose to her feet. Emerging from the tent, she found Craeg, Gunn, and Flora seated around the fire, their faces grim.

Craeg glanced up, his gaze meeting hers. His lips parted as he readied himself to speak, but Coira forestalled him. "Can ye get me a pair of leather gloves?"

His eyes widened, while both Gunn and Flora turned to stare at her. "Aye ... the smithy will have some ... why do—"

"I also need a small, long-bladed knife," she continued. "And some vinegar."

Gunn drew a boning knife from a sheath on his thigh. "Will this do?"

Coira nodded. Meanwhile, Craeg had risen to his feet. "I'll go and get those gloves and vinegar."

Coira swallowed down nausea and held the knife steady.

The gloves Craeg had found for her were too big, making her movements clumsy; yet it was a necessary precaution. She'd not lance these boils without protecting her hands.

She'd cleaned the blade by holding it in the flames till it glowed red. Now she held a small earthen bowl under the boil she was about to lance, ready to catch whatever fluid escaped.

Clenching her jaw, Coira sliced the knife into the boil. Pus and blood burst forth, and her belly roiled. Fighting a gag, she continued her work, cutting open the swelling so that it emptied completely.

Revolting.

Coira had never seen a boil like it. She just hoped that lancing them in this way wouldn't send her patient's body into shock. Once the first had been lanced, she moved onto the second boil—and once that too had emptied, she doused both with the vinegar Craeg had given her.

Her mother had always used vinegar on lanced ulcers and boils, swearing that it prevented them from festering. Coira too had noted how effective it was.

Fenella, who'd been insensible during the entire process, moaned. Sweat slicked her face, and her body still trembled from the chills that wracked her.

Sitting back on her heels, Coira let out the breath she hadn't even realized she'd been holding. No wonder she was starting to feel light-headed. The drained plague boils weren't a nice sight, but they were definitely less sinister-looking than how they'd looked previously.

Gathering up her things, Coira left the tent.

Gunn was standing outside, waiting for her. "Did it work?" he asked. The man's face was haggard with worry, his gaze gleaming.

Coira stripped off the gloves, dropping them onto the ground next to the tent's entrance. "It's too early to tell," she admitted softly. "But what I've done has not worsened her condition." She straightened up and met Gunn's eye. "If she survives the night, ye may have cause to hope."

Heading in the direction of the fireside, Coira removed her scarf and tucked it away in her healer's basket. Her limbs felt heavy, and her temples ached. She wasn't sure what the time was, but she sensed it was growing late.

"We all need to sleep ... like everyone else in this camp," she murmured, her gaze sweeping around at her companions. "There's nothing more any of us can do for the moment."

Craeg nodded, rising from the fireside. "Very well ... I'll be in my tent if anyone needs me." His voice was subdued as well, his gaze shuttered.

Watching him, Coira wondered if he was brooding about what she'd told him earlier. She hadn't expected such kindness, such compassion, from him. It had unbalanced her. She knew his hatred for Duncan MacKinnon ran deep, and she wondered if she'd just added fuel to the fire.

A strange hush had settled over the camp, now that most of the folk here had retired for the night. However, it was a watchful, tense silence, for they all knew what the dawn would bring.

Craeg needed to rest, and Coira wanted to let him retire to his tent, yet she needed to ask something else of him tonight.

"Craeg," she called to him as he turned to go.

The outlaw leader swiveled around. "Aye?"

Coira faced him, her gaze steady. "When ye and yer men ride out to face MacKinnon tomorrow, I want to go with ye."

Craeg tensed. "War isn't for women," he replied, his tone terse now. "Ye will be safer here."

"I can fight," Coira replied, scowling. "All Sisters of Kilbride know how to wield a weapon."

A muscle flexed in Craeg's jaw. Coira was aware that Gunn's gaze was boring into her back, yet she deliberately kept her attention upon the man who stood between her and her wishes.

"As ye all might have guessed, the quarter-staff I carry isn't to help me walk," she continued. "Mother Shona taught me how to do harm with it."

"That may be so," Craeg replied after a pause. "But being able to wield a weapon, and facing a screaming warrior bearing down up ye with a claidheamh-mor is another."

Coira raised her chin, her own jaw tensing. "I'm aware of that."

Their gazes fused. A battle of wills ensued. Although she appreciated Craeg's empathy earlier, she'd not be ordered around by him now.

"Ye are needed here, to tend Fen," Gunn spoke up from behind her, his voice wary.

"Flora will be able to look after her," Coira replied, her gaze still fixed upon Craeg. "I've done all I can for the time being."

Silence settled over the fireside. "I won't get in yer way," Coira continued, stubbornness settling within her. She'd argue this with Craeg all night if he wished. "But ye will have yer vengeance tomorrow. Let me have mine."

20

No Going Back

"MACKINNON ... ARE YE unwell?"

Duncan MacKinnon's head snapped up at the abbess's enquiry.

No, he wasn't. His head hurt. His body ached. And it felt like someone had just taken a stick to him. Not only that, but he was sweating as if he sat next to a roaring fire. Although it was a cool morning, the air heavy with mist, it felt the hottest day of the year to him. There was no doubt about it, he was getting sick. Yet he wasn't about to admit his frailty—not to this bloody woman.

"I'm fine," he rasped and returned his attention to where he was tightening his horse's girth.

"So ye know the location of the outlaw camp?" she asked.

Duncan shot her a hard look. He was grateful she'd changed the subject, but the gleam in the abbess's eyes made him suspicious of her. Mother Shona was taking far too much interest in his affairs. Indeed, Keith and the others had returned with news that they'd tracked the outlaw and nun into the mountains. They'd taken refuge in a hidden ravine.

Still, it mattered not if she knew his intent this morning.

"Aye," he growled. "They're hiding out in the mountains east of Kilbride … and we're heading there to slaughter them."

The abbess appeared to flinch at the brutality of his words, and despite that he felt like death warmed up, MacKinnon managed a grim smile. This pious woman, with her peaceful ways, paled at such violent talk.

He held her gaze for a moment, darkness stirring within him. He hadn't been making idle threats to Coira. He'd meant it when he'd told her that he'd butcher the abbess and her flock of nuns if Coira didn't return to Dunan with him.

But Coira had still defied him. Right now, she was with his bastard brother.

Duncan's already aching belly, twisted. *Anyone but him. She'll pay for disobeying me.*

When he'd dealt with his brother, and his ragged band, Duncan would return to this abbey and slit this annoying woman's throat. Then he'd torch this place.

As if glimpsing the violence in his eyes, the abbess drew back and made the sign of the cross before her.

"Peace be with ye, MacKinnon," she murmured, her voice cowed.

Duncan flashed her a harsh smile. "Aye … it will be."

He swung up onto his horse's back and twisted in the saddle, noting that the rest of his men had also mounted and were awaiting his orders.

A wave of nausea washed over Duncan then, and he clutched the pommel of the saddle. *Satan's cods, I feel wretched.* Fear slithered in the pit of his belly, cold and clammy. *Is it the plague?*

No—he wouldn't entertain the thought. He'd merely eaten something that had made him ill.

"We ride!" He called out, gathering his reins. Turning his horse on its haunches, he urged it toward the open gates.

Mother Shona watched the clan-chief and his men empty out of the yard. One moment the space had been filled with men and horses—the next she stood alone, listening to the drum of hoof-beats as they galloped east.

Murmuring a prayer, she crossed herself once more. *The good Lord protect me ... that man is evil.*

She'd never looked into someone's eyes and feared for her life like she just had. She'd seen his intent, as clear as if he'd spoken the words.

He planned to kill her.

Heart drumming against her ribs, Mother Shona wiped her damp palms on her skirts, her gaze still upon the open gate where the clan-chief had just departed.

MacKinnon was sick. He could deny it all he wanted, yet the pallor of his face, the sheen of sweat upon his skin, and the way he moved as if he'd suddenly aged overnight told a different tale. The sickness had dug its claws into him.

Still, the knowledge didn't make him any less dangerous. He wasn't ill enough to be prevented from spilling blood today.

A chill feathered down Mother Shona's nape. Until now, Kilbride had been a sanctuary against the sickness, yet MacKinnon had brought it here. How many of them would fall ill because of him?

The abbess clenched her jaw, her gaze still upon the empty gateway. She recalled the things Sister Coira had told her, of how MacKinnon had tormented her.

No wonder she's run off. The very sight of the clan-chief must have turned Sister Coira's stomach. Mother Shona's breathing hitched. *Satan rules this land ... and he must be stopped.*

A cool feeling of resolve settled over the abbess then, drilling in the marrow of her bones. MacKinnon's rule of terror would end today, and she would sacrifice her life, if need be, to see it done.

She tore her attention from the gateway and swept her gaze around, taking in the peaceful surroundings of Kilbride. This place had been her home for so long, but it wouldn't be for much longer.

Everything was changing. Father Camron's campaign against her would never end. Even without MacKinnon threatening the abbey, the sanctuary that she'd worked so hard to protect would soon be no more.

That being the case, she'd do what she could to help Craeg and his men bring MacKinnon down.

Turning on her heel, she glanced about her. It was early, just after dawn. She and the sisters had just finished Lauds, the prayer dedicated to recounting the eternal light bestowed on the world by the Risen Christ.

The monks were now at prayer in the kirk. As soon as the nuns exited, the abbot and his monks had filed inside. Father Camron insisted on conducting his own dawn service, in which the nuns were not welcome.

Spying a small figure across the yard, hurrying toward the refectory, Mother Shona called out. "Sister Mina."

The novice halted and turned to her. After the awful scene the day before, in which MacKinnon had strode across the refectory, hauled Sister Mina from her seat, and twisted her arm behind her back, she was surprised not to see the young woman's face gaunt and strained. MacKinnon had come close to breaking her arm. Yet the novice wore a composed, if wary, expression this morning.

She expected a rebuke from the abbess—although none had been forthcoming the day before.

"Come, Sister … help me. We must bar the doors," Mother Shona instructed, striding toward the kirk. "Now!"

Thankfully, although Sister Mina's gaze drew wide at the instruction, the novice didn't question her. A heartbeat later the nun joined her, and they ascended the stone steps to the kirk. There was a heavy iron bar inside the building, in case the nuns ever had to barricade themselves inside during an attack. However, there was also a bar on the outside—one that Mother Shona had never used, until today.

Halting before the closed oaken doors, the abbess listened. Inside, she could hear the low rumble of the abbot's voice.

Mother Shona's mouth thinned. *There's no going back after this.*

Father Camron was looking for something to condemn her for—and she was about to give him an excellent reason. However, this man's meddling could no longer be borne.

For what she planned to do now, he had to be kept out of the way.

Together, the two women lifted the heavy bar and slid it through the iron handles, locking the doors together. Fortunately, there was no other exit from the kirk, for the narrow windows were too high to reach.

Father Camron and his monks were now trapped inside.

Turning to Sister Mina, the abbess saw the novice's gaze was gleaming with excitement. Although she hadn't yet explained her plan, the young woman knew that something was afoot.

"Gather the others. Tell them to don their winter woolen leggings, and collect their weapons and bring them to the stables," she ordered, her voice sharp with purpose. "No time must be wasted."

"Where are we going, Mother?" Sister Mina asked. She was already moving away, intent on doing the abbess's bidding.

"MacKinnon plans to carry out a massacre today," Mother Shona replied. "We must stop him."

Sister Mina's step faltered, her eyes growing huge. "We're going to fight the clan-chief?" The novice's voice trembled, betraying her fear. Mother Shona didn't blame her. Sister Mina hadn't been at Kilbride long, and hadn't spent as long as the abbess had preparing for this day.

But many of the others had. This was the day they'd all hoped would never come.

"Hurry, Sister," the abbess instructed sharply. "Time is against us."

Dawn had barely touched the edge of the ravine as Craeg strode through the ranks of his men. Shouldering quivers of arrows and pinewood shields, their faces were grim, their gazes glinting with purpose.

Craeg met their gazes, his chest constricting as both pride and trepidation filled him.

These men trusted him.

They'd put their lives in his hands—he couldn't fail them.

"We leave shortly," he shouted, his voice echoing about the rumble of conversation. "Ready yerselves." It wasn't a rousing speech, but there would be time enough for that on the battlefield.

Approaching the far end of the ravine, Craeg tensed, preparing himself for the worst. No word of Fenella had reached him for the remainder of the night. He'd slept fitfully and awoken in the pre-dawn, exhausted.

Had Fen died overnight and no one told him? A heavy weight pressed down upon Craeg's breastbone at the thought of losing Fenella; she and Gunn had been with him since the beginning. They were the family he'd always longed for. The fear in Gunn's eyes the night before had been a dirk-blade to Craeg's guts.

He hated to see his friend suffer like this.

Gunn stood before the smoking ruins of last night's fire, his face hewn from stone as he prepared himself for battle. He'd donned a mail shirt and was attempting to lace leather bracers about his forearms.

"Here." Craeg stopped before him. "I'll help ye with that."

"Fen usually does this," Gunn replied softly.

"How is she?" Craeg asked, deftly drawing the laces tight, fastening the leather bracer.

"Still alive."

"Her condition has steadied overnight." A woman's voice intruded then. "And her fever has lowered a little."

Craeg's chin snapped up, his hands stilling.

A woman he barely recognized stood a few feet away.

Coira had removed her habit and dressed in men's clothing: leather breeches, hunting boots, a léine that reached mid-thigh, and a brown vest. The only concession to her former attire was the small wooden crucifix that hung about her neck.

For a moment Craeg merely stared.

He'd spent far too much time in the past days dreaming what Coira's hair looked like. He'd imagined it would be dark, and it was. Yet it wasn't shorn against her scalp as he'd expected. Instead, it hung in a dark glossy braid over one shoulder.

"She's the same size as Fen." Gunn spoke up, when the silence stretched out. "So she might as well borrow some of her clothes. The woman can't go into battle in long skirts, can she?"

Craeg tore his gaze from Coira and saw that his friend now wore a tight smile.

Still speechless, Craeg glanced back at Coira. She seemed taller, leaner, and younger dressed like that.

"Coira." The strangled edge to his voice drew him up sharply. "What weapons do ye have?"

"Just this and a knife," she replied coolly, holding up the quarter-staff with her right hand and slapping the blade strapped to her thigh with the other. "I need nothing else."

Watching her, Craeg's pulse quickened. Coira appeared transformed. The woman's self-confidence stunned him; she wasn't putting on a brave-face. He could see the steely determination in her eyes.

Craeg shifted his attention back to Gunn's bracers. Quickly he finished lacing them, and then he stepped back, turning to face Coira.

"I need to speak to ye," he said firmly.

Her eyebrows arched, her gaze turning wary. "Now?"

"Aye ... follow me."

Craeg walked past the two tents, leading the way to the farthest edge of the ravine, where a thin stream of water trickled down the rock face. The air here was misty and smelled of moss. The light of the braziers and torches down the ravine barely reached here—as such, Coira's face was heavily shadowed when he turned to face her.

"Craeg," she began, her voice husky. "I don't think we should—"

"I know this isn't the time or place for this," he cut in. He was aware of the tension in his own voice, yet he pressed on. "But since we're about to depart for battle, I think there are a few things that need to be said."

21

Remember

COIRA'S JAW FIRMED, although her gaze was suddenly wary. "Go on then."

"The first thing ye need to know is that *nothing* about yer past bothers me," he continued. Her lips parted as she prepared to argue with him, but Craeg pressed on. "Ye forget ... I've seen it all. I was *born* in a brothel ... my mother was a whore. I know what happens there, how many of the women are forced into that life." He paused and drew in a steadying breath. "I also know that Duncan MacKinnon is a pig. He took his perversions, his hatred for women, and made them yer burden. I vow that he'll pay for that."

Coira's throat bobbed, although when she replied, her voice was firm. "We'll *both* make him pay, Craeg," she murmured.

"Aye," Craeg replied, vehement now. "Ye too want reckoning ... I understand that." He took a step closer to her, half expecting her to back away, but instead Coira held her ground. "Once he's dead ... once ye trust men again ... ye will heal."

She swallowed, her gaze gleaming now as tears threatened.

Craeg's throat thickened. He didn't want to make her weep, but the words inside him had to be spoken. "Time moves against us now," he said, softening his tone. "I don't want to go into battle without knowing what it's like to kiss ye."

Her chest heaved, and even though they weren't touching, Craeg felt the tension emanating off her.

"I'm still a nun," she finally managed the words, although her voice sounded choked.

Craeg's mouth curved. "Not dressed like that, ye aren't."

"A habit doesn't make a woman a nun ... but the vows she takes."

"Aye." He moved closer still to her, unable to stop himself. "But ye have left the order, have ye not?" He raised a hand then and brushed the back of his knuckles across her cheek—as he had that night in that moonlit glade. How he'd longed to kiss her back then, and the yearning had not lessened. It had grown to a hunger that now dominated every waking thought.

He felt her tremble, heard the whisper of her quickened breathing. She was fighting the hunger too—he knew it.

Heat pulsed between them, as did an ocean of things unsaid. Words were pointless now though. There were too many reasons why he shouldn't be touching her, shouldn't want her with his body and soul. But none of them would stop him now.

With a stifled groan, Craeg cupped her face with his hands and leaned in, his lips brushing hers. It was a tentative kiss, feather-light. He didn't want to startle her or force this moment.

Craeg brushed his lips across Coira's once more, giving her the chance to pull away, yet she didn't. And when a soft, breathy sigh escaped her, Craeg covered Coira's mouth with his.

Coira had never been kissed before.

The men who'd frequented *The Goat and Goose* didn't kiss the whores. There wasn't any tenderness, any intimacy, in what had passed between her and the men she'd once serviced. They'd disrobed, rutted her, tossed her a coin, and left.

This was completely new to Coira, and when Craeg's lips first touched hers, a dizzying wave of panic rose up within her. He was crossing her boundaries, smashing down the walls that had kept her safe over the years.

But she didn't shrink away.

Despite the blood roaring in her ears, her wildly beating pulse, she forced down her fear. His lips brushed hers once again, and the need she'd been fighting for days now ignited within her like dry kindling to a naked flame.

His lips were soft, and the heat of his body, the spicy male scent of his skin, sucked the breath from her. She couldn't help it; a sigh of need escaped her.

And that was when everything changed.

His mouth slanted over hers, firmer now, and his tongue gently parted her lips.

Aching want swept over Coira, along with a desperation that shoved any lingering fear aside.

He tasted better than the first apple wine of the autumn, better than fresh bread or heather honey. He smelled like summer rain, like crushed grass, like oiled leather. He was life, death, and eternity all in one kiss.

A cry rose in Coira's throat, smothered by his gently exploring lips, his masterful tongue. She heard her quarter-staff thud to the ground, slipping from nerveless fingers. Not caring, she leaned into him, her tongue tentatively stroking his.

Craeg groaned, deep in his throat, his hands sliding down from her face to her shoulders. He drew her against him, gathering her into his arms as his kisses deepened.

Coira was lost. Her hands came up, her fingertips tracing his jaw, his neck—resting in the hollow between his collarbones, where his pulse raced. She couldn't believe she'd lived her whole life till now without this.

His body, pressed against the length of hers, was strong, warm, and exciting beyond measure. Her fingers ached to strip away the clothing that lay between them. She longed to know what his naked flesh felt like pressed up against hers. Hot desire flooded through her, dizzying in its intensity.

It was Craeg who eventually ended the kiss. His breathing came in ragged pants, his eyes gleaming, when he pulled back. His face was taut, his expression feral.

Their gazes fused as the first glimmers of early dawn filtered into this dark corner of the ravine.

"Whatever comes to pass today," he said, a rasp in his voice, "I want ye to know that the shadow MacKinnon has cast over ye will soon lift. Please remember that, Coira." He reached up, stroking her lower lip with the pad of his thumb.

A lump rose in Coira's throat, making it hard to swallow, to breathe, and to speak. His voice was a balm, his touch an anchor. Suddenly, she dared believe he was right. How she wanted to believe that.

She sought his hands with hers, their fingers entangling. Finally, she nodded.

Carr Broderick stood on the walls and watched a damp, misty dawn rise over Dunan.

The village beneath him, still cast in night's long shadow, was eerily quiet. Usually at this hour, he could see smoke rising from stacked stone chimneys, could smell the aroma of baking bannock.

But this morning it was as if ghosts inhabited Dunan.

Even before MacKinnon had ridden out with his men, folk had started to flee the fort, hurrying out into the hills with rolled blankets and packs upon their backs. But in the three days since the clan-chief had departed, so had the bulk of the village's residents.

The streets were now deserted, the markets closed. Sickness had come to Dunan, and its people had sought sanctuary elsewhere. Carr's gaze narrowed at this observation. Of course, they'd just taken the sickness with them, and would likely spread it.

The fortress at Carr's back was also empty. The broch of Dunan hadn't been spared. Most of the servants who hadn't sickened had run off.

Carr heaved in a deep breath and turned, making his way along the narrow walkway to the steep stone steps leading down to the bailey. A grim sight awaited him there: a row of bodies covered by sacking. Three of the stable lads and one of the cooks lay under there. Carr and the few remaining members of the Dunan Guard would have to burn them later in the day.

A knot tightened under Carr's ribcage. He'd been spared so far—but how much longer would it be before he fell ill? He lived day-to-day now, with the Grim Reaper breathing down his neck. Sooner or later, he expected to feel the Reaper's cold touch.

Entering the broch, Carr went first to the kitchens. The only soul there was a lass—the only one of the kitchen staff remaining—frying a large round cake upon a griddle. Carr shouldn't have been surprised really. Kenzie was a tough wee thing and doggedly loyal to MacKinnon.

She glanced up when he entered and favored Carr with a tired smile. "The bannock is ready if ye are hungry?"

"Thank ye, Kenzie," he replied, not returning the smile. His mood was too dark this morning to make the effort. No word of MacKinnon had returned to Dunan. Carr wondered if the clan-chief had indeed managed to track his bastard brother down, and if so, what the outcome had been.

"I'll take some up for Lady Drew first," he added.

Kenzie nodded, relief suffusing her face. There weren't any servants left now to carry out such tasks. Working quickly, she flipped the bannock onto a platter before slicing it up into wedges. She then added earthen pots of butter and honey before lifting up the tray and handing it to Carr. "I'm sorry ye have to be saddled with such tasks, Broderick," she murmured, offering him another smile.

Carr suspected that the young kitchen wench had developed an affection for him of late—feelings which had intensified as the inhabitants of the broch slowly dwindled. Carr had given her little encouragement, yet that did not dim her interest.

"I don't mind," he answered, returning her smile now. It was the truth. Bringing Lady Drew some food to break her fast was merely an excuse to see her. The only good thing to come from this sickness was that he now interacted with Lady Drew far more often than he had in the past.

Climbing the stairs, he made his way to her solar. He knocked on the door.

"Enter," a soft voice called out.

Carr pushed open the door with his elbow and made his way in.

Lady Drew was seated by the fire, a thick shawl about her shoulders. Carr's step faltered a little at the sight of her. It was rare to see MacKinnon's sister with her hair unbound. Long and wavy, and the color of peat, it tumbled over her shoulders.

Drew's grey eyes widened at the sight of him. "Oh ... it's ye, Broderick ... I thought it was Kenzie."

"She's busy downstairs," he replied with an apologetic shrug. "Ye shall have to make do with me, milady."

He moved to the center of the solar and set the tray down upon a table.

"I'm quite at a loss, ye know," she said, her tone rueful. "I'm used to having servants fuss around me in the morning ... it looks like I'll have to dress myself and put up my own hair."

Carr huffed a laugh at this pronouncement. "I would offer to help, but ..."

Drew snorted, before she rose to her feet, drawing the shawl tight. "I'm sure I'll manage. God's bones, Broderick ... it's cold in here. Could ye put some more peat on the fire?"

Carr nodded and went to do as bid. However, he personally found the chamber warm and a little stuffy. He couldn't see how she could feel a chill. "I was going to open a window," he said, "but I take it ye would prefer I didn't?"

"Please don't," she replied, moving over to the table. "Come and join me at the table instead ... I take it the lass didn't expect me to eat all these bannocks?"

After attending to the fire, Carr returned to the table and took a seat opposite Drew. He waited until she had helped herself to a bannock, before he did the same.

Being able to sit at the same table as the woman he longed for was both an unexpected pleasure and a torture—but he'd not deny her.

Spreading some butter upon his wedge of bannock, Carr glanced up, his gaze fixing upon her. This close, he saw her heart-shaped face was pale.

Carr went still. "Lady Drew," he said softly. "Are ye well?"

She nodded, her mouth tightening in annoyance. "Of course ... don't fuss."

Carr watched her, his gaze narrowing. Her sharp tongue didn't bother him. However, her well-being did. Without asking permission, he rose from the table and crossed to her, placing his hand upon her forehead.

It was the first time he'd ever touched the woman he served.

The move was bold, and in other circumstances he wouldn't have dared. But today was different.

"Broderick!" she gasped, twisting away from him. "What the devil are ye doing?"

Carr withdrew his hand, dread twisting under his ribcage. Her brow was burning hot, the skin clammy.

Their gazes fused then, and whatever admonishments she'd been about to utter died upon her lips when she saw the look on his face.

22

Face-to-Face

DUNCAN REINED IN his horse and watched the riders approach, before frowning. He'd sent scouts ahead, to keep an eye on the outlaws, but they'd returned sooner than he'd expected.

"They're on the move," Keith greeted him. The blond man's face was flushed. He'd ridden hard to reach the clan-chief as quickly as possible. "The outlaws are traveling west ... toward us."

"How far away are they?" Duncan barked, trying to ignore the chills that wracked his body and the cough that tickled the back of his throat.

Curse them all, he felt terrible.

Keith MacKinnon's gaze settled upon the clan-chief, and his pale blue eyes narrowed. Duncan could tell by the way his face tensed that he didn't look good. However, the man was wise enough not to comment upon it.

"Around twenty furlongs distant." Keith replied. "Our paths will cross before noon."

This news made MacKinnon scowl. He hadn't expected his bastard brother to ride out to meet him—at least not so soon. He'd wanted Craeg's scouts to spot them and scurry back to their hiding place before chaos and panic ensued. Duncan clenched his jaw; it mattered not. The sooner they clashed the better.

"Did someone let them know we were coming?" One of Duncan's men asked behind him, echoing the clan-chief's own thoughts.

"Who cares," Duncan growled. "The Bastard has saved us all a long ride." His gaze swept right to left, taking in the wide valley they'd pulled up in. Behind him stretched woodland, whereas broom and gorse dotted the slopes of the valley below. "We make our stand here."

They'd been marching for over an hour when the sky above cleared and the sun appeared. Warmth filtered over Coira, and she raised her face to it.

This was the first time in a decade that the sun had shone upon her naked head. She felt strange, lighter, walking without being shrouded by her veil. The sensation had been discomforting at first—she'd felt naked without her habit. It had been her shield for so long. When she'd warn it, men ceased to see her as a woman. But ever since she'd appeared before the outlaws in Fenella's clothing, the world looked upon her differently.

"Can ye really use that quarter-staff?" Farlan's question made Coira lower her face from the sun's gentle caress and glance right. The outlaw walked beside her in the long column that snaked down the mountainside.

Coira's mouth curved in her first real smile in days. "Do ye want a demonstration? I can knock ye flat on yer back, if ye would like."

Farlan raised his hands, dark eyes glinting. "No need for that ... save yer aggression for MacKinnon's lot."

Coira's smile faded. "I intend to."

"So ... the rest of the nuns at Kilbride ... are they like ye? Can they really fight?"

"Aye."

"Why?"

"Mother Shona taught us. Before she came to Skye, she had a hard life. When she was elected as abbess, she decided that the Sisters of Kilbride should be able to defend themselves if the need ever arose."

Farlan gave a low whistle. "And there was me thinking nuns were useless."

Coira's gaze narrowed. "The Lord's work is never 'useless'. Kilbride is the reason the people of Torrin haven't starved over the past years. MacKinnon always raids their stores in autumn."

"So ye have been helping folk?"

"Aye, when we can. It's just one of the reasons why MacKinnon has always disliked us."

Farlan frowned. "And the other reasons?"

The young man was sharp—too sharp. Coira might have confided in Craeg, but she wasn't about to do the same with Farlan. She liked him well enough, yet he asked too many questions.

Coira glanced away then, her gaze traveling down the column to where Craeg strode next to Gunn. The red-haired warrior was easy to spot in a group, and he was never far from the outlaw leader.

Warmth settled in the cradle of Coira's hips, radiating out.

If she'd been alone, she'd have raised her fingers to her lips, allowing the memory of that kiss to flood through her. However, under Farlan's penetrating gaze, she prevented herself.

That kiss had shifted her world. Everything was different in the aftermath. She felt desire for a man—a man that didn't turn her stomach, a man that didn't want to pay her so she'd spread her legs, a man who treated her as if she were something precious, something to be cherished.

A pressure built in her chest as she thought about Craeg, recalled the tenderness in his eyes and the fierceness upon his face as he stared down at her at dawn.

The shadow MacKinnon has cast over ye will soon lift.

He'd said those words with such conviction that she'd believed him. For the first time, she actually had hope. It was something she'd searched for at Kilbride, yet despite her strong faith, she'd never truly found it.

Not until Craeg entered her life.

A soft laugh drew her from her reverie. Coira glanced back at Farlan to find him still watching her, a knowing grin upon his lips. "Ye wouldn't be the first woman to fall for him," he said with a shake of his head. "Craeg wields charm like a blade."

A chill stole over Coira at these words. He made Craeg's behavior seem contrived, practiced—as if he'd put on a show for her. Perhaps Farlan saw the alarm on her face, for his grin abruptly faded. "Sorry, poor choice of words. I could do with some lessons in charm myself. No wonder the lasses prefer Craeg."

Coira huffed a laugh, although underneath it she was now wary of Farlan. "Aye … one day ye will cut yerself on that sharp tongue of yers, Farlan."

He offered her a sheepish smile. "I think I just have."

The two bands met just as the sun reached its zenith in the sky.

Craeg, who walked ahead of his men, caught a glimpse of MacKinnon pennants in the distance. His gaze traveled along the line of horsemen outlined against the dark wall of greenery behind them.

"Stay here," Craeg murmured to Gunn, his gaze never leaving the riders. "I'm going out to talk to him … alone."

"I should come with ye." Gunn's voice held a warning, yet Craeg ignored it. Before the end came, he'd speak to Duncan MacKinnon face-to-face.

"Stay here," he replied, still not glancing at his friend.

With that, Craeg stepped out of the line and walked down the scrubby slope to where the horse and rider had halted at the bottom of the valley.

The sun warmed the crown of his head as he walked, and he was aware that after what seemed like weeks of grey, misty weather, the sky had cleared and summer had returned to the Isle of Skye.

Craeg walked easily, despite the heavy pine shield he wore slung across his back and the claidheamh-mor that hung at his side. Unlike many of his men, he didn't carry a quiver of arrows and longbow, for he preferred to lead the charge of warriors into battle. However, he'd strapped a long-bladed dirk to his right thigh for fighting at close-quarters, should the need arise. And it most likely would.

MacKinnon cut an imposing figure astride the magnificent warhorse. He sat easily in the saddle, and Craeg remembered what a skilled horseman his half-brother was. He'd heard about his prowess as a hunter too—Duncan would be a formidable adversary, mounted or not.

And as he drew near, Craeg finally made out the features of the MacKinnon clan-chief's face.

His breathing quickened.

So many years had passed since the pair of them had met face-to-face, since they'd looked each other squarely in the eye.

He'd heard many folk pass comment on the physical resemblance between them, but since the times were few and far between when Craeg ever glimpsed his own reflection, he would have to take them at their word.

Duncan hadn't changed much over the years, although there were perhaps lines of severity upon his handsome face that made him look sterner, older. Those iron-grey eyes were the same though: cold and shrewd.

But as Craeg came to a halt around eight yards back from the destrier, he realized that something wasn't quite right. Those lines upon his face, weren't from age, but from strain. His skin had a grey tinge and sweat gleamed off his forehead.

"No horse for Craeg the Bastard, eh?"

Duncan MacKinnon's greeting slammed into Craeg like a fist to the belly. In an instant he was transported back to that fateful day in Dunan. The last time he'd heard that voice, he'd been curled up fighting consciousness in an alley that reeked of stale piss.

That arrogant, drawling voice had echoed in his ears for months afterward.

But now all Craeg heard in his ears was the roar of his own breathing. His heart started to race, and he clenched his jaw as he resisted the urge to bare his teeth.

Hatred rose within him, clawing up from his gut like a beast that had been waiting far too long for reckoning.

Finally, after all these years, the time had come.

23

The Yoke Breaks

WHEN CRAEG DIDN'T answer, MacKinnon smiled. It was a cold expression, full of malice.

Of course, his half-brother had waited a long time for this day too.

"Still proud," MacKinnon drawled. "Still believe ye are my equal, don't ye?"

"We're not equals, Duncan," Craeg said finally. The calmness of his voice surprised him. No one would have suspected the turmoil that churned within. "I've always been yer superior ... and ye and I both know it."

The response was inflammatory, designed to anger, and when MacKinnon's smile faded and his gaze narrowed, Craeg knew he'd hit his mark.

"Ye have been a burr up my arse for too long, Bastard," he murmured. "I shall enjoy watching ye die."

Craeg smiled back, showing his teeth this time. "Ye should have killed me that day. Ye have made many mistakes over the years, but that was yer most foolish."

MacKinnon's dark brows knotted together, something feral moving in his eyes. He shifted his attention from Craeg then, just for a few moments, his gaze sweeping the line of warriors upon the brow of the hill behind him. "Coira is with ye, I take it?"

Craeg went still, his fingers flexing as the urge to draw his sword surged within him.

Seeing his reaction, MacKinnon's eyes gleamed. "Enjoying my whore, are ye?"

A taut silence settled between them then. The cold knot of hatred in Craeg's gut drew tighter. The impulse to rush howling at MacKinnon was almost overwhelming, yet Craeg mastered it. Instead, he let those words hang between them, let battle fury kindle in his blood.

Long moments passed, and when MacKinnon realized that Craeg wasn't going to bite, his mouth twisted. "Coira will be mine again soon enough. Get ready to taste steel, Bastard."

Once again, Craeg didn't reply—he didn't trust himself to. Instead, he turned his back on his half-brother and walked away up the slope, back to where his men silently waited. All the way up, the skin between his shoulder blades itched. He almost expected his brother to throw a knife into his back.

Yet no such strike came.

Still, it was a long walk up the hill, and Craeg was sweating when he reached Gunn's side once more.

The big red-haired warrior met his eye and raised a ruddy eyebrow. "Well?"

"He's sick," Craeg replied.

"The pestilence?"

"Could be." Craeg drew his claidheamh-mor, the scrape of steel echoing over the hillside. "But that doesn't make him any less dangerous."

He shifted his attention from Gunn then, back down the valley. MacKinnon was riding away, cantering back to join his men.

Swiveling on his heel, Craeg's gaze swept over the ranks of men who'd joined him from all over the territory. He saw the fierceness on their faces, the glint in their eyes. They were ready to fight for him, to die for him. Craeg's pulse accelerated. He raised his claidheamh-mor high then, drawing their gazes to him.

"Long have we prepared for this day." His voice rang out across the hillside. "Ye all know what ye must do ... I won't remind ye of it." He paused then, his chest swelling. "Ye know of the bad blood between MacKinnon and me ... but remember this fight is about much more than just vengeance ... it's about freedom. Long has MacKinnon's iron fist crushed ye all into the dust. His Guard came to yer villages, took all yer savings, and robbed ye of yer last sack of barley—the only thing between yer families and starvation. And then when ye fought back, he called ye criminals and put a price on yer heads."

Craeg broke off here, breathing hard as fire caught in his veins. He wasn't used to giving speeches like this. But his men needed to hear these words. His gaze swept the ranks then, and there, near the back, he glimpsed a lone woman.

Coira stood watching him, her eyes gleaming, her jaw set. He didn't want her to fight—didn't want her to risk her life. But she had her own score to settle with MacKinnon today, and he wouldn't take that from her.

His belly twisted all the same, when he thought of her facing men swinging claidheamh-mors. Although he'd witnessed Lady Leanna with a longbow, he hadn't seen Coira fight. What if she'd overplayed her abilities to him? What if, in the heat of battle, her nerve failed her?

Craeg swallowed the lump that suddenly rose in his throat. He wouldn't be able to help her. Once the fighting began, Coira would be on her own, and she knew it.

Pushing the realization aside, Craeg forced his attention back to the ranks of warriors watching him.

"The yoke breaks today!" He shouted, thrusting his broadsword high into the air. "Today, we take back our lives!"

A cry went up among the outlaws, rippling out across the hillside.

Craeg's skin prickled at the sound. Turning, he looked back across the valley and saw that MacKinnon's warriors had urged their horses forward. They were now careening down the slope toward the bottom of the valley.

Craeg's heart leaped. "Archers!" he yelled. "Ready!"

And then, as he and his men had planned long before this day, Craeg dropped to one knee. Beside him, Gunn did the same—as did all the warriors in the first three lines.

But the row of men behind them—those bearing longbows—didn't crouch. Instead, they notched arrows and sighted their quarry.

Craeg held his breath, his gaze tracking the line of horses that thundered toward them, and then a shout tore from his throat. "Loose!"

I'm taking them all to their deaths.

Leading the way up a steep hill interspersed with wildling pines, Mother Shona tried to ignore the guilt that dogged every step, yet it hung over her like an oppressive shadow, darkening with each furlong they journeyed east.

She'd made her choice; there wasn't any point in regretting it now.

Although the women traveled fast—alternating between a brisk walk and a steady jog—worry had begun to form a hard knot in the pit of the abbess's belly.

They're on horseback ... we'll get there too late.

Indeed, the urgency that had driven her to call the Sisters of Kilbride to arms had faded, and in its place grew a gnawing worry.

Things hadn't started well at dawn. Once she'd gathered the sisters to her, it had become evident that three of the nuns were unwell: Sisters Anis, Fritha, and Morag had all come down with fevers and coughs overnight. A chill had settled over the abbess as she'd sent the nuns back to the dormitory to rest—she'd feared that MacKinnon had brought the sickness with him to Kilbride, and she'd been right. She'd left Sister Magda to tend them; 'Old Magda' wasn't agile or strong enough to join the others anyway.

Mother Shona frowned as she pushed aside a pine branch. She didn't want to leave the nuns behind with only an aged woman to tend them, yet she had no choice.

She had committed to this now.

Breathing hard, the abbess pushed herself up the last few yards toward the tree-lined brow of the hill. Like the other nuns, she'd adjusted her clothing for this journey. Under her skirts, she wore woolen leggings, and she had knotted her underskirts and habit, tying them around her hips with twine. It wasn't an ideal solution, yet it enabled the nuns a far greater freedom of movement.

Although she was one of the oldest women in the group, she had deliberately led the way. The sisters depended upon her strength and guidance. She could not lag behind.

Fortunately, the hard, physical toil of a nun's life prepared the abbess for this journey. Even so, as she shouldered her way between two embracing fir trees, Mother Shona noted that her legs now ached and her lungs burned from exertion.

However, when she stepped out of the trees, and her gaze alighted upon the valley beyond, the abbess came to an abrupt halt.

Behind her, Sister Elspeth, who'd kept pace with her the whole morning, breathed a prayer.

A pitch-battle was taking place in the valley below. Men on horseback—the Dunan Guard—had engaged a host of warriors on foot. The clang of metal, the meaty thud of weapons connecting with flesh, and the cries of the injured and dying rang out.

"The outlaws came out to meet them," Elspeth gasped.

"Aye." Mother Shona glanced over her shoulder at the nun. She knew an abbess shouldn't play favorites, but she'd warmed to Sister Elspeth far less than many of the other sisters over the years. She could be a troublemaker and a gossip. And yet, this morning she'd shown a different side to her character.

The moment Mother Shona had announced her plan, the nun had swung into action, ordering the younger sisters about and ensuring they were ready to depart as quickly as possible.

There had been no word of complaint from her on the journey east. She had not questioned Mother's Shona's decision—not once.

Meeting the nun's eye now, the abbess saw the trust, the utter conviction that whatever Mother Shona decided was right.

The abbess's breathing hitched. *Merciful Lord, I hope I have made the right decision.*

She'd fought in battles during her time with the outlaws. But the women who followed her had not. She only hoped she'd prepared them adequately for this.

One by one, the sisters emerged from the trees and halted upon the brow of the hill, their gazes sweeping to the fight unfolding beneath them.

Mother Shona searched their faces, her belly clenching when she saw some of the nuns pale, their eyes growing huge as they observed the violence. One or two even swayed a little on their feet, as if they might faint.

What have I done?

"Mother Shona!" Sister Elspeth's voice rang out, drawing the abbess's attention once more. "Look ... it's Sister Coira!"

Following Sister Elspeth's pointing finger, the abbess turned and peered into the fray.

And there, at the heart of it, she spied a tall woman, fighting with a quarter-staff.

Mother Shona's breathing caught. Coira was no longer wearing her habit—her long dark braid flying as she whirled, ducked, swung, and jabbed. Yet she stood out amongst a crowd of men—and as the abbess watched, Coira brought a big man down with a deadly swing to the jaw.

Mother Shona's heart started to pound. *I taught her that move.* Indeed, she had—although she'd never been as deadly with a quarter-staff as Coira was.

"She's magnificent." The surprise in Sister Elspeth's voice jerked the abbess back to the present. Sisters Coira and Elspeth had never been friends, and yet the nun stared at Coira with awe upon her face.

The expression jolted the abbess into action. Heart pounding, she turned to the nuns following her. "MacKinnon has brought nothing but misery to the folk of this land." Her voice lifted above the roar of battle that echoed up from below. "Our own sisters have suffered at his hands. He hunted Sister Ella and abducted Sister Leanna. They would likely still be with us, if not for him."

Breaking off there, Mother Shona saw the gleam in the nuns' eyes, the determination in their faces. Then, inhaling deeply, she continued. "Sister Coira is down there fighting for her life. Are we going to let her do so alone?"

A few feet away, Sister Mina drew the knife at her waist. A slight tremble betrayed her nerves, yet her gaze was fierce. "No!"

"No!" The other nuns echoed, drawing their weapons.

"Those with longbows remain at a safe distance and pick off as many men wearing MacKinnon colors as ye can," Mother Shona instructed. Calmness descended upon her. "The rest of ye, with me."

Her gaze swept over the line of nuns once more. There were only twenty of them: women armed with dirks, longbows, and quarter-staffs. Mother Shona was the only one of their number who wielded a sword. It was a different weapon to the huge claidheamh-mors that the men below used. She'd had a smith in Torrin fashion her a lighter blade not long after she became abbess, one that she could wield one-handed.

Mother Shona drew her weapon. The double-edged blade glinted in the bright sunlight, and a tight smile curved her mouth.

If only Aaron could see me now.

Her lover had taught her how to wield a sword. He'd taught her that speed and agility mattered just as much as strength when it came to swordplay.

It was at the end of one of their long practice sessions that he'd kissed her for the first time.

Aaron and the life she'd once lived had seemed an age ago until now. The walls of Kilbride had sheltered her from her past and kept the memories at bay. Yet at that moment, she wasn't Mother Shona, Abbess of Kilbride— but Shona of Lismore. Wild, brave, and fearless.

With a howl, she fled down the hill and to battle.

24

Legacy

COIRA KNEW THAT Craeg wanted to be the one to kill MacKinnon—but that didn't stop her searching for the clan-chief all the same.

Craeg needed to have his reckoning, yet so did she. However, she couldn't get close to the front. The press of male bodies was too thick.

From early on in the battle, she was glad that the quarter-staff was her weapon of choice. Although tall and broad-shouldered compared to many women, she still lacked a man's brute strength. Those massive broadswords that even a warrior had to wield two-handed would never have suited her.

Instead, the iron-tipped quarter-staff cut a path through the ranks of the Dunan Guard. She'd just knocked two men off their horses, when a warrior came at her, sword swinging.

Blood coursing down one cheek, he had a maddened look upon his face, an expression that warned her the man had passed the point where he cared about his own mortality. If he died bringing her down, so be it.

Coira spun the quarter-staff, using a two-handed under-arm spin. The weapon flew so fast that it became a blur. Leaping forward, she struck the warrior across the face with the staff, before his blade could reach her. He reeled back, kept his feet, and lunged for her.

She spun the staff once more and struck her opponent again, felling him this time, before stabbing him through the throat with the pointed end of her weapon.

Breathing hard, Coira turned quickly to face another warrior and blocked his attack. She then delivered a downward strike, hitting him hard across the ribs. The man hissed a curse and attacked once more, but this time Coira ducked and swept low, knocking the warrior's feet out from under him.

Sweat trickled down Coira's back, heat pulsing through her as she struck, swept, and thrust her way through the fray.

And then, through it all she caught a glimpse of black and white on the hill above.

Three nuns, spaced around half a dozen yards apart, were firing arrows into the fray.

Coira gasped.

The Sisters of Kilbride were here, fighting alongside the outlaws.

A few feet away, a MacKinnon warrior went down, a feather-fletched arrow embedded in the back of his neck.

Coira's attention snapped back to the fighting then, as another man launched himself at her, dirk drawn. He was trying to get under her guard. Coira gritted her teeth and struck hard, bringing the staff down on his hand. She felt the bones crack under the impact. The warrior howled, the sound choking off when Coira swung her staff into his face.

Whirling away from the fallen man, Coira peered through the fracas and spied the abbess.

Mother Mary ... she can fight!

Coira had sparred with the abbess often over the years, but had always known the woman was holding herself back.

She just hadn't realized how much.

The abbess moved like a woman half her age, striking like an adder and dancing away from any attack that came near her. She toyed with the big men who swung at her with their claidheamh-mors. She made them look like lumbering giants as she escaped the reach of their blades again and again.

Blood splattered across Mother Shona's face and her snow-white wimple. Her delicate features were set in hard lines, and her brown eyes gleamed. An instant later Coira recognized Sister Elspeth fighting at the abbess's side. The woman wielded a dirk, its long blade dripping with blood. Coira remembered that Sister Elspeth was as good with blades as Sister Ella had been. Nonetheless, it was a shock to see the nun fighting with such savagery. The left sleeve of her habit was torn, and blood oozed from a long cut to her upper arm, yet Sister Elspeth paid it no mind.

Coira's fingers tightened around the ash quarter-staff.

She wouldn't let them face the Dunan Guard alone.

She resumed her path through the press of MacKinnon warriors and horses. Eventually, her breathing coming in short gasps, she staggered from the press to join the nuns.

Mother Shona yanked her sword free of a fallen warrior and favored Coira with a savage smile. "Thought we would leave ye out here on yer own, did ye?"

Coira shook her head, too exhausted to answer. The battle was starting to drain her, and she realized this was where men held a distinct advantage. Their stronger, more muscular bodies withstood battle for longer. They had greater endurance. It was just as well she now stood with the Sisters of Kilbride, for her arms had developed a slight tremor as she spun her staff and readied herself to face a man on horseback who now charged at her.

This wasn't the time for her body to fail her.

She widened her stance, anchoring herself on the ground. And then, an instant before she swung her staff at the warrior bearing down upon her, she caught a glimpse of two men fighting with claidheamh-mors in the heart of the melee: Craeg and MacKinnon.

Craeg slashed his way through the fray, searching for his half-brother. It seemed that MacKinnon had done the same, for when they finally found each other, the two men paused amongst the chaos, frozen for a moment.

We share the same blood, Craeg thought, a strange heaviness settling within him, *and yet he's my mortal enemy.*

Craeg knew he shouldn't be surprised by the hatred between them. How many siblings had turned against each other over the centuries? There seemed to be no greater hate than that between brothers.

Half-brothers.

Aye, that was the root of it. Craeg was a bastard, spawned by a whore, while Duncan was the rightful heir and ruler of these lands. And yet it had never stopped him being threatened by Craeg.

He circled MacKinnon, shrugging out the knots in his shoulders. Years of hiding, years of slowly whittling away at the man who'd nearly killed him—and here they finally were.

MacKinnon attacked first, with an aggressive lunge that nearly took Craeg unawares. His brother was ill—he could see it in the rictus of pain and effort in his face, the wild look in his eyes, the pallor of his skin, and the sweat that poured off him. But his sickness had turned him vicious.

Yet reckless behavior also made a man careless.

Craeg only had to bide his time.

"Bastard," MacKinnon hissed, repeating the word, again and again, as he attacked. "Baseborn. Son of a whore. Misbegotten. *Bastard.*"

"Save yer breath," Craeg grunted as he brought his sword up to counter a violent overhead swing. "I am who I am ... the whole world knows about it but only *ye* care."

MacKinnon's eyes burned with loathing. It had all begun that day Jock MacKinnon brought Duncan to *The Goat and Goose* so he could meet his half-brother. The clan-chief had known what he was doing—but it pleased him to sow the seeds of hate.

And that hate had grown into something monstrous, something that risked destroying both men. It didn't matter to Jock MacKinnon anymore. He was dead, nothing but bones in a crypt. Yet his legacy lived on.

MacKinnon's onslaught was growing wearing. He attacked relentlessly, not giving Craeg the opportunity to counter. Around and around they went, Craeg's teeth jarring with each blow.

Craeg bided his time, waiting for the opening that would surely come. MacKinnon was a formidable swordsman. Even sick, his brother was the best he'd ever fought.

And then as Craeg shifted backward to block another overhead swing, he slipped on a patch of gore.

His feet flew out from under him, and he reeled back.

MacKinnon was on him in an instant, slicing downward in an attack designed to split his skull asunder.

Only Craeg's quick reflexes saved him. He dropped his sword, rolled, and drew his dirk.

MacKinnon lunged again, the blade of his claidheamh-mor whistling through the air. Craeg rolled once more, a chill sweeping through him as he realized that his half-brother now had the advantage.

Craeg was down, and MacKinnon's relentless attack made it impossible for him to rise to his feet.

Duncan was going to kill him. He swung his sword toward Craeg, in a deadly arc.

And then MacKinnon froze, his blade stilling. Craeg stared up at him, raising his dirk in an attempt to deflect the blow.

Yet the strike never came.

Instead, his opponent staggered forward, and then sank to his knees. MacKinnon grasped at his right armpit, his fingers coming away slick with blood. He gave a pained wheeze, color draining from his already pallid face, and slumped sideways onto the ground.

Behind MacKinnon stood a small figure swathed in black, an iron crucifix gleaming upon her breast: Mother Shona.

Breathing hard, the abbess lowered the sword she'd just plunged into him.

Duncan MacKinnon could no longer hear the fighting.

It was as if his ears were suddenly filled with wool. Lying upon the ground, he stared up at Craeg. The man's mouth was moving. He was speaking, saying something to him. But Duncan couldn't hear the words.

He was grateful for that.

He didn't want the last thing he ever heard to be Craeg the Bastard's voice.

Damn his half-brother to hell. He couldn't believe it had come to this. He couldn't believe someone had attacked him from behind, had stabbed him in the armpit while his arms were raised.

Despair clawed its way up his throat, yet he fought it. His body ached, and his throat felt as if it were on fire, as if he were lit up by a furnace within. Pain ripped through his chest. Duncan fought it all. For a few moments, he tried to convince himself that he could defeat everything: the sickness, his enemies, death itself.

And then he saw her.

His angel of mercy. His angel of death. The woman stepped up behind Craeg, those vibrant violent eyes fastening upon him.

Coira's face was flushed and blood-splattered, and her chest heaved from exertion. In one hand she held a quarter-staff, and in the other a dirk. She no longer wore a nun's habit. Instead, she was dressed as an outlaw.

She's one of them.

Outrage pulsed through Duncan, its heat puncturing the agony that dimmed his vision. His mouth moved, and he tried to speak. Yet he couldn't hear if any sound came out.

Suddenly, it hurt to breathe. It felt as if he were drowning.

Duncan reached up, stretching out for the woman, his fingers clawing the air as he imagined they were fastening around her neck. She was just like all the other women who'd disappointed him. His mother. His sister. Ella. Leanna. Traitorous bitches, the lot of them.

Coira stared down at him, a nerve ticking in her cheek. And then she knelt, bringing her face close to his.

Duncan sagged back, his hands lowering. Maybe she was sorry after all. Perhaps she would comfort him.

But there was no comfort for Duncan MacKinnon.

Another woman, her blood-splattered face taut with ruthless determination, knelt down and whipped the dirk from Coira.

The last thing he witnessed before his life ended was the flash of a knife blade.

25

In Yer Debt

"HE'S DEAD." CRAEG'S voice was flat, disappointed.

"And not before time," Mother Shona replied. She sat back on her heels, her gaze moving to where both Coira and Craeg stared at her. "The man was a scourge upon this earth."

Coira gaped at the older woman. She couldn't believe the abbess had killed MacKinnon. "Mother Shona," she finally gasped. "I wanted to be the one to slit his throat. Why did ye take that from me?"

The two women's gazes fused. Around them the battle was dying. The outlaws had finally managed to overcome the Dunan Guard. The remaining MacKinnon men had wisely cast aside their weapons, dropped to their knees, and raised their hands in surrender.

Mother Shona cocked an eyebrow. "Ye think I've stolen yer reckoning?"

"Aye, ye have," Craeg rasped. He was still breathing hard from his fight with MacKinnon. He stared at the abbess, gaze narrowed. "I had a few more things to say to him, before ye interrupted us."

The abbess huffed. "He couldn't hear ye anyway."

"What makes ye sure of that?"

"He had that look dying folk get sometimes. The glazed eyes, vacant expression ... I doubt he heard a word ye said."

A muscle bunched in Craeg's jaw. "All the same, they were things I needed to say before *I* cut his throat."

Coira clenched her jaw at his words. Curse them both, *she'd* intended to slay MacKinnon.

"And that's why I stepped in," Mother Shona replied, her voice soft yet with steel just underneath. Her gaze swept from Craeg back to Coira. "Revenge is a poison. I couldn't let it blacken yer souls. I know what ye have both suffered at his hands, but he's dead now. Be content with that."

Coira realized that Mother Shona wasn't going to apologize. She wasn't sorry in the slightest.

"This was personal to ye too," Coira pointed out, still fighting down anger. "Ye couldn't stand him either."

A bitter smile twisted the abbess's blood-splattered face. "No ... few could."

"Then surely, revenge drove ye as well?"

Mother Shona shook her head. "No ... for me his death was simply necessary."

Craeg heaved a deep breath, shattering the mounting tension between the two women. He raised a bloodied hand and raked it through his sweat-tousled hair before rising to his feet. "Well, it's done now," he said wearily. "Thank ye, Mother Shona ... ye saved my life."

The abbess's smile gentled, and she favored him with a nod, accepting his thanks.

Retrieving his claidheamh-mor, Craeg swept his gaze around the valley floor. Coira did likewise, her skin prickling at the sight of so many bodies littering the ground.

Not all of them belonged to the Dunan Guard.

Her breathing hitched when she spied a small crumpled form, swathed in black, lying a few yards away.

Picking her way through the carnage, Coira went to the nun. An ache flowered across her chest when she saw that it was Sister Mina.

"Lord, no," she whispered, hunkering down next to the novice.

Sister Mina didn't stir. Her grey eyes stared sightlessly up at the sky, and when Coira checked her for wounds, her hands came away bloody. Someone had stabbed her through the chest with a wide blade—a claidheamh-mor. Her end had been swift.

Coira's vision blurred then, the ache under her breastbone intensifying.

She couldn't believe that Mother Shona had brought the Sisters of Kilbride to the outlaws' aid.

Lifting her chin, she saw the abbess limping toward her. Now that the fighting had ended, Mother Shona's face was slack with exhaustion and sorrow.

The abbess halted before Sister Mina, and Coira saw that she was weeping, tears running silently down her face.

The sun made its lazy progress across the sky, slowly dipping toward the western horizon. Meanwhile, the survivors had the grisly task of clearing the battlefield.

MacKinnon and his dead men were placed upon a pyre and burned at the southern end of the valley, whereas the outlaws and the five nuns that had fallen were placed upon biers to be buried back at Kilbride. There were a number of injured, including Farlan, who'd taken a nasty gash to the thigh, and Sister Elspeth, who bore a cut to her arm. Gunn, however, had come through the battle relatively unscathed.

Despite that they were the victors, it was a somber party that made their way west to Kilbride, following the course of the sun. Few of the men or the nuns conversed. Instead, they trudged onward, their heads bowed and their steps wary. Once the madness of battle had faded, exhaustion set in.

Coira walked apart from her companions, her thoughts turning inward.

MacKinnon is dead.

The realization kept hitting her, so sharply at times that her breath would sometimes catch. It seemed strange, almost like having a limb amputated. Her loathing for that man had become part of her. Knowing that he was dead, and could no longer threaten her, was a relief. And yet, her belly still clenched as she recalled the abbess snatching the dirk from her hand and finishing the deed.

He was mine to kill.

"Coira." Craeg dropped back halfway through the journey and fell in step next to her. "Are ye well?"

She nodded before forcing herself to meet his eye. Craeg looked as exhausted as she felt, his mouth and nose bracketed with lines of tension. "Curse the abbess," she said softly. "I hate it when she's right."

His mouth quirked. "I take it that she often is?"

"Aye ... I lose count of how many times she's counselled me over the years. She's wiser than anyone I know."

"Then perhaps she did us both a favor," he murmured. "Revenge has a way of taking ye over, of making ye forget what really matters."

Coira glanced up, and their gazes fused. For the first time since before the battle, Coira became acutely aware of him—like she had in that shadowed corner of the ravine before he'd kissed her.

Warmth rose within her, smoothing out the nausea that still stung the back of her throat, the tension in her muscles, and the hard knot that clenched her belly. Mother Mary, the man had a gaze that could melt a frozen loch.

When he looked at her in that way, it was like she was the only woman alive.

Eventually, the tension got too much. Clearing her throat, Coira glanced away. "Mother Shona says that MacKinnon was sick."

"Aye ... I noticed it too."

"She also tells me that three nuns back in Kilbride have fallen ill ... and one of the men we've taken captive has a fever."

When she glanced back at Craeg, she saw he was frowning. "Aye … the sickness is upon us. How long before the rest of us fall prey to it?"

The warmth his gaze had caused ebbed away at these words. Nonetheless, his question was valid. All of them could now be on borrowed time.

"I wonder how Fenella is faring?" Coira said, voicing her thoughts aloud.

"Gunn has ridden back to the ravine to fetch her and the others," Craeg replied. "They will join us in Kilbride … we shall find out soon if she lives."

The shadows were long, the afternoon sun gilding the hills, when the bloodied band reached Kilbride Abbey at last. Old Magda opened the gates to admit them, her wrinkled face tensing when she saw that five of the nuns who had left that morning—Sister Mina among them— now returned as corpses.

The elderly nun's gaze filled with tears, and she made the sign of the cross before her. "Dear Lord have mercy, what happened?"

Mother Shona went to Sister Magda and placed a comforting arm around her shoulders. "There was a battle," she murmured, her voice brittle. "MacKinnon fell … but so did some of those opposing him."

Watching the two women embrace, Coira's throat started to ache.

Kilbride was a tight-knit community. The sisters might not have been related, but they were as close as if united by blood.

Tears streamed down both Mother Shona and Sister Magda's faces when they drew apart.

"How are the others?" the abbess asked.

Sister Magda's mouth trembled. "They steadily worsen," she murmured. "Sister Morag has started vomiting blood."

This news brought gasps from the surrounding nuns.

"I shall go to her," Sister Elspeth announced. The woman's face was strained and pale, and she favored her injured arm. However, Coira knew that Sisters Morag and Elspeth were close friends.

"No, Sister." The abbess turned to Sister Elspeth and held up a hand, forestalling her. "Sister Magda and I will be the only ones to tend the sick. We can't risk the rest of ye falling prey to this plague."

Sister Elspeth's thin face went taut, and she opened her mouth to argue. But Coira spoke up, preventing her. "*I* will tend to them." All gazes swiveled to her, including Sister Elspeth's. Coira held the older nun's eye, before her mouth curved into a weary smile. "I am a healer and have already dealt with the sickness. Mother Shona is right ... the rest of ye should keep yer distance."

Her gaze fused with Sister Elspeth's then, a look of understanding passing between them. The irony of the moment wasn't lost upon Coira. For years, she and Sister Elspeth had barely tolerated each other. Coira had never been one of the circle of nuns who'd hung on Sister Elspeth's every word, and the nun had resented her for it.

But all of that was behind them now.

"Thank ye," Sister Elspeth replied, her voice unusually flat and heavy. "Peace be with ye ... Coira."

Coira. Not Sister Coira.

Coira was suddenly aware then that she was no longer one of them. For the first time, she felt as if she stood on the outside looking in. This abbey was no longer her home.

My time at Kilbride has truly come to an end.

Looking about her, Coira realized how quiet the abbey seemed, especially after all the visitors they'd had of late. Craeg's men were putting up tents outside the abbey walls, for the abbess had warned him that there were sick nuns inside. Only Craeg had entered the yard with the nuns, and now he stood silently at Coira's side, observing the exchange between the abbess and her flock.

Coira tensed then, realizing exactly why the abbey seemed so quiet. It wasn't just the absence of MacKinnon and his rowdy warriors—besides Craeg, there weren't *any* men here. Her gaze swept back to the abbess. "Where are Father Camron and his monks?"

Mother Shona released a weary sigh. The abbess then glanced over at the kirk, where Coira noted that the doors were barred shut.

26

There Will Be Consequences

THE ABBOT BURST from the kirk, purple-faced and seething.

"Ye will pay for this, Mother Shona!" he raged, rounding on the abbess. She stood at the foot of the steps, awaiting him. "How dare ye lock me up!"

Suddenly, he stopped short, taking in the abbess's appearance: her leggings, bunched up skirts, and the sword she wore at her hip. "What. Is. This?" he demanded.

"It was for yer own good, Father," the abbess replied, ignoring the question. Looking on from a few yards distant, Coira was surprised at how calm Mother Shona sounded. "Things have gone ill … I was trying to protect ye."

The abbot gaped at her, torn between rage and concern. Finally, he drew himself up, fisting his hands at his sides. Meanwhile, his monks exited the kirk and gathered in a frightened knot behind him. "Protect me? From what?"

"The plague has entered Kilbride," the abbess informed him, her tone flattening. "Three sisters are ill with it."

At this news, Father Camron took a few rapid steps back from Mother Shona, alarm flaring in his dark eyes.

"That's not all," the abbess pressed on. "The outlaws clashed with MacKinnon today … the clan-chief is now dead."

The abbot's eyes widened at this news, his throat bobbing. "MacKinnon's dead?"

The abbess nodded.

Father Camron's attention shifted then to where Craeg still stood, a few yards back, at Coira's side. The abbot frowned, clearly trying to place him. "Who's this?"

"I'm Craeg the Bastard," Craeg replied as he observed the abbot with a cool stare. "Surely ye have heard of me?"

Father Camron's gaze widened, before his face went taut. "Ye have brought the outlaw leader here?"

"Aye … we fought on his side, Father," the abbess continued. "We helped bring MacKinnon and his men down."

The abbot's mouth worked soundlessly at this news. Watching him, Coira forced down the urge to laugh. The words sounded ridiculous, and yet they were the truth.

When Father Camron finally crossed himself, she noted that his hand shook. His face, which had momentarily slackened in shock, twisted, his cheeks growing an even darker shade of purple.

"Unnatural, wicked … godless!" he spluttered, barely able to form a coherent sentence, such was his rage. "This will be the end for ye, Mother Shona. The Pope will excommunicate ye. I will see to it personally."

A chill settled over the yard in the wake of these words. Coira glanced over at Craeg, to see that he was scowling. "The abbess doesn't deserve yer condemnation, Father," he said, his voice a low rumble in the ominous quiet. "She is a good woman."

"She is an abomination. She has sinned against God," the abbot rasped. His attention swiveled to Coira then, pinning her to the spot. "As ye all have."

It was an effort to hold the man's eye. The hate on his face made Coira want to avert her gaze. Yet, she'd faced sword-wielding warriors today. She'd not let one self-righteous bigot intimidate her.

"I was right about this woman too." He spat out the words. "Look at her ... dressed as a man with her hair uncovered. Ye have no right to wear that crucifix about yer neck."

Father Camron took a threatening step toward Coira. "Take it off, before I rip it from ye."

"Touch her, and ye shall lose yer hand, Father." Craeg's warning was uttered softly, yet there was no mistaking the menace in it. He rested his right hand upon the pommel of his claidheamh-mor, his fingers flexing.

The abbot's eyes bulged. "Bastard ... are ye threatening me?"

"No ... I'm making things clear. If ye touch this woman, there will be consequences."

Father Camron's heavyset body started to tremble then—not from fear but from fury. Glaring at Craeg, the abbot raised a hand to the heavy iron crucifix around his neck, his knuckles whitening as he squeezed. His gaze flicked from Craeg to Coira then, his lip curling.

"Fornicators."

Coira tensed. The abbot was taking his insults too far now. If he didn't put away that forked tongue, she wouldn't be held responsible for her actions.

She took a step forward, her fingers flexing around the quarter-staff. In just one move, she could bring him to his knees. Outrage pulsed within her. Just one more word from the abbot and she'd strike.

Sensing how fragile the leash was on her self-control, Craeg reached out and placed a cautioning hand upon Coira's arm.

"Father Camron," he said, the calmness of his voice at odds with the steel that lay just beneath. "I do believe ye have somewhere to go?"

For a long moment, the abbot didn't move. He just glowered at Craeg, as if a black look could strike the man dead.

But if that were the case, the abbot would have been dead ten times over—for now all the nuns surrounding them were glaring at Father Camron.

The abbot eventually drew in a deep, shuddering breath and twisted on his heel. "Ready my mule!" he snarled at one of the monks cowering behind him. "Now!"

Four of the monks broke off from the group and scurried away across the yard toward the stables to do his bidding. Then, gathering up the skirts of his robe with as much dignity as his offended pride allowed, the abbot followed, the rest of his flock trailing behind him.

Coira watched them go, as did Craeg. And when Father Camron had passed out of earshot, Craeg glanced over at Mother Shona. "That man has the power to ruin ye, Mother."

The abbess's shoulders slumped. "Aye ... assuming we haven't just given him the plague ... but I knew that when I locked him inside the kirk."

"Do ye want me and my men to go after him ... ensure he never sends word to Rome?"

The abbess huffed a bitter laugh. "No, Craeg. As much as I'd like ye to cut out that man's tongue, I won't allow it."

"I was actually thinking of slitting the shit-weasel's throat."

"Again ... tempting." Mother Shona drew herself up, her shoulders squaring. "But no." Her gaze swept around the yard, at where the nuns all watched her, worry etched upon their faces. "I'm sorry, Sisters ... but our time here has ended."

"No!" Sister Elspeth burst out, her face blanching. "Ye can't—"

The abbess raised a hand, cutting her off. "Father Camron will indeed write to the Pope, and I will be removed as abbess and excommunicated. There is nothing left at Kilbride for ye." Mother Shona's eyes glittered with unshed tears as she continued. "Return to yer quarters and pack yer bags. Ye must all leave with the dawn."

Coira stifled a gasp. "But where will they go?"

Mother Shona glanced her way, her expression bleak. "To Inishail Priory on the mainland. The prioress there … Mother Iseabal … will welcome them."

"But we don't want to go." One of the nuns spoke up. Sister Robena had only been at Kilbride two years, and had just recently taken her vows of perpetuity. "We wish to stay here."

"Ye can't, Sister." Mother Shona met the younger woman's eye, her features hardening. "I made a mistake, thinking that teaching ye all how to wield weapons would aid ye. I was arrogant, and my hubris has brought this abbey to ruin." The abbess paused there, her gaze guttering. "It's too late for me, but not for the rest of ye. Tomorrow, ye will leave Kilbride and make a fresh start elsewhere … that is my final word on the subject."

A solemn air settled over Kilbride Abbey with the dusk. Emerging from tending to the three sick nuns in the infirmary, Coira raised her face to the sky and whispered a prayer for them.

Sister Morag was close to death. She was older and weaker than Sisters Anis and Fritha. Coira had left Sister Magda to tend to the sick. Now, she'd bathe and join Mother Shona and Craeg for supper in the abbess's hall.

Frankly, Coira didn't feel up to it, but Mother Shona had insisted. It would be the last time they'd break bread together—it was goodbye.

Outdoors, the air was warm and scented with the sweetness of summer. The world didn't know of the turmoil of the current days. It didn't care.

Coira circuited the complex of buildings and went to her cell. A little of the day's tension ebbed from her when she saw that some kind soul had left her a bowl of water, soap, and drying cloths with which to bathe.

The water was still warm.

Stripping off her clothes—which was far easier now that she no longer dressed as a nun—Coira washed away the grime, sweat, and blood. She even washed her hair, teasing out the tangles with her fingertips.

The same individual who'd left her the soap and water, had also given her clean clothes—not men's clothing but a faded blue kirtle and cream-colored léine to wear under it. The cloth was poor, the hems frayed in places, yet Coira sighed with relief as she slipped on the garments.

Lord, it felt good to be clean again.

As before, she placed her crucifix around her neck; somehow, she felt naked without it. No matter what happened in the future, she would take her faith with her.

Quickly braiding her damp hair into a single plait, Coira then left her cell and made her way to the abbess's hall.

Craeg was already there, seated in one of the high-backed chairs near the hearth, opposite Mother Shona. His shaggy hair was loose and looked damp—it seemed that he too had bathed before joining the abbess.

The outlaw leader—who'd been talking to the abbess in a low voice, his hands wrapped around a goblet of wine—glanced up at Coira's arrival. His gaze rested upon her, lingering for a heartbeat longer than was necessary, and heat rushed to Coira's cheeks in response. Fighting down the instinct to adjust her clothing or check her hair, she crossed the flagstone floor to the hearth and lowered herself onto a stool.

"Good eve, Coira," Mother Shona greeted her with a tired smile. She rose to her feet, placed her goblet on the mantelpiece above the fire, and poured a third goblet, passing it to Coira. "How are yer patients?"

"They all worsen," Coira replied. "I don't think Sister Morag will last the night." Her words were bald in their honesty, yet she was too weary to soften them. "The illness has attacked her lungs."

Coira's attention shifted to Craeg then, to find him watching her. The warmth in her cheeks intensified. She hadn't gotten used to being 'seen'. Indeed, her habit had provided a shield from men's eyes. "Have Gunn and Fenella arrived yet?"

He shook his head. "It's too soon … they'll be here tomorrow morning at the earliest."

Coira glanced back at the abbess. "I tried out a new treatment with an outlaw woman … if it was successful, I should like to try it here."

Mother Shona nodded. "We are lucky to have yer skills, Coira. The Lord has indeed blessed us."

Coira offered the abbess a weak smile in reply and lifted the goblet to her lips, taking a gulp of wine. It was rich and smooth, not at all what she expected. Her eyebrows raised. "This is good."

The abbess's mouth quirked. "Aye … I was saving it for a special occasion. Now seems appropriate."

Coira's smile faded. "I can't believe ye are sending the nuns away … it seems so … drastic."

Mother Shona sighed. "Drastic … but necessary. If there had been another path, I'd have taken it."

"But—"

"Enough talk of this." The abbess waved her silent. "I've already gone over and over this with Sister Elspeth. My mind is made up … and it's for the best. Now, ye must focus upon yer own futures."

27

Undone

"KILBRIDE WILL CLOSE for the moment," Mother Shona continued. She crossed the hall to her desk, where a platter of food awaited. It was simple fare—bread, cheese, and boiled eggs—yet Coira's mouth watered at the sight of it.

She was starving, so hungry in fact that she couldn't summon the effort to argue with Mother Shona. It was clear the woman wouldn't be moved.

I'll speak to her alone tomorrow.

The abbess carried the platter across to them and set it on a low table within easy reach of them all. She then helped herself to some food and took her seat. Mother Shona ignored her companions as she began to peel an egg.

Wordlessly, seeing that the conversation had halted for the moment, Craeg and Coira helped themselves to supper. Coira took a large bite of bread and cheese, forcing herself to chew properly before swallowing. Likewise, Craeg ate with the appetite of a famished hound, inhaling two huge slices of bread and cheese, before he eventually broke the silence between the three of them.

"Someone will have to let MacKinnon's kin know he's dead," Craeg said, his voice heavy. "I suppose I should send word to his sister in Dunan."

The abbess glanced up, her gaze spearing him. "*Yer* sister. This land needs a new clan-chief, Craeg … and ye are MacKinnon's closest surviving male relative."

Craeg's face went taut, his gaze shuttering. "What?"

"Don't pretend ye don't understand me or that ye haven't thought on the possibility before." The abbess lowered the slice of bread she'd been about to take a bite of. Her face developed that steely look Coira knew only too well. "Ye are a born leader … and the people of the MacKinnon territory need someone to guide them, especially now when times are bleak."

"I can't become clan-chief." Craeg's voice turned rough, his green eyes hard.

However, the abbess wasn't a woman easily intimidated. "Why not … ye are MacKinnon's brother?"

"I'm his *bastard* brother."

"It matters not. Blood is blood."

"It matters to me!"

Coira cleared her throat. She sensed an argument brewing; something she really didn't have the stomach for tonight. "Would the folk of Dunan ever accept Craeg as heir?" she asked the abbess.

Mother Shona met her eye. "The people of this land *hate* Duncan MacKinnon … but they love his brother. Craeg knows this, but for some reason he's afraid of taking on the role, afraid of facing his destiny." Her gaze swung back to Craeg. "Yer enemy is dead now. It's time for ye to take his place."

"Ye make me sound a lot nobler than I actually am," Craeg countered, his handsome face taut. "It was revenge, Mother Shona. I did it for me … no one else."

The abbess shook her head, a rueful smile curving her lips. "Aye, ye had a score to settle with MacKinnon … but ye also drew men from every corner of this territory to yer cause. Ye inspired them in a way yer brother never could."

A brittle silence fell. Craeg continued to glare at the abbess, a nerve flickering in his cheek. And when he didn't contradict her, Mother Shona added. "If ye don't take Duncan MacKinnon's place, someone less worthy will, I'm sure. Would ye put this land ye love in peril again? Would ye let yer pride override good sense?"

Craeg swallowed. Watching him, Coira sensed his turmoil, his conflict. With a jolt, she realized he wasn't being falsely modest; he really didn't want to take Duncan MacKinnon's place. He couldn't see past the name that had defined him his entire life.

Craeg the Bastard.

Coira's breathing quickened. She wasn't sure what she thought about the abbess's idea either. Frankly, the suggestion had come as a shock. However, as the moments slid by, she realized that Mother Shona was, indeed, an excellent judge of character.

"The abbess speaks wisely," she said finally, her voice subdued. "No one would make a better clan-chief than ye. Please consider it."

Craeg's gaze widened. Mouth flattening, he looked away, staring at the glowing lump of peat in the hearth. He was so tense, she expected him to leap up at any moment and stride from the hall.

Yet he didn't.

The abbess finished her supper and brushed crumbs off her lap. Her attention then focused upon Coira.

"Craeg isn't the only one who needs to consider their future," she said softly. "What will *ye* do?"

Coira swallowed her last mouthful of bread and cheese and stalled by taking a slow, deliberate gulp of wine to wash it down. "I don't know," she admitted.

She was aware then that Craeg had shifted his gaze from the fire. She could feel him looking at her, awaiting her answer.

"Ye aren't staying here," Mother Shona reminded her. "Will ye go to Inishail Priory with the others and take up the veil again?"

Coira shook her head. The definitiveness of her refusal surprised her. She'd been too occupied over the last few hours to give her future any thought. However, she knew she wouldn't be going to Inishail Priory.

"I'm not sure where my path will lead me," she murmured. "But one thing I do know is that I won't be returning to the order."

The abbess's gaze shadowed. She looked almost disappointed. "Why not?"

Coira sighed. She glanced over at Craeg then, her chest constricting. "For years I've sheltered behind the walls of Kilbride … have tried to erase my past with prayer and penitence, and shrouded my body in yards of black cloth so that no man would ever see me as a woman again," she admitted softly. "God will always remain in my heart, but I don't want to hide anymore. I want to live."

Coira slipped through the gates into the make-shift camp below, her heart pounding like a battle drum.

A full moon hung over Kilbride, its friendly face casting a hoary light over the world. A perimeter of torches flickered around the clusters of tents, and a man standing guard greeted Coira with a nod. Neither of them spoke. He allowed her to pass through into the outlaw camp without questioning where she was going.

Maybe he already knew.

There was only one person here she'd have any reason to seek out. Only one person who dominated her every waking thought.

Coira's breathing quickened, and she did her best to slow it, to calm her thudding pulse.

She'd tried to go to her cell, where she'd spend her last night at Kilbride. She attempted to stretch out upon her narrow pallet and let sleep claim her.

She was certainly tired enough.

But sleep hadn't come. All she'd been able to think of was that time was slipping like grains of sand through her fingers. And she didn't want to waste one more moment.

Eventually, she'd risen from her pallet, donned her clothing, and left the abbey. Her feet carried her toward her destination of their own accord. She moved on instinct now, not questioning her decision.

Craeg's tent was easy to find. It rose above the others surrounding it, and sat at the heart of the camp.

Coira halted before the entrance, her heart racing so fast now that she felt sick.

This is it.

Until now, she and Craeg had danced around each other, but once she took this step, life was bound to get messy, complicated. She risked getting hurt, risked having her heart ripped to pieces.

But she hadn't lied at supper. She was done hiding from life.

It was now time to embrace it.

Coira pushed aside the tent flap, stooped low, and entered the tent.

To her surprise, Craeg was still awake. He sat propped up on a pile of furs, staring moodily up at where shadows danced upon the roof of his tent. A small brazier burned next to him, the orange light burnishing the planes of his chest.

Coira's mouth went dry when she realized that apart from a form-fitting pair of leather breeches, he was naked.

For a moment she merely gazed at him, taking in the beauty of his tall, strong body, his broad chest.

And then his gaze flicked to her, and she struggled to catch her breath.

Suddenly, the impulse that had driven her here felt reckless and ill-advised. She'd deliberately avoided thinking on the consequences. After years of steering clear of men, she'd now walked straight into one's lair.

And yet, this man wasn't a predator. He'd only ever been gentle with her.

Craeg stared at her, surprise flickering over his face, before he favored her with a slow smile that made her belly somersault. "Couldn't sleep either?"

Coira swallowed. "No."

"I should be exhausted," he said, giving a slow, languorous stretch. "I *am* exhausted."

"So am I," Coira admitted. She couldn't take her gaze from his brawny arms, from the play of muscles across his sculpted chest. He'd removed the bandage from around his torso, and despite that she stood a few feet away, Coira could see that the injury looked healthy enough. The battle hadn't split it open as she'd feared. "But I couldn't sleep ... not without seeing ye."

Craeg pushed himself up into a sitting position upon the furs. His mouth quirked. "And what can I do for ye, Coira?"

Heaving in a deep breath, Coira reached up and began to unlace the bodice of her kirtle.

"I want to lie with ye, Craeg," she murmured.

His gaze widened, his lips parting as he stared at her.

"Our world's in turmoil," she continued, "and there's every chance either of us could succumb to the sickness. That being the case, I want to live for the moment. I want ye."

She pushed down the sleeves of the kirtle and shrugged it off; the garment fluttered into a pool around her ankles, and she stepped out of it. Underneath, she wore the long sleeveless léine.

"Are ye sure this is what ye desire?" he asked. His voice came out in a rasp, very different to the confident tone he'd used earlier. His naked chest now rose and fell quickly. "Some things can't be undone, mo chridhe."

Coira, who now reached for the hem of her léine, stilled a moment.

My heart.

Did he mean those words, or was it merely an endearment?

What did it matter? The fact remained that her legs now trembled from wanting him, the pulsing ache between her thighs too much to bear.

"I know that," she whispered. "But I want to be undone."

And with that, she grasped the hem of her léine and drew it up over her head.

Standing naked before him, she was aware of the warm air inside the tent feathering over her sensitive skin, of the rasp of both of their breathing—and of the searing heat of his gaze.

"Come here," he said softly, the catch in his voice betraying him.

Coira obeyed. She moved slowly toward the furs, noting the sudden flush across his cheek bones and the huge tent in his tight breeches.

Coira's breath caught. She couldn't believe she was actually doing this, that after so many years, she wanted this.

She'd never lusted after a man. Those years at *The Goat and Goose* hadn't been about pleasure for her. No encounter she'd had there ever left her breathless and aching. It had been a mere transaction: flesh for silver.

But with Craeg, everything was different. With this man, she was willing to give up her soul.

Coira lowered herself onto her knees beside Craeg, and then, gathering her courage, straddled him. She bowed her head, gazing deep into his eyes.

"Sweet Lord have mercy," he murmured. "Is this a dream?"

Coira's mouth curved. "If it is, then it is a good one."

And with that, she lowered her lips to his.

28

Tainted Blood

CRAEG FELT AS if he'd died and gone to heaven.
Strange really, since after everything he'd done over the
years, he was sure he'd have ended up with Satan and all
his demons.

Coira's mouth, tentatively moving over his, was
divine. The nearness of her luscious, naked body, made
his groin ache. She was long-limbed and lean, yet with
large, high breasts that begged to be touched.

He was going to go insane if he didn't.

And when her tongue parted his lips, he knew this
woman was going to make him lose his wits altogether.

He'd longed for this, hadn't been able to sleep tonight
for wanting her.

Craeg hadn't enjoyed taking supper with the abbess.
Mother Shona had brought up subjects he'd have
preferred to ignore. And every time he'd shifted his
attention to Coira—clad in a simple blue kirtle that
hugged her long, supple body—he'd found it difficult to
keep his train of thought.

It had been awkward when they'd bid each other
goodnight outside the abbess's hall. He'd watched her
walk off toward the nun's lodgings, and had almost

called out to her, almost asked her to spend the night with him.

But after everything Coira had been through, it seemed too aggressive.

Although it frustrated him, he had to let this woman come to him. If they lay together, he wanted it to be Coira's choice. She needed to leap the abyss between them and take the initiative—as she did now.

Coira cupped his face with her hands as she deepened the kiss. Their tongues danced and tangled, and when she gently bit his lower lip, the dull ache in his groin grew unbearable.

Reaching up, Craeg unfastened the heavy braid down her back, his fingers tangling in the waves, still damp from bathing. Then he stroked the curve of her back. Her skin was so smooth, so soft. He could hardly bear it. And when his hands moved to her breasts, his fingertips brushing across her nipples, Coira groaned low in her throat.

It was too much. Craeg tore his mouth from hers, took hold of her hips and pulled her against him as he buried his face in her breasts.

His mouth fastened on a nipple, and he suckled, lust exploding through him when Coira gave a voluptuous moan. She arched back, pressing her breasts hard against him.

They were both breathing hard when she finally drew back and their gazes fused once more.

It was an intense moment, almost too much.

The want he saw in those violet eyes made an ache rise in Craeg's chest. This woman completely unraveled him, stripped away the mask he'd worn his whole life. Aye, since becoming an outlaw he'd amassed a loyal band of followers. Craeg knew folk were drawn to him, that they looked to him as if he was their savior. For years, he'd played the role and enjoyed it even.

But Coira saw past all that. She saw into his heart, understood his loneliness, the belief he held deep down that he was as worthless as Duncan MacKinnon had told him.

He didn't need to explain himself to her, for when she looked into his eyes, she saw it all.

Coira's hands explored the planes of his face before sliding down his neck, to his shoulders and then his chest. She traced the lines of his body with rapt attention, as if she was committing them to memory.

The turmoil of the world they lived in made this moment even more intense.

Coira was right—all of them now possibly lived on borrowed time.

But for one night, death wouldn't touch them. This night belonged to them.

Leaning back against the furs, Craeg let Coira explore his body, let her take control. He sensed that was what she wanted, and although he longed to reach for her, roll her under him, and plow her senseless, he knew that this union was a gateway for her.

He gazed up into her face, his throat tightening when he saw the wonder there.

Desire was something new for this woman, despite her past. Having grown up in a brothel, Craeg knew why. He'd seen the men who'd visited *The Goat and Goose* on a regular basis, he'd witnessed how they'd treated the whores—treated his mother.

Tonight, he'd let Coira take the lead, take what she wished from him.

Nonetheless, when her fingertips trailed down his belly to the waistband of his breeches, Craeg wondered how much longer he'd be able to bear it.

Her slow exploration was driving him mad.

He watched Coira unlace his breeches and heard her sharp intake of breath when his shaft sprang free to greet her. Swollen and quivering, its tip slick with want, his rod was making his need for her clear.

A sultry smile curved her lips as her slender fingers curved around him, stroking him.

A strangled cry escaped Craeg, and his hands clenched at his sides. He wasn't sure how much longer he could restrain himself.

And then when she rose up on her knees and shifted so that his rod pressed up into the damp flesh between her thighs, Craeg caught his breath.

He'd thought she'd lower herself onto him, but instead Coira began to stroke herself with the tip of his shaft, taking her pleasure. He watched wonder suffuse her face, watched her head fall back while soft gasps escaped her.

"Coira." His voice sounded strangled, as if someone was choking him. "Ple—ease."

She ignored him, continuing to slide herself against the length of him now, her body quivering as she lost herself in the sensation.

Craeg was enraptured. He'd never seen a woman act like this before. Coira had no idea how lovely she was when she let herself go and followed her instincts. And when she finally lowered herself onto his engorged rod, her head snapped forward, her gaze widening.

Taking hold of her hips, Craeg guided her down so that she was fully seated upon him. He could feel the tremors that wracked her, the trembling that increased when he took hold of her hips and moved them in a slow, sensual circle.

"This is wonderful," she whispered, her voice full of awe. "Why is it … oh … Craeg!"

He felt her core tighten around him, sweat beading upon her naked skin. Craeg favored her with a slow smile as he continued to move her hips while he arched up, grinding against her. He loved that this was all new to her, loved watching her discover the pleasure that coupling could bring.

He started to rock Coira her back and forth, in a sensual rhythm that made her gasp. Craeg groaned, arching up once more as he sought to drive deeper. She was so slick now, so hot, that it was stretching his self-control to the limit.

Leaning forward, Coira grasped hold of the furs, the tips of her lush breasts brushing his face. This altering of position allowed him to thrust deeper, allowed her to push back harder against him.

Coira started to cry out, soft mewing sounds that excited Craeg beyond measure. His belly muscles tightened, and the world darkened. His release now charged toward him; there was no stopping it—not when this beautiful woman rode him, writhing and shuddering as she lost herself in her pleasure.

Breathing hard, her body damp with sweat, her core still pulsing in the aftermath of their lovemaking, Coira lay against Craeg, her face buried in his chest.

She could feel the thunder of his heart against her cheek. Like her, his skin was wet with sweat and his chest rose and fell sharply.

"God's bones," he rasped finally. "Where have ye been all my life, woman?"

Coira huffed an exhausted laugh, tracing her fingers down his breast bone. "I wish I'd met ye years ago," she answered honestly.

"Aye." His voice was soft when he answered. "Although ye might not have liked me then ... I was insufferably arrogant."

Grinning, Coira propped herself onto an elbow. "Even more so than now?"

His mouth quirked. "Aye ... if ye can believe it."

Their gazes held, and warmth spread through Coira's chest. Did this man have any idea how devastating he was? Arrogant or not, she'd have fallen under his spell.

The moment drew out, and, reaching up, Craeg stroked Coira's cheek. "I've been thinking," he said eventually, "about what the abbess said tonight."

Coira cocked her head. "About ye taking MacKinnon's place?"

"Aye." His gaze shadowed as the outside world intruded once more. "The abbess was right. I'm not going to pretend that I've never entertained the thought ... that those who follow me haven't mentioned it before."

"So why the reticence?"

Craeg's mouth twisted. "I don't rightly know ... maybe the fear I have tainted blood?"

"What?"

He gave a bitter laugh. "I'm not proud of the man who sired me ... nor of my half-brother. What if I end up like them?"

Coira stared at him, surprise filtering through her. He was serious. "Ye are as different to Duncan MacKinnon as the sun is to the moon," she said, vehement now. "The fact that ye even worry about such a thing shows just how different ye are. Ye would make a wonderful clan-chief. Ye would rule these lands justly, and ye would treat those who live here with the same respect ye show those who already follow ye."

Craeg's eyes widened. Her intensity had taken him aback, she realized. Yet she couldn't let him think for a moment that he was like MacKinnon.

"So ye think I should go to Dunan and take his seat in the Great Hall?" he asked finally.

Coira's breathing slowed. Not trusting herself to answer without betraying her sudden nervousness, she nodded.

"But what if I don't want to rule alone?" Craeg's mouth lifted at the corners, and his hand cupped her cheek. "It's not power I crave, Coira. None of it matters without ye."

Coira stilled. What was he saying?

"I'll go to Dunan tomorrow," he continued softly, his gaze never straying from hers. "But only if ye agree to come with me."

29

Together

"COME WITH YE?" Coira breathed, her pulse accelerating.

"Aye," he replied, his expression growing serious. "And when we get there ... will ye become my wife?"

Coira's mouth fell open. She knew it wasn't an attractive look, yet his words had completely taken her by surprise. Her mind spun at the enormity of what he was asking.

"Life is short, mo ghràdh," Craeg murmured, his mouth curving into a half-smile that made something twist deep within Coira's chest. "We must take it by the horns while we have it."

"This is so sudden," Coira replied, finally finding her tongue. Her voice was higher than usual, brittle. "Are ye sure?"

"Surer than I've been about anything in my life." Doubt shadowed his green eyes then. "I love ye, Coira ... but do ye feel the same way about me?"

The sudden vulnerability on his face, the fear that he'd just exposed himself only to risk being pushed away, made a lump rise in Coira's throat.

"Aye," she whispered, her vision blurring. The realization barreled into her with such force that she struggled to draw breath. "I love ye so much that it frightens me."

Indeed it did. She'd learned years earlier what it was to lose those she loved. After her parents had died, she'd been utterly alone in the world. She'd missed them so much that a permanent ache had lodged itself in her chest for many years afterward. She wasn't sure she could bear such heartbreak again.

"It scares me too," he admitted. There was a rough edge to Craeg's voice, and his eyes now gleamed. He reached down to where her hand still lay upon his chest, his fingers wrapping around hers. "But isn't it time we both faced our fears?"

"Good morn, fair Coira," Farlan greeted Coira with a cocky smile. She'd just ducked under the awning, where he and three other badly injured men were laid up. Coira was pleased to see that all of them looked better than they had the night before. Farlan was sitting up, eating a wedge of bannock.

"Morning." Coira stopped before him and raised an eyebrow. "How's the leg?"

"Burns like the devil."

"Let's take a look at it then."

Hunkering down, Coira unwrapped the bandages, her gaze taking in the wound that slashed down his right thigh. She'd hastily sewn it shut the day before. Despite her exhaustion, she'd done a surprisingly neat job of it. She'd cleaned the wound first with vinegar and then packed it with woundwort. This morning, although it was red and angry-looking, there wasn't any sign of souring.

"It's going to take a while before ye can walk," she warned him, sitting back on her heels and meeting

Farlan's eye. "But ye were lucky … the blade just missed a large vein."

Farlan nodded, his throat bobbing as a little of his earlier arrogance dimmed. "So I'll keep the leg?"

Coira smiled. "Aye … I'd say so."

Voices, raised in excitement, drifted through the encampment then, drawing their attention. Stepping out from under the awning, Coira spied a stocky horse approaching from the east. A big man with wild red-hair rode it, and a woman wrapped in a fur cloak perched side-saddle before him.

Coira's heart started to pound. *Fenella.*

Picking up her skirts, she hurried through the camp, skirting around smoking fire pits and men packing up tents, to greet the newcomers.

And she knew, the moment she saw Gunn's face clearly, that the warrior brought good news.

Reining in the horse, he smiled. "Yer treatment worked," he rumbled. "Fen is on the mend. God bless ye."

Gently, he drew back the hood of his companion's fur mantle, revealing a pale face. Fenella peered out, and even managed a wan smile of her own when she spied Coira.

Excited chatter went up around them, joy rippling through the camp. Many of the folk here hadn't expected to see Fenella alive again.

A wide smile split Coira's face. The relief that flooded over her made her legs wobble. So much so, that she was grateful when a strong male arm fastened around her waist.

"It's so good to see ye back, Fen. I was wondering when ye two would get here," Craeg greeted them. "Lucky for ye, there are still some bannocks left. I know ye have the appetite of a half-starved hound, Gunn."

Laughter rose up into the balmy morning air. Coira joined in, the tension she'd been carrying around all morning, as she'd waited for Gunn's arrival, releasing.

Gunn grinned. "Speak for yerself, man." His gaze then lit up as he took in the sight of Coira and Craeg standing together.

Meanwhile, Coira leaned into Craeg, her arm snaking around his chest. She was aware of the curious looks, the stares, around them. If any of them had suspected the developing relationship between their leader and the woman who'd recently joined them, they were now vindicated.

Warmth suffused Coira as she realized she didn't care who knew. Nothing in the world felt as right as Craeg's arm around her.

"I don't want to leave ye here alone, Mother." Sister Elspeth's voice cracked as she spoke, betraying just how upset she was.

The nun faced the abbess at the foot of the steps to the kirk. Like the group of nuns behind her, she wore a leather pack upon her back. However, Sister Elspeth's right arm was in a sling.

"I won't be alone, Sister Elspeth," the abbess replied, favoring the nun with a tired smile. "Sister Magda is with me ... and so will be Sisters Anis and Fritha ... if they live." She paused then. Sadly, Sister Morag had passed away during the night. Earlier that morning, Coira had shown the abbess how to lance plague boils, a vile task but a potentially life-saving one. "We won't tarry here for much longer either. As soon as we can, we too shall move on."

Hope flared in Sister Elspeth's eyes. "Will ye join us at Inishail Priory?"

The abbess shook her head.

Sister Elspeth's gaze guttered. "Why not?"

"I don't know where I shall go after this ... perhaps Sister Magda and the others will join ye, but I will seek solitude."

A brittle silence followed these words.

Looking on, Coira saw that Sister Elspeth was now close to tears. She was an odd woman, Coira reflected. Watching her now, Coira realized just how much Kilbride meant to Sister Elspeth. It tore her up inside to leave it.

The nuns filed out of the abbey, solemn black-garbed figures. They carried a defeated aura about them—so different from the fierce women of a day earlier. They wielded no weapons now, and probably would never do so again.

A dull sensation settled in the center of Coira's chest. She glanced across at where Craeg stood, watching the nuns leave. She was happy to stand at this man's side, to go with him to Dunan. But at the same time, the situation here at Kilbride filled her with regret.

Not for herself, but for the Sisters, for Mother Shona.

Turning to the abbess, she met her eye. "None of this is yer fault, Mother," she said softly. "Please don't blame yerself."

Mother Shona's mouth pursed, her gaze narrowing. "Isn't it? There's a reason why men go to war and women keep the home fires burning. For years I fought against the natural order of things ... I wanted to make ye all strong. Ye put yer trust in me, but I put yer futures all in jeopardy. I should never have taught ye all how to fight."

Coira drew back. "Ye did a good thing."

The abbess shook her head, her jaw tightening. "Father Camron wouldn't have returned here to investigate me, if I'd run the abbey as I should have."

Coira tensed. "That bigot? He—"

"Hush, Coira. I like the man no more than ye do, yet he's an emissary of the Pope. For years I thought myself above following the rules. I can play games with my own life, but not with the lives of others."

Coira heaved in a deep breath. The abbess seemed intent on shouldering the responsibility for Father

Camron's meddling. Although Coira didn't share her view, she could see that there was little point arguing with her.

One thing she'd learned over the years was just how stubborn Mother Shona could be. The harder you pushed, the more she dug her heels in.

"So ye will go off to some forgotten isle and find yerself a hermit's hut?" she asked finally.

Mother Shona snorted. "Perhaps." She gave Coira a shrewd look then. "And what of ye, lass?"

Coira's cheeks warmed at the question. Although she hadn't minded standing with Craeg in front of his outlaws, being so bold with Mother Shona wasn't as easy. Embarrassed, she lowered her gaze.

"There's no need to look ashamed," the abbess murmured, a note of chagrin in her voice. "Do ye think I'm in a position to pass judgement upon yer choices?"

Coira lifted her chin, aware that Craeg had stepped close, his hand taking hers. The warmth and strength of his fingers made the awkwardness ebb a little. Even so, it was difficult to meet Mother Shona's eye.

"I took vows," she replied softly. "And I have broken them."

"Aye ... but none of that matters now," the abbess replied. Her expression turned wistful then. "Ye never belonged here, not really. Like Sisters Ella and Leanna, ye used these walls as a refuge. But like it or not, our past catches up with us eventually, just as mine has. The Lord has other plans for ye, as it had for yer friends."

Mother Shona's attention shifted to Craeg then, and a soft smile curved her mouth. "Plus, love is hard to fight. I once gave my heart to a man like ye, Craeg MacKinnon ... I know how difficult ye are to resist."

30

Ghosts

THE BULK OF Dunan appeared in the distance, lit up in red and gold by the setting sun.

The sight of it, rearing up against a backdrop of dark pine forest, made a host of unwelcome memories slam into Coira. The skin of her forearms prickled, and her breathing quickened.

This was going to be harder than she'd thought.

Glancing left, she saw that Craeg was staring at the fortress, his handsome face strained.

The pair of them walked at the front of the column of warriors, alongside the gurgling River An. However, when they were around four furlongs from the walls, Craeg halted and turned back to his men, his gaze sweeping over them. "Watch yer backs," he called out, his voice carrying down the line. "They will be expecting Duncan MacKinnon to return to them. Not us."

"He will have left a few of the Dunan Guard behind to guard the broch," Gunn pointed out. The warrior had put Fenella on one of the wagons and ridden forward to join Craeg. "They might put up a fight."

Craeg nodded. "Aye ... draw yer weapons, but don't use them unless I say so," he ordered. "Enough blood has been spilled of late … but if we have to use force, we will."

Coira's gaze shifted over the faces of the outlaws before them. They were weary, their eyes hollowed with fatigue, yet their faces were set in determination.

The gates of Dunan would only hold them for so long.

The column moved on. They skirted the locked South Gate, taking the road to Dunan's main entrance, the North Gate. On the way, Coira saw the blackened embers of what looked like funeral pyres.

A chill stole over her.

The sickness.

The gates were open, and the arable fields before them were empty, the rows of vegetables left untended.

"Where is everyone?" Craeg breathed, looking around.

"They've fled," Coira replied. "For fear of getting sick." She met Craeg's eye then. "Ye may find that only ghosts now inhabit Dunan."

A lone guard met them before the archway leading into the broch's bailey. He was a broad, brawny warrior with short blond hair and a face that might have been handsome, if it hadn't been set in such a severe expression.

A heavy claidheamh-mor hung from the man's waist, but he hadn't yet drawn it.

Craeg, who'd led the way up the cobbled street from the North Gate, halted a few feet from the guard.

The men's gazes fused for a few instants, before Craeg spoke. "Do ye know me?"

The guard's mouth thinned. "The family resemblance is uncanny … Craeg MacKinnon I take it?"

The note of grudging respect in the man's voice surprised Coira. He'd not addressed him as 'Craeg the Bastard' as they'd all expected.

Another heavy silence stretched between the two men, before the guard spoke once more. "MacKinnon is dead, then?"

"Aye," Craeg answered, his voice flat. "As are his men, save the survivors we bring with us. If ye'd like confirmation that he's gone ... ye can ask them if ye wish?"

The guard swallowed, the only sign that this news moved him at all.

"And ye are?" Craeg asked, when the man didn't answer.

"Carr Broderick," the man replied gruffly, "Captain of what's left of the Dunan Guard."

Craeg inclined his head, taking the man's measure. "So, what will ye do now, captain? Deny me access?"

Broderick's mouth twisted into a humorless smile. "I could ... but we both know how that would end."

"How many of ye are left?"

"Twenty ... three of whom are sick."

Craeg glanced over at Coira, and they shared a long look. They both knew surrender when they saw it. However, it was also clear that this was costing Carr Broderick dearly.

"Ye were loyal to my brother?" Craeg asked, his attention swinging back to Captain Broderick.

To Coira's surprise, the man's mouth pursed, as if Craeg had just said something distasteful.

"Aye," he replied after a pause, bitterness lacing his voice. "Like a hound."

"And can a man change loyalties?"

Broderick frowned, his jaw tensing as he sensed a trap. Tension rippled between them, and when the warrior finally replied, his voice was rough with suppressed anger. "I didn't like yer brother," he admitted. "But I still served him ... not like Ross Campbell, who took a stand."

Craeg's gaze narrowed. "Ye knew Campbell well?"

"Aye ... and I was sent to track him down. I caught up with him too, just before he and Lady Leanna escaped from Skye ... yer brother never learned about that meeting though. I'd have swung for it, if he had."

Craeg raised an eyebrow. "Ye let Campbell and Lady Leanna go?"

Broderick nodded, his features tightening.

"Then ye weren't MacKinnon's hound after all," Craeg replied. "Ye are glad he's dead. I see it in yer eyes."

The captain dropped his gaze, his hands, which hung by his sides, clenching into fists. He then shifted to one side, making it clear that Craeg and his men could pass.

Craeg moved forward, drawing parallel with Broderick. "Is Lady MacKinnon at home?" he asked coolly.

The captain's chin snapped up, and Coira, who'd stopped just behind Craeg, drew in a sharp breath when she spied the anguish in Broderick's grey-blue eyes. "Aye," he rasped. "Although ye won't want to see her ... Lady Drew is gravely ill."

Coira followed Captain Broderick up the stairwell to the uppermost level of the broch. The emptiness they'd seen in the narrow streets and alleyways of 'The Warren' had continued within the broch itself. Apart from the odd scurrying servant or skulking guard, the fortress was deserted.

"Surely, not all the servants fell ill?" she asked, hurrying to keep pace with the warrior's long strides as he led her along a hallway. There were no windows in the corridor; instead, a row of flickering cressets illuminated the cool space.

"A few did," the warrior replied, his tone as gruff as it had been at the entrance to the bailey. "The rest fled like rats ahead of a flood."

Coira took this news in, her mouth thinning. His words didn't surprise her, although it was concerning. How many of those who'd fled had been ill already, and had merely taken the sickness with them and passed it on to others?

Broderick led her halfway down the hallway, and into a dimly-lit bed-chamber.

The first thing Coira did—before even going to the figure lying on the bed—was walk to the window and unlatch the shutters. She then pushed them wide, breathing in the pine-scented evening air with relief.

Turning back to Broderick, she saw that he was glowering at her. "Don't look so worried," she chided him. "I told ye that I'm a healer."

"The last one told us to close the shutters," he replied, his voice edged with suspicion.

"And where's he?"

Deep grooves bracketed Broderick's mouth then. "He fled with the others."

Coira sighed. "Well then … it's just as well I'm here." She gestured to the open window. "Fresh air clears out the ill humors. Plus, it'll help me to see." Placing the basket she'd brought on a desk, she pulled out her scarf and gloves and put them on.

When she shifted her attention back to the captain, he was staring at her as if she'd just sprouted horns.

"It's for my own protection," she told him, moving toward the bed. "I'm not much good to the sick if the plague gets me, am I?"

Approaching the bed, her gaze fixed upon the woman reclining there. One glance, told her that she was possibly too late.

The woman, around five years her elder, lay there, dressed in a sweat-soaked léine. Her dark hair fanned across the pillow, although her delicate features were gaunt with sickness and pain. The eyes that watched her were eerily familiar—iron-grey—marking her as Duncan MacKinnon's kin. Her clammy-looking skin was ashen and marked with dark spots, huge swellings visible under the arms.

Despite her scarf, Coira took in a shallow, measured breath. *The Lord have mercy on us all.*

"Can ye help her?"

The desperate edge to Captain Broderick's voice drew Coira's attention. Her gaze swiveled to him. She wondered why the man was so obviously upset, before realization dawned.

He's in love with her.

Coira's throat tightened, and she shifted her attention back to Lady Drew. Even if the woman had been well, anyone could see that such a love-match would be impossible. She was a lady and he a guard. Society would not allow it.

And would society allow a union between ye and Craeg? A voice needled her.

Underneath her scarf, Coira's mouth curved. A woman who'd lived as both a whore and nun, and an outlaw with a price on his head—they were a perfect match indeed.

"She is in the latter stages of the illness," Coira said softly. "But I will do all I can ... even if the shock of the treatment may be too much for her." It was true, Lady Drew's weakened state made this procedure a risky one. Coira then reached for the knife she carried at her waist. "Can ye get me a bowl?"

31

Make Ye Mine

IT WAS AFTER dark when Coira joined Craeg in the clan-chief's solar.

He stood by the window, a lonely figure looking out at where a dark line of trees met an indigo sky. Even from the doorway, she could see the tension in his broad shoulders. He wasn't comfortable here.

She didn't blame him. Neither was she. However, she'd had plenty to occupy her since her arrival at Dunan. It had taken her a while to tend to Lady Drew, and to adequately clean the lanced boils. But after seeing to her patient, Coira hadn't gone to Craeg directly. First, she had gone down to the kitchens and found a bucket of water and lye soap to bathe with.

Tending the sick left a taint behind it. She wanted to scrub it off, before she spent time with her love.

Hearing the thud of the door closing behind her, and the light pad of her footsteps, Craeg turned. His gaze was shadowed. "How's my sister?"

"In a bad way," Coira replied softly. "But I have treated her like the others ... if she survives the night, there may be hope for her."

Craeg watched Coira, his throat bobbing. "I never met Drew, ye know," he said after a pause. "Our father thought it fitting to bring Duncan to the brothel to meet me ... but it would have been unseemly to bring the bastard into the broch itself."

"So ye have never set foot in here before today?"

He shook his head.

Coira reached Craeg's side and linked her arm through his, leaning against him. "And how does it feel?"

"Odd," he huffed. "Like I'm trespassing."

"Well, ye aren't."

Craeg drew Coira close, his hand sliding up her back. "I feel as if the moment I step outside this room, a servant is going to appear, point at me and shriek '*Bastard* ... what are ye doing here'?"

Despite herself, Coira laughed, burying her face against the warmth of his neck. "No need to worry ... there are no servants left to heckle ye."

"Ye mean we shall need to fix our own supper?"

"Aye ... if we can find any food."

Coira drew back from him then, lifting her chin to meet his gaze. The look on his face—both tender and fierce—made her heart leap, her breathing quicken. When he looked at her in that way, her limbs melted like butter in the noon sun.

"Mother Shona was right, Craeg," she said softly. "This is yer destiny. Ye might feel like an imposter right now, but no one could rule these lands better than ye. I am proud to stand by yer side."

Craeg gazed down at her, his expression suddenly vulnerable. "I'm glad ye are here with me, Coira," he murmured. "This broch is a tomb. I feel as if my brother's ghost is breathing down my neck."

Coira huffed. "Yer brother will be too busy trying to outrun the devil and his pitchfork in the depths of hell," she replied.

Craeg's mouth quirked at the image. "Aye." He reached out, his fingers tracing the line of her jaw, to her cheekbone. "Long may he burn there." He lowered his head then, his mouth slanting over hers.

His kiss was hungry, demanding, and Coira answered in kind. Reaching up, she linked her arms around his neck. Her mouth opened beneath his, heat rising in the pit of her belly.

She couldn't get enough of Craeg. His taste, his touch, swamped her senses.

It only took moments for the kiss to spiral out of control, for all thought to dissolve from Coira's mind.

Nothing else but this man mattered.

She reached down and unlaced his léine, her fingers sliding against the warm flesh beneath. Frustrated, she unbuckled the belt that prevented her from ripping the tunic off him.

Breathing hard, Craeg broke off the kiss, stepped back, and pulled off his léine. A soft sigh escaped Coira then, as she leaned forward and tasted the skin where his neck met his shoulder, her fingers sliding over the breadth of his chest and the crisp, dark hair there.

She'd been aching to do this all day. Last night had been but a taste of what she hungered for. Had circumstances permitted, she'd have locked them away together for a week so she could feast on him. Her lustiness shocked her. After years of numbness, yearning like this was unexplored territory.

Craeg groaned as she worked her way down his chest, her fingers plucking at the waist band of his braies.

"No, mo ghràdh," he growled. "Tonight is my turn to take the lead. Tonight, I will make ye mine."

Excitement fluttered low in Coira's belly, and delicious anticipation shivered through her.

Craeg undressed her swiftly, stripping off her kirtle and léine. He then gathered her to him, pressing Coira up against the wall next to the open window. A cool breeze feathered in, caressing her naked skin. Outside, it was completely dark now, and a moth fluttered by, seeking the flames of the fire burning in the hearth and the cressets upon the walls.

Bracing his hands either side of her head, boxing her in, Craeg's mouth ravaged Coira's once more. His presence overwhelmed her, yet she gave into it. Her eyes fluttered shut as his lips shifted from hers, and he trailed kisses down her jaw and neck.

Mother Mary have mercy.

His mouth was hot, seeking, and when he reached her breasts, she let out a shuddering groan. Her hands fastened upon his shoulders, holding him fast as he stroked and suckled.

And then when he slipped farther down her body—and lifted one of her legs over his shoulder as he went down on his knees before her—Coira let out a soft cry.

Never had a man touched her like this.

During her time at *The Goat and Goose*, the men never took time to pleasure her—they risked catching the pox from a whore after all. As such, the intimacy of what Craeg was doing to her now made tears sting Coira's eyelids, made her chest tighten in a strange blend of tenderness and abandon.

Pleasure crested swiftly, making her cry out again, yet he didn't halt his ministrations. Coira's thighs started to tremble, and if he hadn't been holding her up, she'd have slid down the wall and ended up in a quaking heap upon the floor.

Coira was aware then that she was moaning his name, her fingers tangling in his hair.

Eventually, Craeg rose to his feet—the movement so swift that Coira's eyes flew open and she smothered a gasp.

Their gazes met. Craeg's face was all taut angles, and his eyes had deepened to a dark green. Not shifting his attention from her, he reached down and unlaced his breeches. Then, almost roughly now, he took hold of her hips and raised her up against the wall, kneeing her thighs wide.

An instant later he entered her, in a slow, deep thrust that made Coira buck against him. The sensation of him sliding into her, of how she stretched to accommodate his girth, caused an aching pleasure to ripple through the cradle of her hips.

Last night, she'd reached her peak with a man for the first time—had marveled at how pleasure had set her loins on fire.

But this was even more intense. It was a pleasure that throbbed deep inside, radiating out like ripples in a pool, suffusing her whole body with a languor that made her feel reckless and wild.

Nothing in the world mattered except this. Nothing.

Craeg's body trembled, while he held himself leashed. He moved slowly, holding her pinned against the wall as he took her.

And all the while, his gaze held hers.

It was almost too much, too intense, too intimate. Coira felt stripped bare, as if all she was—her heart and soul—was displayed before him. But she didn't look away. Instead, her hands clung to his shoulders, her fingernails biting into his flesh as wave after wave of aching pleasure rippled through her.

And when Craeg finally exploded inside her—his groan shuddering through the cool night air—tears flowed down Coira's cheeks.

A grey dawn rose over Dunan. Curtains of fine rain swept across the valley, obscuring the surroundings. It made the broch a grim place indeed, yet there was a lightness to Craeg's stride as he descended the steps into the bailey.

Gunn was there, checking over one of the horses from Duncan MacKinnon's stable. It was a fine beast, a huge bay stallion.

"His name is Curaidh," Gunn greeted Craeg. "Apparently, he belonged to yer brother."

Craeg smiled. *Curaidh—Warrior—a mighty name indeed.*

"He's recovering from a foot abscess," Gunn continued. "The old man who looks after the stables— one of the few folk left in this place—tells me that's why MacKinnon left him behind."

MacKinnon.

Soon folk would start referring to *him* by that name. For years now, the clan-chief's name had brought sneers and grimaces to the faces of the people of this land.

"He's a beauty," Craeg murmured. He stepped close and stroked the stallion's neck.

"Well, he's yers now," Gunn replied with a grin. He leaned down then and ran practiced hands over the stallion's hind-quarters, checking for any lameness.

Craeg was observing him when suddenly, something cold and wet pushed against his hand.

Startling, Craeg glanced down to see a large charcoal grey wolfhound sitting at his feet. The hound stared up at him with soft, dark eyes, its tail beating out a tempo on the flagstones.

"What's this?" Craeg said, addressing the dog. "No use looking at me like that … I'm not yer master."

"The hound's been pestering me all morning too," Gunn replied, glancing up. "The old stable hand tells me that the dog's name is Bran. He too belonged to MacKinnon … so that means he's yers as well."

Craeg sighed, before he reached out and ruffled the dog's soft ears. The hound looked a bit lost. A pang went through him then. Duncan MacKinnon had been such a vile individual—the only one who'd truly mourn him was his dog.

"How is Fen this morning?" Craeg asked.

Gunn straightened up and slapped the stallion on the rump. "Much better. She's starting to get her appetite back." The relief on his friend's face was evident. His eyes gleamed, and his throat bobbed. "And we have Coira to thank."

Craeg smiled. Stepping forward, he placed a hand on Gunn's shoulder. "Ye are the first to know that as soon as we can find a priest … I'm going to make Coira my wife."

A grin stretched across Gunn's rugged face. "That is good news indeed."

"How is she?"

The rawness in Carr Broderick's voice made Coira tense. His face looked as if it were hewn from stone, yet he betrayed himself when he spoke.

"A little better, I believe," she replied cautiously. Coira's gaze narrowed as she examined the boils she'd lanced the day before. Although they had a raw appearance, she was pleased to see that they were clear of pus and blood. It also seemed that Drew's fever had lowered a little.

Indeed, the lady herself was awake and now observed Coira, her grey eyes clouded with pain and confusion. "Who are ye?" she croaked.

"My name's Coira. I'm a healer."

"And why do ye wear a scarf over yer face?"

"Ye have the plague, Lady Drew ... as ye know, the illness passes quickly from person to person."

Drew licked her dry lips. "I'm so thirsty."

"Here." Coira picked up a wooden cup of water, not an easy task when wearing leather gloves, and held it to her patient's lips. "Just take a few sips mind ... yer belly is still tender."

Drew did as bid before settling back against the mound of pillows. Her gaze shifted then, over Coira's shoulder, to where Captain Broderick stood, still and silent now that his mistress had awoken.

"Did ye fetch this healer, Broderick?" she asked weakly.

He shook his head. "She arrived here with Craeg, milady."

Drew's gaze widened. "The outlaw ... he's here?"

Coira stilled. Was that how Lady Drew saw Craeg? *The outlaw ... he's yer brother.*

Straightening up, Coira met Drew's eye. "I am Craeg MacKinnon's woman," she informed her softly, her breath catching a little as she said the words out loud. "Ye should know that there was a battle between the Dunan Guard and the outlaw band two days ago. Duncan MacKinnon is dead."

Drew stared at her for a long moment. Watching her, Coira's throat tightened. She wasn't going to apologize. When it came to MacKinnon's demise, she couldn't bring herself to show any regret. Not only that but, despite her weak state, she sensed that the woman before her was no whimpering maid. There was strength in the set of the lady's jaw and the steely glint in her eyes.

Silence stretched out, and then Lady Drew let out a long sigh. "It's over then," she whispered weakly.

"Aye, milady," Broderick spoke up. "Worry not, Craeg MacKinnon will allow ye to remain here."

Drew's mouth thinned. "That's generous of him." Her eyes fluttered shut then, the tension going out of her. "Well ... he can't be any worse a clan-chief than Duncan was I suppose," she rasped.

"He won't be." The vehemence in Coira's voice surprised her. "Craeg is a thousand times the man Duncan MacKinnon was."

Drew MacKinnon's eyes opened and then, surprisingly, she favored Coira with a tremulous smile. "That is a relief to hear."

32

Destined

Two weeks later ...

STANDING IN FRONT of the slender mirror, Coira surveyed her appearance. She'd never seen her reflection like this before—having only ever caught glimpses in a still pool or the polished sheen of metal.

She barely recognized the woman before her.

Dressed in a sky-blue kirtle with a violet over-gown, meadow flowers entwined through her hair, she looked like a princess.

It was hard to believe she'd once been a fallen woman, and then a Bride of Christ. Both those identities were behind her now.

Coira's throat thickened then, and she glanced down at the ring she now wore upon her left hand—soon she would wear Craeg's ring upon her right. How she wished her parents were still alive to witness this day.

"That shade is perfect," a woman's voice intruded. "It matches yer eyes."

Coira smiled and turned from the mirror, her gaze settling upon Fenella. Once her fever had abated, the outlaw woman had recovered swiftly. Now, only the thinness in her face hinted that she'd recently been ill.

Usually, Fenella favored a more masculine style of dress, striding about the broch in braies and a form-fitting leather vest. Yet today she'd donned a dark-blue kirtle. Her wild mane of blonde hair, which usually tumbled over her shoulders, had been tamed and piled above her head.

Inhaling a shaky breath, Coira then smoothed out the silken material of her over-gown. "I'm nervous, Fen … what a goose I am."

Fenella's mouth curved, her blue eyes twinkling. "As all brides are. Come on … everyone's waiting in the kirk. Craeg will soon think ye have changed yer mind."

Coira's breathing hitched. *Never.*

Ever since Craeg had sent out men in search of a priest, she'd been looking forward to this day. The plague had ravaged parts of the isle while leaving some areas untouched, yet men of the cloth were hard to find. However, finally one of the men had returned with a priest from Dunvegan in MacLeod territory. He had arrived with the carcass of a prize stag and Malcolm MacLeod's best wishes.

It appeared that the folk of these lands weren't the only ones pleased by the news of Duncan MacKinnon's passing.

"Let us go to him then," Coira replied. She retrieved a posy of flowers from the sideboard—aromatic sprays of purple heather—and led the way out of the women's solar.

Outdoors, the sun bathed Dunan in warmth. The bailey was still quiet. Although the sickness had passed, folk were slow to return to the fortress. Even so, Dunan no longer had the desolate air of when they'd arrived here.

It still didn't feel like home, although Coira could now envision a time when it might. These days, she was just happy that the sickness had spared her and those she loved. Each night, she knelt by the foot of the bed and thanked the Lord for it.

The two women skirted the base of the broch and headed toward the South Gate.

Two men wearing MacKinnon sashes stood guard there. They both bowed to the women, smiles stretching their faces. Those of the Dunan Guard who'd not wished to serve Duncan MacKinnon's bastard brother had been let go—only those who willingly followed Craeg remained.

Passing under the archway, Coira and Fenella made their way through the kirk yard. The path led between haphazard clusters of gravestones. Ahead, loomed the open door of the kirk.

Coira swallowed hard, sweat suddenly beading upon her back.

This was real. She was about to become Craeg MacKinnon's wife.

Only a handful of people awaited them inside. With the threat of sickness still lurking in Dunan, Craeg preferred to keep the gathering small. Still, those who mattered most to them both were there—even Lady Drew.

Seated by the doors, Craeg's half-sister turned to look at Coira as she stepped inside.

The two women's gazes fused for an instant, and Coira noted how much better Drew was looking. Color had returned to her cheeks, although she was still painfully thin. Behind Drew stood Carr Broderick.

The man had barely left the lady's side over the past two weeks. With Craeg's arrival, he'd become her shadow. Gunn was now Captain of the Dunan Guard and Broderick had taken on the role of Lady Drew's personal guard.

The moment drew out, and then Drew MacKinnon's mouth lifted at the corners, warmth showing in her grey eyes. It had been a strange time for Drew. When she was strong enough, Craeg had gone to her solar, and the pair of them had spoken for a whole afternoon.

Coira wasn't sure what had passed between them, but in the days that followed, when Drew joined them at mealtimes, she noted that brother and sister got on well, and even laughed together on occasion.

The family Craeg had never known wasn't completely lost to him after all.

However, Drew only occupied Coira's attention for a few instants. She shifted her gaze then to the tall dark-haired man who awaited her before the altar.

A squat individual with ruddy cheeks, garbed in priestly robes, stood next to him.

Both of them watched her approach.

Gunn sat upon a bench a few yards away from the altar, Farlan next to him. The latter favored her with a grin and a wink. A walking stick sat next to him; the outlaw's leg had recovered well, although he would be lame for a while yet.

Both men shuffled to one side, making room on the low bench for Fenella.

Craeg ignored them all. His attention never shifted from Coira, not for a moment. Dressed in a charcoal pair of braies and a snowy-white léine, with a sash of pine green and red across his chest, he'd never looked more handsome. His hair, although long still, had been trimmed. The striking green of his eyes stood out against his lightly-tanned skin.

Coira couldn't stop smiling. With every passing day, she loved this man more—his strength, warmth, kindness, and courage. He was constantly surprising her. Since taking control of Dunan, Craeg had swung into action, clearing up the mess created by the plague and his half-brother's poor management. Crops had been tended, and the broch's stores of grain were now being used to bake bread for the locals. Folk were returning to 'The Warren' in a steady trickle now word had spread that Craeg MacKinnon was clan-chief.

Looking at him, it dawned on Coira that this had always been Craeg's destiny. Mother Shona had told her once that the Lord had a plan for everyone, and although he'd spent many years as an outcast, Coira now believed that Craeg was always meant to end up here.

Which meant that she was also destined to be his wife.

Coira's throat constricted. The joy within her brimmed so full it risked spilling over. She didn't know it was possible to feel this happy, to shine like the sun. She'd heard folk say that there were few as radiant as a woman on her wedding day, but she hadn't believed the tales till today. Now, she understood—if the match was between two people who loved each other, there was no happier moment.

Coira's step slowed as she approached the altar. She wanted to draw this moment out, wanted to imprint it forever upon her mind.

Smiling, Craeg held out a hand to her, his gaze shining.

And reaching out, Coira entwined her fingers through his and squeezed tight.

Epilogue

Belonging

Dunan broch
MacKinnon Territory

Yuletide
Four months later …

"THE DRUIDS OF old used to swear by mistletoe, ye know?" Coira said as she hung the garland above a doorway. "It was seen as sacred … a symbol of life in the dark winter months."

"I've always thought mistletoe a dull-looking plant," Leanna answered from across the room. "I prefer holly—the red berries are so cheerful."

Coira frowned, examining the sprig with dark green leaves and tiny white berries she'd just hung up. She disagreed. There was something timeless and wise about mistletoe—maybe it was the fact she was a healer, but she loved the plant.

"It's the scent of pine I look forward to every year," Ella spoke up then. "The Great Hall at Scorrybreac resembles a forest glade this time of year."

"Duncan never liked me to make a fuss over Yuletide decorations," Drew said, her voice oddly subdued. "It feels strange to see this broch so … festive."

Coira turned then, her gaze traveling to where the three women sat near the fire in the chieftain's solar. Together, they'd decorated this chamber with all three of the seasonal plants. The only thing missing was the Yule log—the massive oaken log that they would try to keep burning for all twelve days of Yuletide—that burned downstairs in the hearth of the Great Hall.

A warm aura of contentment spread over Coira as she looked upon Drew and her two friends. Drew had recovered swiftly over the past months. She now had a bloom in her cheeks and a gleam in her eye as she peeked under the lid of the pot of mulled wine that sat keeping warm by the edge of the hearth.

A few feet from Drew, Ella looked well, although a little tired, for she held a swaddled infant in her arms. Wee Anice was three months old and had arrived just as the plague swept through the north of the isle. Fortunately, Scorrybreac had been only lightly touched by the sickness.

Coira's belly tensed as her attention shifted to the bairn's thatch of thick copper-blonde hair and rosy cheeks. They were so lucky that the illness had spared her and Ella.

All of us here today are fortunate.

Indeed, they were, for many upon the isle had died. Word had reached Dunan that whole villages had perished. Those who survived emerged into a much more subdued world. Whenever she went into 'The Warren', Coira was struck by just how quiet it was these days.

The Goat and Goose had shut its doors permanently. It appeared the sickness had torn through the brothel, and once Old Maude succumbed to it, the few whores still alive fled Dunan.

Coira's thoughts returned to the present, and she glanced over to where Leanna sat making a large holly wreath. It would be the center-piece on the table for tonight's Yuletide feast. Coira noted how well Leanna looked. Her eyes were bright, her smooth cheeks pink with excitement.

Leanna had always loved Yule, even at Kilbride, where the celebrations had been considerably limited. Coira was glad she and Ross had made the trip from Barra to spend Yule with them.

After word of Duncan MacKinnon's death spread, a missive had arrived in Dunan around a month later. Coira had been sharing her morning bannocks with Craeg in this solar when Carr Broderick brought up a message.

It was from Leanna.

She and Ross were wed and farming a tract of land upon the Isle of Barra, where they raised sheep. Leanna had never been happier but admitted that she missed her old friends terribly.

Afterward, Coira had decided that she would invite both Leanna and Ella to stay. Now that the ravages of the plague were behind them, it was safe to travel again. While Duncan MacKinnon ruled, Ella and Gavin weren't welcome in Dunan either. In fact, he'd longed to have a chance to get his revenge against them.

Now, they no longer had to worry about him.

The rumble of male voices, punctuated by a burst of laughter out in the hallway beyond, drew Coira's attention then. Smiling, she met Leanna's eye. "Sounds like the men are back from hunting."

Leanna gave a squeal of excitement, cast aside her half-finished wreath, and leaped to her feet.

At that moment, the door to the solar flew open and three men entered.

The first was tall and broad-shouldered, a grey brindled wolfhound loping at his heel. Around his shoulders the MacKinnon clan-chief wore a heavy fur cloak. Snowflakes dusted his shoulders and peat-brown hair.

Behind him another dark-haired man strode into the solar, his piercing blue eyes sweeping around as he took in the decorations. "Good grief ... ye have all been busy."

"Do ye like it?" Leanna rushed to her husband and launched herself at him. With a laugh, Ross caught her before lowering his lips to his wife's for a kiss. "Aye ... it's bonny."

"I don't suppose there's any mulled wine, is there?" A blond man entered behind Ross. Gavin MacNichol blew on his chilled hands. The clan-chief had warm blue-grey eyes and a boyish grin that Ella responded to with a smile of her own. "Aye ... the servants have just brought up some. It's still hot ... help yerself."

Gavin went to the cast iron pot sitting at Drew's feet and lifted off the lid. The heady scent of plum wine and costly spice—cinnamon and clove—wafted through the solar.

Coira breathed in the rich aroma with pleasure. This was her first experience of such a drink. She had grown up relatively poor, and her life in the brothel and then at the abbey had never given her the opportunity to try mulled wine.

Gavin ladled cups for everyone and handed them out. Coira took hers gratefully, wrapping her fingers around the cup as she took a sip.

Glancing up, she saw Craeg approach her. The pair of them shared a smile.

"Did ye enjoy the hunt?" she asked. Behind them, Bran had settled down in front of the fire and was licking his wet paws.

"Aye ... we brought down two red deer," he replied. He took a sip from his own cup, his gaze widening. "Lord, this is good."

"Mulled wine is as new to me as it is to ye then?" Coira asked.

"Of course ... outlaws don't live like lairds."

Coira laughed, stepping close to him. Around them, the chatter of conversation punctuated with bursts of laughter filled the solar. Ross was teasing Leanna over her messy wreath, Gavin had picked up his daughter and was tickling her, while Ella and Drew debated whether or not it was too early to bring out plum and apple cakes to feast on. It was a happy scene, one that gave Coira a true sense of belonging.

A feeling that eluded her until recently.

She was happier too, since she'd received word from Shona. A message had arrived just a few days earlier. The former abbess of Kibride had found a new home far to the north of Scotland, upon one of the Isles of Orkney, where she lived as a hermit. And although it saddened Coira that Shona blamed herself for the events that had torn their lives at Kilbride apart, she was relieved to know that the woman was well. Maybe, one day, she'd realize the good she'd done them all. Coira knew she had much to thank Shona for.

"Ye have a smile to light up the world this afternoon, mo ghràdh," Craeg murmured, moving nearer still. "I love to see ye so content."

"I am," she admitted, her smile fading just a little. "I only wish I could make this moment freeze in time ... that all of us could remain exactly as we are ... that nothing could ever touch us."

"Aye, but it's the very fact that these moments are fleeting that makes them so precious," he replied, favoring Coira with that soft smile he reserved only for her. He reached out then and gently cupped her chin, raising it so that their gazes met. "Just remember that we will have other days like this in the years to come. I plan to spend many more Yuletides with ye, Coira. Many, many more."

The End

From the author

FALLEN was a real adventure to tell. I tend to plan my entire series before I write it, but there were still elements about this novel that surprised me. Coira and Craeg's relationship was less angsty than I'd expected. He ended up being far more of a gentleman with a real soft side. Despite his rough upbringing, Craeg is a guy of true class—just what Coira needed after everything she'd been through!

Of course, this novel does have a few heavy themes in it. Coira's past experiences had really damaged her, and the Black Death—which I'd been building up to in the previous two books—features prominently in this tale.

I planned FALLEN nearly a year before I wrote it, although it was an eerie feeling to be writing about the ravages caused by the Black Death when, in March 2020, a pandemic threw our world into chaos. History, indeed, has much to teach us.

The Bubonic Plague devastated Europe in the mid-14th Century, although the Scottish Highlands weren't as badly hit as more densely populated areas. The plague arrived in Scotland in late 1349 and reached its full, devastating heights in 1350. However, I tweaked the time-frame by a couple of months as it hits the Isle of Skye earlier in 1349 when my story takes place.

We now know that the Black Death was caused by the spread of deadly bacteria from fleas—and from person-to-person through bodily contact and fluids—but at the time everyone was mystified by it. Healers had no idea how to deal with the plague, and some of the treatments such as bleeding and rubbing excrement on lanced 'plague boils' just quickened the patients' demise! As such, I had to be careful with just how much knowledge I gave Coira. In many ways, thanks to her very wise mother, she is 'ahead of her time'.

Later, healers did discover that people could recover from the illness if the buboes (enlarged lymph nodes), commonly known as 'plague boils', were successfully lanced. However, some patients went into shock after such a procedure and died anyway. Coira's discovery of this practice helps her save a few lives!

I hope you enjoyed this emotional trilogy, and the happy endings for Ella, Leanna, and Coira. I teared up as I wrote the last lines of FALLEN, as I really didn't want to leave this world behind. I hope too that you love CLAIMED, the wee extra where you'll find out what happens with Drew and Carr!

Jayne x

About the Author

Jayne Castel writes Historical Romance set in Dark Ages Britain and Scotland, and Epic Fantasy Romance. Her vibrant characters, richly researched historical settings, extensive world-building and action-packed adventure romance transport readers back to forgotten times and imaginary worlds.

Jayne is the author of the Amazon bestselling BRIDES OF SKYE series—a Medieval Scottish Romance trilogy about three strong-willed sisters and the men who love them. In love with all things Scottish, she also writes romances set in 4th Century Isle of Skye ... sexy Pict warriors anyone?

When she's not writing, Jayne is reading (and re-reading) her favorite authors, learning French, cooking Italian, and taking her dog, Juno, for walks. She lives in New Zealand's beautiful South Island.

Connect with Jayne online:
www.jaynecastel.com
www.facebook.com/JayneCastelRomance/
Email: contact@jaynecastel.com